Death

Island

A Postcard from the Gilded Age

Carol Tonnesen

ISBN-13: 978-0-9992130-6-3

To Karl

I would fly in a plane with you.

To William

My Dragon Master

Acknowledgments

I would like to express my appreciation to Jill and Rosemary for all of their hard work as editors of this novel. Between the two of them, they kept me focused and provided the encouragement I needed.
I would also like to thank William for bringing life to this book with his special mix of optimism and imagination.
My very dear friend Barbara deserves a special thank you for taking the photograph featured on the cover of this book.
A special thanks goes to Jackie, Taylor, and Teresa and all my friends on Jekyll Island.
Thank you all so very much.

This book is a work of fiction. Though the postcards are real, the story, the characters, and the plot within these pages are completely fictional. Any resemblance to actual events, people, or places is purely coincidental. The postcards found in this book are from my collection.

As always, I have tried to be as historically accurate as possible. Historical events related to this book have been researched, represented, and portrayed accurately to the best of my ability. Much of my research comes from personal interviews, letters, diaries, books, newspapers, photographs, and postcards from the era. Though it is not easy to find older material, I prefer it that way. It's much more fun to dig about in musty cellars, airless attics, and dusty minds. The Internet is efficient but rather sanitary and soulless when compared with written and oral histories.

As I do for all my books, I make lengthy visits to the places I write about. During these visits, I soak up local culture and talk to everyone I meet. I am often asked if I prepare extensive outlines for my books. The short answer is: yes. But truth be told, the process is more complex than that. A writer takes an idea and begins to mold it into a book. As the words take the form of paragraphs, the book starts to take whatever shape the author had in mind. Sometimes along the way, the words and characters sort of take over and do their own things. Sometimes, the author writes something into the book that he or she hadn't intended in the beginning. Characters can be especially difficult, each taking on their own complex personalities. What begins with the tilt of a head or the position of an arm can eventually become a completely different person. Often unintentionally, a single word can take the writer and the book off in a totally unexpected direction. When this happens, the author often has no choice but to sit back and enjoy the ride.

‘The most essential elements of success in life are a purpose, increasing industry, temperate habits, scrupulous regard for one’s word---courteous manners, a generous regard for the rights of others, and, above all, integrity.’

W.A. Clarke
Copper Magnate and philanthropist

‘The golden gleam of the gilded surface hides the cheapness of the metal underneath.’

Mark Twain

Author of the Gilded Age

Author notes:

While writing this book, I researched the men responsible for shifting the United States from an agrarian society to an industrial giant. One such man was born in the small town where I have spent my entire adult life. What follows is a brief description of his connection with Lebanon, Ohio. It also goes a long way to explain why I chose to portray the men in this story in a positive light.

William E. Harmon made his money by offering land for sale on an installment plan. In other words, in the 1880s, he set up the first home mortgage system in the United States. By the time he was 38 years old, he had loan offices in 40 cities. At the time, he operated the largest real estate operation in the world. Besides being clever, he was a good man. He once wrote to a friend:

'I have a very deep conviction that one owes something tangible to the place of his nativity.'

-William Elmer Harmon
Real estate mogul and philanthropist

Born in Lebanon, Ohio, he lived up to his words. In 1903, when Andrew Carnegie provided the funding to build the Lebanon Library, it was Mr. Harmon who bought the books and furniture to fill it. During his lifetime, Mr. Harmon, using his grandfather's name, Jedidiah Tingle, in order to anonymously help people in need. He established parks in small towns in thirty-four states across the United States including, in 1912, the eighty-eight-acre Harmon Community Golf Course and Harmon Park in Lebanon. He built Harmon Hall in 1913 as a community recreational center for Lebanon's young people. Later, when a larger facility was built, this became the Harmon Museum featuring the art and history of Warren County, Ohio. In 1915, he established the Harmon Civic Trust to provide money for community improvement projects. The trust still exists today!

'Serving one's own people, transcends duty... and becomes a privilege.'

-William Elmer Harmon

Timeline

1852 Marshall Field creates Marshall Field's Department Store in Chicago

1861 The Civil War begins on April 12

1865 The Civil War ends on April 9

1869 Cornelius Vanderbilt acquired and consolidated the Hudson River Railroad and the New York Central

1870 John D. Rockefeller created Standard Oil on January 10

1871

1872 Andrew Carnegie begins construction of his first steel mill

1873 Ulysses S. Grant elected for second term as president

1874 American Jennie Jerome weds Randolph Churchill, 8th Duke of Marlborough

1875

1876

1877 Rutherford B. Hayes takes office as president

1878

1879

1880 James A. Garfield elected as president

1881 Chester A. Arthur serves as president when Garfield dies in office after being shot by an anarchist on July 2 (He died September 19)

March 13: Czar Alexander II is killed by a bomb planted under his carriage by an anarchist

1882

1883 Andrew Carnegie acquires the Homestead Steel Works

1884

1885 Grover Cleveland takes office as president

1886

1887

1888

1889 May 31: Johnstown Flood, caused by the failure of the South Fork Dam, kills thousands in Pennsylvania

1890 Benjamin Harrison takes office as president

1891

1892 Grover Cleveland takes office as president

Anarchist movement begins to gather strength

Golden Age of Assassinations begins (1892-1901)

Andrew Carnegie forms Carnegie Steel Company

July: Homestead Steel Works employees riot and strike

Anarchist attempts to assassinate Andrew Carnegie's second in command, Henry Clay Frick

New water tower constructed at the Jekyll Island Club

1893 May: Financial panic follows bankruptcy of the Philadelphia and Reading Railroad

Panic deepens with run on gold reserves as people exchange silver certificates for gold

World's Columbian Exposition (world's fair held in Chicago) celebrates the 400th anniversary of Christopher Columbus' arrival in the new world. It runs from May 1 to October 30.

Yellow fever epidemic strikes Brunswick and surrounding areas. Jekyll Island Club virtually closed for 1893-1894 season

1894 French President, Marie Francois Carnot, assassinated by anarchists

1895 November 6: Consuelo Vanderbilt marries the 9th Duke of Marlborough

Jekyll Island Club clubhouse expanded: enlarged dining room, billiard room, barber shop, toilet room, staircases, additional fireplaces

1896 William McKinley takes office as president

1897 August 8: Prime Minister of Spain, Antonio Canovas del Castillo, killed by an anarchist

1898 February 15: Battleship Maine explodes and sinks in Havana Harbor

April 25: U.S. declares war on Spain

Summer: First golf course set up at Jekyll Island Club

September 10: Empress of Austria-Hungary, Elizabeth Hapsburg killed by anarchist

October 2: Hurricane swamps Jekyll Island with four feet of water

December 10: War with Spain ends

1899 March 20-22: President McKinley visits Jekyll Island

1900 July 29: Assassination of King Umberto I of Italy

1901 President McKinley assassinated by anarchist (shot on September 5, died September 14)

Electrification of Jekyll Island Clubhouse begins with building of a power plant

J.P. Morgan buys Carnegie Steel for $480 million

1912 President Theodore Roosevelt is shot by an anarchist while waving from his car. The bullet is deflected by his speech which he carried in his pocket. He refuses medical treatment until after he delivers his speech

That's all a man can hope for during his lifetime—
to set an example—
and when he is dead, to be an inspiration for history.
William McKinley
President 1897-1901

*Photograph of William McKinley and permission to use it thoughtfully provided by the Warren County Historical Society as part of the Warren County Historical Society Collection. All other photographs were taken by the author.

Chapter 1
Tiffy Rose

Tifton Rose Baldwin had never seen the sea before. Rivers, lakes, ponds, yes, but never anything as magnificent as the Atlantic Ocean. She gazed out to sea. The vastness of the ocean stunned her into silence. So empty, and, except for the sound of the birds in the air and the murmur of the surf—so quiet. Tearing her eyes away from the horizon, she watched the perfection of the waves rolling in to meet the sand. She reveled in the rightness of it. Taken in by the magic of the sunlight dancing on the waves, Tifton Rose Baldwin fell in love with Jekyll Island.

How lucky she was to be on Jekyll Island in March. She shaded her eyes from the bright morning sun. The air was unbelievably fresh and clear after last night's thunderstorm. Tifton Rose drew in a deep breath. How fortunate she was to be here, at the edge of the world—or so it seemed to her. To the east, as far as she could see, there was nothing but an empty expanse of water.

Shifting her attention to the beach, she watched the restless, storm-tossed tide come ashore and wrap itself around a large dark object floating at the water's edge. What could it be, this thing rolling over and over in the brown surf on the beach? Was it a sea creature that had gotten caught by the receding tide? From a distance, she could not tell.

Tifton twisted in her side-saddle and looked toward the north end of the beach. Far away, a group of riders splashed and romped with their mounts in the surf. How had she managed to get separated from the riding party? If her mother found out how far she had strayed, she would never hear the end of it. She knew her mother's lecture on lady-like deportment by heart.

Tifton, Tiffy Rose to her friends, contemplated waiting for the others to join her before investigating further, but, as usual, her curiosity got the better of her. She turned back toward the object which now lay as if suspended between the sand and the sea, neither in nor out of the water. As she closed the distance, her normally calm horse began to snort and dance about, almost unseating her. An accomplished horsewoman, Tiffy Rose righted herself on her side-saddle and took command of the animal.

"Hush," she said soothingly as she stroked the horse's neck. "There is nothing to be upset about. It's probably a big old pile of trash washed overboard from one of the ships that cruise up and down the coast. The storm last night was a nasty one. This morning, there is debris all over the beach. Hush, now, hush."

The horse quieted, allowing Tiffy Rose to take a closer look at the shapeless black lump. Recognition dawned, followed by a sharp intake of breath. Shoes! It wore shoes! It wasn't some sort of sea creature. It wasn't a pile of garbage that had floated to shore in the storm. It was a man!

Tiffy Rose leaned over the neck of the horse and took a closer look. Suddenly, the bracing morning air seemed cloying, the bright morning sun much too hot. Normally unflappable, Tiffy Rose swayed in her saddle.

"Careful there," said a masculine voice.

Tiffy Rose snapped her head up and found herself looking at a man on horseback who had appeared magically at her side. She stared at him, speechless. Good looking in a dashing sort of way, he appeared to Tiffy Rose as someone from a dream.

Gently, he placed a steadying hand on her arm. "You're all right. Take a couple of deep breaths."

But his words did little to quiet her pounding heart. Whether because of her discovery on the beach or the stranger's presence, Tiffy Rose felt light-headed.

"You mustn't faint, Miss. I have enough to deal with just now." His words came out as a command.

Something about his tone sparked a rebellious streak of pride in Tiffy Rose. She mustered her strength and sat up straighter. She adjusted her riding habit and secured her hat more firmly to her head. The effort cost her. She swallowed hard to keep her breakfast in her stomach where it belonged. Tiffy Rose found her voice and remarked caustically, "Sir, I have never fainted in my life."

The stranger, his clean-shaven, tanned face lit by the early morning sun, merely looked at her, his expression unreadable. He let go of her elbow and replied without emotion, "Good. You will need to have your wits about you when you ride for help."

Noting that the man was studying her, Tiffy Rose did some inspecting of her own. What she saw before her, pleased her. He had a good face—intelligent and kind. Despite his taciturn behavior, there was something vital and alive about him.

"Miss Baldwin!" called a young man as he cantered his horse toward where Tifton and the stranger stood. "Miss Baldwin! Is this man accosting you? Unhand her!"

Tifton realized how things must look. She turned her horse to face that of Randolph Patterson Chatsworth III, who, for better or worse, was to be her fiancé.

Willing herself to sound nonchalant and in control of the situation, she said politely yet firmly, "No, Mr. Chatsworth, you are mistaken. This man has only asked if I needed assistance. He has no intention of harming me. He came to my aid. I have made a most unpleasant discovery."

"What the lady says is true. It is I who needs assistance. Send your faster riders to the club for help." Though the stranger spoke softly, his voice carried the force of one used to giving commands.

The club that he referred to was the exclusive Jekyll Island Club. This private club counted among its members the wealthiest men in the United States—perhaps the wealthiest in the world. The Jekyll Island Club maintained its selective membership roster by enforcing stringent rules in order to join. Besides having substantial financial resources, anyone interested in membership in the club needed to be sponsored by a business associate, a close friend, or perhaps a relative who was already a member. After completing a formal application, the candidate had to be elected by the board of directors. Only two negative ballots were necessary to vote down an individual's application.

"You'd better rejoin your friends," suggested the stranger when neither Randolph Patterson Chatsworth III nor Tifton Rose Baldwin moved. "Send for help—a wagon, strong men, a doctor."

His words caused Tiffy Rose to snap out of her reverie. She kicked her horse with startling force. The horse seemed surprised by her sudden urgency to return to her companions. Gamely, he picked up a loping canter. Tiffy gripped the saddle as she tried to follow the rocking gait of the horse. Normally, she preferred to ride astride since it was so much more secure. This morning, however, she had bowed to convention and accepted the sidesaddle on the quiet horse. As a guest at the Jekyll Island Club, she knew the members wouldn't approve of her outlandish choices. Heaven help her if they ever found out that she had long ago stopped wearing a corset.

Though he lagged behind, Randolph Patterson followed her.

In the space of a few minutes, she reached her friends; the Maurice family, the Rawlins sisters, and her chaperone, Miss Flora Goodwin. Tiffy Rose reined in her horse and it skidded to a halt. Unprepared for her sudden stop, Randolph Patterson crashed his mount into hers. Tiffy Rose squealed with alarm when she almost lost her seat.

Before she could right herself, Randolph Patterson asked proprietarily, "Miss Baldwin, were you or were you not speaking with a stranger on the beach, just now?"

"Tifton! You spoke with a man?" asked her horrified chaperone, Miss Goodwin.

Her companions on the ride, the Barnes sisters and the Maurice sisters, looked on in mock horror at the implications of Tifton's inappropriate behavior. Behind their hands, they tittered over Tifton's social disgrace. The Maurice brothers gathered around behind Randolph Patterson, instinctively taking his side.

Tifton Rose ignored their questions and unsaid accusations. Instead, she cried, "Someone's been hurt! There on the beach!" She pointed down the beach to where the stranger stood with his gruesome discovery. "Get help, a doctor and a wagon quickly!"

She purposely withheld any information about the man's true condition. Death wasn't a topic easily broached in polite society. And the Jekyll Island Club was, without a doubt, the epitome of polite society.

"Come on, men! We must tell the others!" shouted an over-excited Randolph Patterson as he spurred his horse. From the back of his rearing horse, he commanded, "Tifton, leave this beach immediately with your chaperone, Miss Goodwin. This is no place for a lady!"

Never one to be ordered about, Tifton Rose Baldwin pointedly ignored him. Instead, she encouraged the men to return to the club. "Hurry! A man needs help! Get help!" she repeated.

The urgency in her voice rather than Randolph Patterson's shouting brought about immediate action among the young men present. They spurred their horses and bounded over the dunes in the direction of the Jekyll Island Club.

Once they were gone, Margaret Maurice put her horse close to Tifton's and asked, "You didn't really speak to a strange man on the beach, did you?"

Tifton Rose sighed at the unfairness of the world. Knowing that her reputation would be besmirched if she admitted that she spoke a total of two dozen words with a stranger. She bit back her anger at how speaking with a stranger outweighed finding a dead body on the beach. She chose an oblique answer to Margaret's question.

"No, not really."

Realizing that they weren't going to learn anything else from Tifton, the women chose to return to the club at a much more sedate pace. Torn between returning to the stranger on the beach and risking another encounter with the dead body on the otherwise pristine beach, Tifton Rose hesitated. Above her, seagulls swirled in the sky and cried piercingly as if they, too, recognized that something was amiss on the beach that day. As she left the beach, Tifton Rose glanced over her shoulder at the distant figure standing alone with his unpleasant burden. She shivered. Randolph Patterson was right. This was no place for a lady. Reluctantly, she turned back to her companions and fell into line behind the other women as they made the slow trek back to the club stables.

Chapter 2
Burke

"Anarchist! I tell you the man's an anarchist!" shouted Mr. Rawlins, a self-made man with a wife and three daughters.

"Keep your voice down! Do you want everyone to hear you?" asked Mr. Maurice. A well-respected member of the Jekyll Island Club, his words carried weight with the men present. Charles Maurice, one of the club's original members, took a deep interest in the welfare of the Jekyll Island Club. He was none too pleased about the presence of a dead man on the beach this morning.

"There may be others!" said Ernest Grob, the club's superintendent. He was a conscientious man who ran the Jekyll Island Club like a large country estate. The safety and well-being of the club's guests was paramount to him.

"He may not be working alone!" Frederic Baker, the owner of Solterra cottage, had good reason to be concerned. President McKinley would soon be a guest in his home. "We must protect the president!"

"We need to protect our families!" said Gordon McKay, at seventy, the club's oldest member, pointed out a concern that was foremost in most men's minds at that moment. A logical and talented inventor, McKay had made his fortune during the Civil War. He created, built, patented, and sold a machine that forever changed the process of stitching boots and shoes.

"We need to increase our patrols!" said Superintendent Grob.

"We must make sure that there are no others. Anarchists usually work alone, but that might not be the case this time." Mr. Rawlins voice was high-pitched with excitement.

"How do we know the man is an anarchist? We haven't even viewed the body yet." J. P. Morgan's authoritative voice cut through the noise and confusion. Everyone grew silent and nodded their head in agreement. To disagree with the powerful financier, was something few would dare to do.

Though Burke had never met the man, J.P. Morgan, with his distinctive nose, round face, and white mustache, was easily identifiable. The financier, standing quietly to the side, exuded authority and intelligence.

"All we know is what this gentleman has told us, which so far is very little." Morgan frowned and turned his piercing stare toward the stranger. "I don't believe I know you, sir."

Burke Thayer stepped forward and extended his hand toward J.P. Morgan. "Burke Thayer, Captain, United States Navy, lately attached to the Battleship Maine."

At the mention of the battleship, nearly prayerful murmurs rippled through the crowd. "Remember the Maine."

The Maine. The worst catastrophe outside of war ever to occur in a decade full of catastrophes. The sinking of the Battleship Maine in Havana Harbor had touched nearly everyone and paved the way to a declaration of war with Spain. It wasn't supposed to happen.

In January of 1898, riots had broken out throughout Cuba. In an attempt to win independence from Spain, Cuban revolutionaries resorted to guerrilla warfare. The Cuban cause generated much sympathy in the United States. The battleship, Maine, with its crew of 354 men, arrived in early February with the task of safeguarding United States interests in its southern neighbor. Secretary of the Navy, John D. Long, insisted that the Maine had been sent to Havana Harbor on a friendly call. The Spanish officials were not so sure.

On February 15, 1898, an explosion rocked the ship. Severely damaged, it quickly sank, taking the lives of 266 men with her. Of the ninety-four survivors, only sixteen were uninjured.

Naturally, such an unprovoked act of terrorism launched a passionate response against both anarchists and Spain. On March 28, a United States Naval Court of Inquiry blamed the sinking of the Maine on a submerged Spanish mine. Less than a month later, on April 25, the United States declared war on Spain. The hugely popular president, William McKinley, sided with American Imperialists and declared that the United States had an obligation to assume the responsibility for the "welfare of an alien people."

Mercifully, the war with Spain had been short, concluding with the signing of the Treaty of Paris on December 10, 1898. Despite winning the war, tempers in the United States, and in particular, the men present in the Jekyll Island Club stable, remained touchy about the subjects of American imperialism, colonies, and annexing the Philippines.

After a respectful moment, Burke handed J.P. Morgan a letter of introduction. "I was sent by the United States government to provide protection for President McKinley while he is visiting Jekyll Island." Actually, that wasn't strictly true and Burke knew it. Though his physical injuries had healed, emotionally Burke Thayer was a troubled man. Recently, the Navy assigned him to protect the President whenever he traveled. To say that the Navy foisted Burke on the members of the Jekyll Island Club would state his position on the island more accurately.

"Ah, yes. Captain Thayer." J.P. Morgan looked pained when he realized who Burke was. The financier had been one of the more outspoken members against accepting Burke into their tightly knit island society. However, the great man rose to the occasion and said politely, "I understand that you acquitted yourself very well during the sinking of the Maine." J.P. Morgan's steely eyes looked carefully at Burke as if searching for signs of injury.

Let him look, thought Burke angrily. People often stared when they met him and learned of his connection to the Maine. One of the few survivors of the disaster, he often wanted to escape the glare of publicity. He had learned to keep his left hand behind his back to hide his burns. He also wore his hair unfashionably long to hide the wounds at the hairline at the back of his neck. His taciturn expression hid the deeper, emotional scars and discouraged intimacy or even friendship. Instead of responding to Morgan's comment, he said stiffly, "Thank you for your concern. I have fully recovered."

"Please, tell me, Captain Thayer, what were you doing on the beach this morning?" J.P. Morgan asked imperturbably, matching Burke's aloofness with a coolness of his own. "I had assumed that you would meet with the club directors before exploring the island."

The rebuke the words carried rang in Burke's ears. However, he was ready for such a question. He was well aware that he had over-stepped the boundaries. He had chosen to break protocol because he wanted to get to know the island and its strengths and weaknesses before attending what was bound to be a long, drawn-out meeting with the Jekyll Island Club board. His desire to always know the lay of the land before taking on a task was what had saved his life on the Maine. After a few hours spent exploring Havana, he had reached the ship's side just as it exploded. He had been hurled into the water by the force of the explosion. Flying debris struck him in multiple places. The critical documents that he had been commissioned to deliver to the Cuban government lay decomposing on the bottom of the Havana harbor.

Burke forced a small self-deprecating smile onto his face and said, "The ferry from Brunswick arrived early this morning. Since I had some time before my meeting with the Jekyll Island Club board, I reasoned that a knowledge of the island would help me with my undertaking. I borrowed a horse from the stables and went for a ride. Naturally, I didn't expect to make such an unpleasant discovery."

"I understand that a young woman was present," frowned Mr. Maurice. With four daughters, he understood the importance of maintaining social proprieties.

"Yes. Fortunately, I was able to turn her back to her companions before she saw anything," Burke lied to shield the reputation of the young lady.

"Yes, the weaker sex must be protected," harrumphed Mr. Rawlins. He was naturally very upset about the proximity of his daughters to the deceased. Though they had not gone anywhere near the body, they had invented lurid stories about their experience. He was as much annoyed by their behavior as he was by the inconvenience of a dead man being found on the island.

"This is the man that the board hired to provide extra protection for President McKinley during his visit?" asked Gordon McKay disdainfully. The inventor's eyes raked over the thirty-five-year-old Burke, taking in his disheveled appearance and his unfashionably long dark hair sprinkled with gray.

Burke withstood the inspection calmly. He could do nothing about his hat which the brisk wind had whisked away while at the beach. Though he had taken the time to shake the sand out of his jacket, he knew some still remained. He also knew that, barring a return to his room, nothing could be done about his surf dampened pantlegs or his waterlogged boots. He took comfort in the fact that he didn't care what others thought about him. Actually, it had been quite a while since he had cared about anything.

"Gentlemen, gentlemen, if I may have your attention." J.P. Morgan waited until the men around him quieted down. He addressed the larger audience who had not heard the words exchanged between himself and Thayer. "As you are aware, things have not proceeded as planned this morning. Therefore, I would like to take a moment to explain how things stand with Captain Thayer and to learn more about his discovery."

A few men murmured agreement. Most patiently waited to hear what else the wealthy financier would say.

"The board decided some weeks ago that President McKinley should be provided with extra protection while visiting our island. Anarchists have been very active recently. Though the president will be accompanied by his own secret service men, we, that is the Jekyll Island Club board, thought it wise to engage the services of Captain Thayer." He nodded toward Burke. "Captain Thayer comes highly recommended from the Department of the Navy where he has been on special assignment for several months. We expect all of you and your families to welcome him to the Jekyll Island Club." Morgan's penetrating eyes swept the room. Though it was unthinkable for the very wealthy to rub shoulders with a mere naval Captain, no dissenting voice was heard.

"Good. Captain, I expect you to conduct yourself with dignity and appropriate deportment while you are a guest here on the island. I also expect you to resolve this current situation quickly and quietly." He gestured to the body covered by a blanket and resting in a wagon.

"Yes, sir," answered Burke politely with a slight nod of his head. Privately, Burke wondered if he would be successful fulfilling either command. Murder was a messy business and this was murder. Someone had deliberately destroyed the man's face before dumping his body in the surf. He had his reasons for this surmise; however, he wasn't ready to share them with anyone just yet.

So instead of saying anything more, he waited patiently until J.P. Morgan chose to speak again.

"Captain Thayer, of all of us, you have had the greatest opportunity to study the dead man. What are your conclusions? Is the man an anarchist like Mr. Rawlins claims?"

"Of course, he is an anarchist!" protested Mr. Rawlins. "With his dark hair and swarthy complexion, he looks like one."

Burke waited for someone to ask the obvious question. He didn't have to wait long.

"Mr. Rawlins, when did you have the chance to examine the body?" asked Mr. Cyrus Hall McCormick of McCormick Tractor. "Even Dr. Martin has not yet had the opportunity." McCormick named the physician who attended club members during their stay on the island.

Dr. Martin, who was present, made a small gesture of agreement.

Mr. Rawlins opened his mouth and shut it multiple times before stepping back out of the circle of men surrounding the blanket shrouded body resting in the bed of the small delivery wagon.

"Well, that is neither here nor there. As unpleasant as this will be, it is time that we examine the body." J.P. Morgan gestured to the wagon.

Burke moved forward and pulled the blanket from the dead man's face. Several of the men present brought handkerchiefs swiftly to their mouths. The someone had done a thorough job of erasing the man's face. All that was left was a pulpy mess.

The men in the barn took one look at the body in the wagon bed and spoke all at once.

"He had no face!" Superintendent Grob choked out the words.

"Who is he?" asked Mr. Rawlins, obviously perturbed.

"How could we possibly know? His face is gone," said Mr. Maurice.

"What do you think, Dr. Martin?" asked J.P. Morgan.

Before answering the man's question, Dr. Martin took the opportunity to introduce himself. "Many of you don't know me. I am Dr. Thomas Martin. I am taking the place of Dr. Merrill this season. Dr. Merrill has been unavoidably detained in Rhode Island."

"What is your professional opinion, doctor?" asked Mr. Rawlins.

Dr. Martin took a quick look at the body. "I don't have much experience with the damage that can be caused by a body's immersion in salt water, however, I am fairly confident when I say that this man's face was scrubbed away by the sand as it rolled in the incoming tide." Dr. Martin reached over and pulled the blanket back over what was left of the man's face.

Murmurs of agreement drifted through the crowd. Others began to chime in with their own opinions.

Instead of joining in on the discussion, Burke focused on the task at hand. He knew he would only have a few moments to gather information before being interrupted. He lifted a corner of the blanket and studied the remains that lay before him in the wagon. Much of what he could see now he had already seen at the beach, though closer inspection revealed that the man's face had been crushed with a heavy blunt object. The movement of the surf against the sand had only managed to soften the edges, rather like what sandpaper does to a piece of lumber. The sea had also washed away any clues as to whether or not the damage to the man's face had occurred before or after death. Burke knew that the critical question was: why did the killer want to keep the man's identity a secret?

Sadly, it was his experience on the battleship Maine that enabled Burke to make such judgements. Despite being injured himself, he had assisted in the rescue and later, the burial of his fellow crew members.

Some of the bodies, torn apart by the explosion had to be carried in baskets to get them ashore. Others were brought to the beach by the tide. An unfortunate few were blown into oblivion by the blast, their bodies never recovered. Even in death, his fellow seamen taught him the difference between man-wrought horrors and those caused by nature.

As to whether or not the man was an anarchist, Burke had opinions on that, too. He examined the fabric of the man's suit and shirt, and the quality of his shoes. Efficiently, he withdrew the contents of the pockets; a silver pocket watch which no longer ticked, a soggy first-class, round-trip railroad ticket for New York, a handful of change and a few sodden dollar bills, a once white handkerchief with no monogram, a pair of binoculars, and a small box compass.

Around him, the men continued to speak.

"Why would an anarchist carry a compass?"

"Or a pair of binoculars?"

"To find his way around the island, of course."

Mr. Rawlins stroked his goatee before speaking. "A boat probably dropped him off. He must have planned to swim ashore and hide on the island until President McKinley arrives."

Suddenly tired of useless and patently incorrect suppositions, Burke spoke decisively. "Swam ashore planning to stay in the wilds of the island for three days in order to kill the president? Not very likely."

"I don't like your tone, sir," protested Mr. Rawlins.

"I mean no offence. My tone has nothing to do with it," responded Burke. Privately, he knew that it did. His tone suggested his fatigue, his lack of tolerance for time-wasting activities, his general withdrawal from the world. Anyone who listened could hear it. The explosion of the Maine had exploded his patience with life, too.

Realizing that he had an audience, Burke continued, "Consider what the gentleman said. According to him, our man swam ashore fully dressed in a business suit and dress shoes but without any supplies. He plans on hiding on an island full of alligators, mosquitos, and wild boar for three days. After that time, he intends to murder President McKinley. With what? What weapon is our man going to use to kill the president? No weapons were found on the body."

"He could have brought his gun or dynamite on shore and hidden it," protested Mr. Maurice.

"And then gone back into the water to continue swimming?" asked Burke with a weary sigh. "Here are two additional questions to consider. What condition would the man's clothing and personal appearance be in after spending three days hiding out in the woods? Who would let such a scruffy individual near the president?"

Despite his obvious lack of enthusiasm, Burke noted that J.P. Morgan was watching him with approval in his eyes. This startled Burke. He felt a sudden urge to do a good job—to not let J.P. Morgan down.

Chapter 3
Tiffy Rose

"Tifton Rose Baldwin, what will people say?" exclaimed her mother, Henrietta Baldwin, after learning the role her daughter played in the discovery of a body on the beach that morning. "Finding a dead body floating in the surf! Speaking with a man on the beach! A complete stranger, I might add. Unchaperoned!" Henrietta, Etta to her friends, wrung her hands. "I know you haven't been out in society very much, Tifton, however, even you know the basics of comporting oneself like a lady. I honestly don't know which is worse—finding a body or your lack of a chaperone!"

"Mother, it isn't as if I went out searching for a body or a man. Don't forget, my chaperone and my friends—friends that you approve of—were nearby," protested Tiffy Rose.

Etta Baldwin, a pretty, feminine woman with a surprisingly strong will, raised a forefinger at her errant daughter. "Don't sass me, young lady."

"No ma'am." Tiffy Rose back-pedaled and apologized. "I'm sorry."

Mrs. Baldwin wrung her hands in despair. "I did so hope that we would be accepted as Jekyll Island Club members. You have blighted our chances and we've only been here a few days! How could you?" she wailed.

Her mother was quiet for a few moments, as she studied the state of affairs from all angles in hopes of finding a way to rectify the situation before it got any worse.

The moments of silence gave Tiffy Rose time to gather her rebellious thoughts. What had she done wrong? The only thing she was guilty of was allowing her horse to wander away from the others. Tiffy Rose hadn't wanted to participate in the splashing in the surf. Despite it being mid-March in Southern Georgia, the ocean water was cold, especially after the previous evening's violent thunderstorm. Besides, the Atlantic Ocean had captured her attention.

She risked a glance at her mother. Tiffy Rose could almost see the steam coming out of her ears. Her mother's next words came out with the hint of a hiss.

"Tifton Rose Baldwin, I am surprised at you. You know how hard your father and I have worked to be accepted in society. You know what it means to us to be here at the Jekyll Island Club. And what about Randolph Patterson Chatsworth III? What will he and his family think of us? Don't you understand how important it is to conduct yourself with care when out in society?"

Of course, Tiffy Rose knew how important it was to behave in public. How could she forget? Her parents were always drumming it into her how they must rise above their humble beginnings. That she must make an advantageous marriage went almost without saying. The fact that she had charmed her way into an 'understanding' with the eldest son of a prosperous and well-connected family from Atlanta went a long way to support her mother's hopes for the future. It was due to Randolph Patterson Chatsworth's invitation that Tiffy Rose and her family were on Jekyll Island. His parents had proposed the Baldwins for membership in the Jekyll Island Club.

Raised by her father to think for herself, Tiffy Rose was remarkably independent for a woman her age. Despite, or perhaps because of her education at Bryn Mawr, the premier university for women, she wasn't really sure about her place in society or her plans for the future. She was even less sure of the marriage market and its resulting unions. She loved her parents and tried to do as she was told, however, the idea of marrying the man that they had chosen for her, Randolph Patterson Chatsworth III, didn't sit well with her willful nature. To put it mildly, she was a very confused young lady of twenty.

As for the people she had met so far on Jekyll Island, she found herself in awe of these individuals who had amassed vast fortunes through their own hard work, motivation, and initiative. At twenty, Tiffy Rose had yet to accomplish anything. She felt that she should at least have one or two small successes to her credit by now. She had no idea what kind of successes were appropriate, but she knew that she should have some. Tiffy Rose sighed with something akin to despair over her predicament.

"Don't sigh, Tifton. Try to remember that your father's family, as well as mine have worked hard to make a place for ourselves in this world. Both of our families managed to create a comfortable lifestyle for themselves. Unfortunately, the Civil War changed all that. We are very fortunate that your father's father came up with a solution."

Her mother looked over at Tifton Rose and saw that her daughter was listening.

Tiffy Rose didn't really need to listen to her mother. She knew the story by heart. Rather than accept a life of poverty, after the war, her father's father—brave man that he was—traveled north looking for work. Instead, he landed in southwestern Ohio where the religious group known as the Shakers made their home near Lebanon. It was there that James Baldwin learned how to easily plane wood. The Shakers had developed a process and the machinery to support it that enabled logs to be sawn consistently into uniform planks of wood with smooth sides and square corners. Up until then, logs were hand-hewn into boards with something that resembled a flat surface on one side.

Excited by his discovery, James Baldwin returned to Georgia, bought a sawmill, and began to implement process improvements and install updated machinery to make this relatively new product. His timing was right. The South was in desperate need of lumber in order to rebuild. These smooth flat boards were so much easier to produce that they cost much less. More productivity plus lower costs equaled increased sales and thus, increased profits. Baldwin's business grew by leaps and bounds. One sawmill soon became a dozen. Amassing a small fortune for himself and his family, James married a distant relative of the wealthy timber and sawmill family, the Tifts. His son, Franklin, married the socially ambitious Henrietta Clark. Tifton Rose was the product of that union.

Wanting to strengthen the fragile Tift family connection, Etta Baldwin named her only daughter Tifton Rose, after the family and the Georgia State flower, the Cherokee Rose. She followed up this wise move by sending a birth announcement to the Tift family patriarch.

Her forward-thinking strategy must have worked because the Baldwins began to be invited to Tift family gatherings. As her father became a successful merchant in his own right, the number of invitations increased. Believing that the people who really made money were merchants, Franklin Baldwin established a chain of stores that sold nearly every tool a man needed to get a job done—any job. Baldwin's Hardware Stores were now present in nearly every Georgia town of reasonable size. While not on the merchandizing scale of the 'Merchant Prince', Marshall Field, in Chicago, Tifton's father had done quite well for himself. Now comfortably well off, the Baldwins hoped that their application for the Jekyll Island Club would be approved.

Tifton Rose Baldwin sat before her outraged mother and held her tongue. She knew better than to defend herself. She knew that silence and forbearance were the best defense against her mother's tirade. Tifton Rose knew that regardless of her own opinions in the matter, any show of defiance would lead to certain disaster. Instead of responding to her mother's well-deserved tongue-lashing, she fervently prayed that this incident would not result in her family being expelled from this wonderful island.

Her mother's voice receded into the background as Tifton Rose daydreamed about Jekyll Island. As soon as she stepped off the ferry from Brunswick, Tiffy Rose had succumbed to the island's potent charms. Jekyll Island had bombarded all of her senses at once. Orange trees perfumed the air. Bright Cherokee roses bloomed everywhere. Stately palms stood tall and erect, contrasting with the twisted limbs of the live oak trees. Spanish moss hung from the live oaks whose leaves whispered secrets as they swayed in the breeze. And there was nearly always a breeze to keep the heat and bugs away.

With the advent of the Jekyll Island Club, man had made an impact on mostly untouched Jekyll Island. The clubhouse featured many elegant guest rooms which were available on a first-come, first-serve basis to visiting club members. The club facilities were the finest available and included a new golf course and new tennis courts. Six large cottages owned by individual club members—Brown, Furness, Maurice, Baker, Fairbank, McKay—lined the waterfront. Set back across a green sweep of lawn sat *San Souci*, a large building containing six apartments. To Tiffy Rose, the island was nearly perfect.

Chapter 4
Burke

"Excuse me, Captain Thayer. I believe that Mr. Morgan and the rest of the Jekyll Island Club board are in the smoking room at the end of the hall. Mr. Morgan asks that you join him there. The room is right down this hallway. Shall I bring you a drink before dinner?" The steward led the way out of the lobby and down the wide carpeted hallway graced with large mirrors.

Reaching their destination, the steward pointed to the doorway of a tastefully appointed meeting room. Men sat in comfortable leather chairs scattered around the perimeter of the room. Cigar smoke hung thick in the air. The conversation in the room came to an abrupt halt when Burke stepped through the doorway and onto the plush rug. All eyes focused on him. He stared back, unfazed by their perusal.

"J.P., you certainly chose a cocky one," intoned one of the men, chomping on his cigar.

"I prefer to believe that Captain Thayer is quietly confident," responded Morgan with a slightly amused smile.

Burke took time to study the faces of each of the twelve men in the room. He could see the self-assurance in their eyes. These men were at the pinnacle of their careers. It was they who were confident—they who were powerful. Burke knew that he currently lacked both confidence and ability. This realization was enough to make him want to jump on the next ferry to the mainland.

Willing himself not to be intimidated by so much power concentrated in one small space, Burke stepped deeper into the room. "Good evening, Mr. Morgan. I hope I have not kept you and the board waiting."

J.P. Morgan smiled as he acknowledged Burke's decorum in handling the situation. "Thank you, Captain Thayer. I am glad that you find our hospitality pleasing."

Both men bowed slightly to each other.

Morgan continued, "May I introduce you to some of our club members. I am certain that you have met many of them at one time or another during the day, however, due to the circumstances, proper introductions were overlooked."

Burke followed J.P. Morgan around the smoke-filled room and shook hands with each man present. Most of their faces, if not their names, were familiar to him by now. He had met many of them during his investigation of the murder. Without the benefit of a formal introduction to give him legitimate standing, Burke had felt ill-at-ease. The meeting this evening would go a long way to lessen his discomfort. He felt his confidence increase.

"So, tell us, Captain Thayer, what do you think happened today out at the beach?" asked Charles Lanier.

Burke felt like Daniel in the lions' den. These men were every bit as powerful as lions and they were just as ruthless. Burke cleared his throat uncomfortably. "I spent the better part of the day seeking clues to the man's identity. As I am sure you all know, his face was destroyed so other methods must be used to determine who he was. Please allow me to summarize what we know.

"The victim was a white male approximately five feet eight inches tall. He was nearly bald. What hair he had was dark, straight and well-barbered. He wasn't a young man. His dark hair had flecks of gray in it. He was overweight with a noticeable paunch. His suit and shirt are made of good material and are well-constructed. The contents of his pockets revealed nothing of interest besides a pocket watch, a round-trip first-class train ticket to New York, binoculars, and a small compass." Burke did not mention that he had obtained permission from the Glynn County sheriff to keep the watch when the victim and his belongings were transported to the mainland.

"Have you been able to draw any conclusions from this?" asked Charles Lanier, the club president.

"While his identity still eludes us, I think we can eliminate the theory that he is an anarchist," proposed Burke.

His statement met with incredulity. The men jumped to their feet, protesting loudly.

"Of course, the man is an anarchist!" cried Mr. Rawlins.

"Explain yourself!" said Mr. Maurice.

"Who else could he be?" asked Dr. Martin. The clean-shaven, raven-haired man reached up and stroked his lips as if expecting to find a mustache there.

"How could you possibly come to such a faulty conclusion?" asked Mr. Barnes.

"And this is the man you hired to protect President McKinley? What were you thinking, J.P.?" asked Mr. Baker, the owner of Solterra.

"The same could be asked of you, Captain Thayer. What were you thinking when you came to this conclusion?" asked Mr. Barnes, his tone unfriendly. "If he isn't an anarchist, then who is he?"

Finally, thought Burke, a sensible question. He waited for the hullaballoo to calm down before he ventured to explain himself. He caught J.P. Morgan's eye and with a crisp nod from the older gentleman, received the man's permission to speak.

"I think that based on the man's age and his clothing we can draw certain conclusions."

"I'd like to hear you explain yourself and your crazy conclusions," said Mr. Maurice.

Burke went on as if the man had not interrupted. "Let's consider the victim's age first. The amount of gray in his hair tells us that he was not a young man. His paunch tells us that he was regularly well-fed. Combined with his rather flaccid muscles, it also tells us that he did not partake in regular exercise. Except for calluses on his right index and middle fingers—the type that accompany the regular use of writing utensils—his hands were soft. They were certainly not the hands of a working man."

"An anarchist can be anyone!" exclaimed Mr. Barnes.

"Yes, they can," agreed Burke. "However, rarely is an anarchist so well-dressed. It is also important to remember that the murderer struck the man hard enough in the face to erase his identity. Would someone have taken the trouble to do that if the man were an anarchist?"

The men grumbled their reluctant agreement with this comment.

"Captain Thayer, you have explained what he is not. Can you answer the question: what or who do you think he is?" asked Charles Lanier.

"A prosperous, middle-aged, banker or financier. He could even be some sort of government employee."

Burke could have sworn that someone in the room took an involuntary breath. Someone in the room knew something about the dead man. Though he glanced swiftly around the room, Burke couldn't identify which of the men had given himself away.

Chapter 5
Tiffy Rose

Tiffy Rose fiddled with the lemon-yellow bows on the front of her pale-yellow satin off-the-shoulder evening gown. She twirled the ends of the ribbons around with her fingers. Dinner could be such a trying time. There were so many rules of etiquette to remember: which fork to use, which wine to drink with what foods, which topic of conversation was acceptable at the dinner table and which was not. She had accumulated such a large amount of trivial information that Tiffy Rose felt as if her head would burst.

Mrs. Eunice Chatsworth, Randolph Patterson's mother, sat next to Tifton Rose at dinner. Tiffy Rose found her rather intimidating. Her domineering personality combined with her preoccupation with wealth and family lineage made her difficult to cope with sometimes. Tiffy would have preferred to sit next to her mother as she normally did. Her mother was smaller and less imposing than the formidable Mrs. Chatsworth. This did not mean that her mother was weak or unsure of herself. Tiffy Rose inherited her brave approach to life as well as her generosity of spirit from her mother.

Tiffy Rose tried hard to follow the conversation that her father and Mr. Randolph Patterson Chatsworth II, known to all as Patterson, were carrying on. She knew her mother expected her to pay attention. She tried to focus on her father's words, but the hustle and bustle of the Jekyll Island Club dining room was too interesting to ignore. Aware that her mother's eyes were upon her, Tiffy Rose struggled to concentrate on what the men were saying.

While his son sat quietly by his side, Patterson was deeply immersed in one of his favorite topics: the rise of American businessmen. In his booming voice, he pontificated. "The United States is still a relatively young country when compared to nations like France and England. Even after one hundred years, we continue to test the meaning of democracy and try to understand what it means to be a republic. Many people living in the States came to the country penniless—in search of the American dream."

Tiffy Rose's father added to the conversation. "I read recently in the *New York World* newspaper that in this decade alone, as many as nine million people came drawn here by the opportunity to make something of themselves—to live a better life—a life that includes enough wealth to never be hungry again. That's exactly what my grandparents did. My wife's parents immigrated, too."

Nodding his head in approval, Patterson, a hardworking man in his late-forties, gathered steam as he continued his speech. "Men like Rockefeller, Morgan, and Vanderbilt used their intelligence, nerve, ambition, passion, and belief in their own abilities to make something of themselves. Some people say that their chief characteristic is ambition."

Franklin Baldwin managed to slip a sentence in while Patterson Chatsworth took a bite of his meal. "Personally, I believe their important characteristic is their strong work ethic and how hard they applied themselves at a very early age."

Nodding his head in agreement, Patterson picked up his train of thought and continued. "For the Vanderbilts it all began with steamships. Cornelius Vanderbilt started with one steamship and in time owned so many ships that he was given the honorary title of 'Commadore'. Then, in the middle of his career, he sold all of his steamships and invested in railroads! Can you imagine selling the very thing that made you wealthy in the first place and then investing everything you had into a new, untried, business?" he asked.

Mr. Baldwin jumped in with an answer. "Only a man sure of his own vision of the future would have the nerve—the audacity—to do so. Remember for these men, failure is not an option."

Before continuing, Randolph Patterson Chatsworth II made eye contact with his son to make sure he was listening. Randolph Patterson dropped the spoon he was fiddling with and sat up straighter in his chair. Frowning, his father continued. "What a leap of faith! What a risk-taker the Commadore must have been. Imagine his confidence in his view of the future and how to adapt to it. Vanderbilt recognized long before the rest of us that railroads would provide the nation with cheap, efficient shipping. Do you agree with me, Randolph Patterson?"

"Yes, Father. He must have been quite a man," answered Randolph Patterson, with a marked lack of interest. He looked down at the unfinished meal on his plate.

Barely hiding his disdain for his son, Patterson turned his attention to Franklin Baldwin, who was at least an appreciative audience. "His son

William is a member of Jekyll Island Club. He has continued with his father's investments in railroads."

Mr. Baldwin sipped his drink and mused, "Yes, that is how the money-making began—first steamships, then railroads, followed by oil, then steel, and most recently, electricity. It makes you wonder what will be the next big thing. Do you realize that it is through the efforts of these men that the United States has changed from an agrarian society to an industrial one in a matter of a mere fifty years?"

"If I hadn't lived through it, I wouldn't believe it." Patterson focused on his food which to this point he had largely ignored.

"Please, Mr. Chatsworth, tell us about other members of the club," Tiffy Rose ventured, trying hard to at least pretend to be interested in what the men were saying.

Randolph Patterson Chatsworth II gave Tifton Rose an approving smile. "Of course, my dear. I would be delighted. We may see John D. Rockefeller here tonight. He made his money in oil—kerosene oil for lamps. He named his company Standard Oil. He got the idea for the name because his employees found a way to ensure high quality kerosene with each and every can purchased by the consumer. He set a standard for the industry. Get it? Standard Oil. Very clever of him, wouldn't you say?"

"Oh, yes." Tiffy stifled a yawn only to feel the sharp kick of her mother's shoe under the table. She bit back a cry of protest.

Unaware of the brief altercation between the two women, Chatsworth II continued his lecture. "Andrew Carnegie made his money in steel. He, Rockefeller, and Vanderbilt have some sort of on-going feud. Something about trying to run each other out of business. From what I understand, Carnegie refused to join the Jekyll Island Club. Instead, the Carnegie family bought all or part of Cumberland Island, just to the south of here. They plan to build a mansion on the island. Can you imagine owning an island?" he asked.

"It boggles the mind, dear," answered Eunice Chatsworth.

Abruptly, Franklin Baldwin entered the conversation. "Time. That's the important thing. We are all given twenty-four hours in a day. It's how we use the time allotted to us that matters. Time is out most valuable resource, squandering it is unacceptable. Remember that, Tifton. Time. Time must never be wasted."

"Yes, Father. I will," she promised.

Patterson took the reins of the conversation again. "We live in an amazing time. Despite pockets of dissent, the depression following the financial panic of 1893, and the Spanish American War, prosperity has returned to the United States. Look around us! Productivity is up. Consumer prices are down. New products are coming onto the market every day. Domestic comfort has improved, as has personal hygiene. Affordable electricity and telephones are changing the way people live and work. Can you imagine a life without the telephone and electricity? Look at the changes to public transportation. Tram lines, omnibuses, and underground subways are now common in every major city. The United States is growing, both in production capabilities and population."

"Why is there no electricity on Jekyll Island?" asked Tiffy Rose innocently. She looked pointedly at the kerosene lamps set on wall sconces.

Randolph Patterson grinned suddenly when he realized that her question had caught his father unprepared.

Frowning at her, the elder Chatsworth recovered quickly. "Generators are required to produce electricity. Very expensive generators, I would imagine. The time will come for a change. The time will come, my dear, the time will come."

"Perhaps it is because Mr. Rockefeller is a member of the Jekyll Island Club. Everyone knows he makes his money selling kerosene. Perhaps he is standing in the way of progress," said Tiffy Rose, showing that she was more aware of current events than her parents or the Chatsworths suspected.

Patterson Chatsworth chose to ignore her comment and return to his original topic. "As I was saying, despite the unprecedented population increase brought about by the influx of more than nine million immigrants, there still exists tremendous opportunities for those willing to work hard."

Patterson Chatsworth paused to consider who he would speak about next. Having made his choice, he continued. "Take for instance, J.P. Morgan. Born into the banking business, he followed his father's footsteps and went into the banking and finance industry. After making his name in those areas, he decided to build his own empire. They say Morgan thinks of the future in terms of decades, not years. Suffice it to say, he has become a key player in the electrification of the United States. In 1882, his home was the first to be electrified. Never one to do things on a small scale, he had four hundred lightbulbs installed at his home on Madison Avenue in New York."

"Please excuse me for a few minutes, " said Randolph Patterson Chatsworth III. He rose and left the table without further explanation.

His parents exchanged glances that did not bode well for young Chatsworth when they got him alone later. Despite her ambivalent feelings about the man she was nearly betrothed to, Tiffy Rose longed to escape with him.

Tiffy Rose's father turned to his wife and said, "Etta, do you remember what it was like at the 1893 World's Columbian Exposition in Chicago? Remember when they threw the switch and 100,000 lights came on all at once? Remember how dark it was that night and then, suddenly, there was light?" Flushed with happy memories, he picked up his wife's hand and kissed it.

Etta blushed becomingly, enjoying her husband's attention. Despite their twenty-five years together, theirs was a loving relationship unlike so many wealthy couples whose marriages ended in divorce. She held onto his hand and said, "Yes, I do, dear. It was magical night."

"It certainly was," agreed her husband.

Tiffy Rose watched the loving interaction between her parents and yearned for someone to call her own. She craved a relationship like her parents had: trusting, respectful, and admiring. Above all, they loved each other and it showed in how they treated each other. Tiffy Rose vowed that her relationship with her future husband would be a loving one.

Once again, Patterson Chatsworth took command of the conversation. "Tifton, from what I understand, you have made the acquaintances of the Rawlins sisters and the Maurice sisters," said Patterson Chatsworth, addressing her directly.

Tiffy Rose's mind snapped back to the present. "Yes, sir, I have."

"What do you think of them?" he asked, genuinely curious.

"Our time together was short, but on first impression, I liked them all. They are friendly, well-read, and cultured young women."

"I am glad that you are meeting young women of quality here. Mr. Maurice is a very successful bridge builder. My colleagues tell me that he is a devoted family man. I know less about Mr. Rawlins. I believe he makes his money from oil wells." Patterson Chatsworth paused for a moment before adding in a low voice, "He is said to be quite ruthless in business."

Chapter 6
Burke

Burke entered the dining room with J.P. Morgan. He stopped dead in his tracks, overwhelmed by the elegant surroundings. It was as if he had stepped into a fantasy world. Tables adorned with crisp white linen tablecloths and comfortable cane-back armchairs were artfully arranged on the richly patterned carpet. Chairs were placed at the tables to accommodate two, four, six, eight, or ten diners. Highly polished silver and crystal reflected the lights from the wall sconces. A large fireplace served as a focal point for the beautifully decorated room. Coffered ceilings and elegant light fixtures added to the diners' visual delight.

Against this backdrop of elegant furnishings, thick draperies, and glittering surfaces, powerful men and elegant women made conversation and ate gourmet food. Never in his life had Burke seen so many well-dressed patrons in one space—men in black-tie and women in beautiful gowns of satin and velvet. Never before had he seen so much impressive jewelry—bracelets coated in sapphires and diamonds, tortoiseshell combs covered in diamonds, long pearl necklaces with diamond clasps. Candlelight reflected off of the brilliant stones on every woman's jewelry, capturing every pinpoint of light and reflecting them back to the viewer. The effect was dazzling.

"Well, Captain Thayer, what do you think of our little rustic hideaway?" asked J.P. Morgan expansively.

Burke didn't quite know how to answer that question. Anything he said would reveal how limited his contact with extreme wealth had been up to this point in his life. His roots were deep in the Southern aristocracy, however, the war between the States had dramatically reduced his family's circumstances. Only the hidden proceeds from his father's days as a blockade runner during the Civil War kept them comfortably afloat.

"Very nice, sir. Very nice." Burke wished he had invested in a better evening suit. He felt underdressed in his serviceable black tie and tails that had been the height of fashion four years ago.

"Good, I am glad that you like it," said J.P. Morgan gruffly. "Tonight, you will be dining with me. I am sure that you will see many familiar faces. While several of our members have their own homes on the island, nearly everyone on the island takes their meals in the clubhouse. It is the best way to visit with friends."

Burke could imagine that all of these people on the island were friends or at least acquaintances. Just looking at them now, all gathered in the same room, he could see that they knew each other well and had much in common. They behaved toward each other in the comfortable manner that comes from long acquaintance. In many ways, the people in this room were like a large and extended family. They were contemporaries; all of similar age, experience, and expectations. And as such, they shared similar interests and lives.

Outwardly, they shared a certain resemblance in their attire and personal grooming. Dinner jackets cut from expensive cloth, snowy white shirt fronts and bow ties, elegant shoes, and gold accessories, mustaches, beards, or goatees. The women dressed in their finery in the latest style. Their hats, adorned with feathers, flowers, and fruit were works of art. Their jewelry glowed and sparkled in the light from hundreds of candles.

Although they were physically unalike, it was as if they had been made from the same mold. They were men from the same background united by shared beginnings of poverty and strife. These were robust, self-made men with strong competitive streaks who turned their own ingenuity and hard work into vast fortunes. Their well-dressed wives, sons, and daughters were emblems of their wealth.

Burke didn't feel the need to express his thoughts to J.P. Morgan. The older man almost certainly knew this instinctively.

Chapter 7
Tiffy Rose

"Look Father, isn't that J.P. Morgan standing in the entrance to the dining room?" said Tiffy Rose when she recognized the financier. She caught her breath when she realized that the man standing behind the financier was the stranger from the beach.

For the first time in her life, Tifton Rose wished she was prettier than she appeared in the mirror above the fireplace that reflected her image. She wished she wore a lovelier dress. She wished she wasn't so tall and thin. She wished she possessed a softer, more demure manner. She wished that she wasn't an old maid of twenty. She wished her heart would stop beating so wildly in her chest at the sight of the stranger.

"Tifton Rose, are you alright?" asked her mother. Filled with concern, she laid her hand against her daughter's cheek. "You're all flushed. Perhaps you had better go to your room to lie down."

Tiffy Rose struggled to control her racing pulse.

"I'm fine, mama," Tiffy Rose managed to choke out. Truth be told, she wasn't fine. She was light-headed and breathless at the same time. She wanted to take her eyes off the mysterious stranger, but couldn't. Who was he? Why did she feel so weak in the knees? What was happening to her? She looked across the table at the empty seat. Perhaps more importantly, why didn't Randolph Patterson Chatsworth III make her feel this way? She didn't even know the name of this stranger, yet she felt flustered and unnerved just seeing him stand there looking very dashing in evening clothes. Did Randolph Patterson look good in evening clothes? Though she sat across the dinner table from him all evening, she hadn't formed an opinion. Perhaps it was her very familiarity with Randolph Patterson that made her long to know more about this attractive stranger. He appealed to her sense of adventure. By comparison, Randolph Patterson was the safe choice that her parents approved of.

Her betrothed chose that moment to reenter the dining room. For the briefest of moments, he stood next to the stranger. Tiffy Rose couldn't help but compare the two men. One was tall and rather well and strongly built. The other tall but not as athletic. One was dark and the other fair. She knew from experience that Randolph Patterson was not particularly unattractive or uninteresting. He was just Randolph. She did not know how charming or interesting the stranger was, but his pleasant yet remote face matched the detached manner that he had exhibited that morning. It was his very reticence—the mystery of him—that made her want to know more about him. She wondered what color his eyes were. She paused for a moment. Did she even know the color of Randolph Patterson's eyes? Had she ever known?

Randolph Patterson Chatsworth's eyes traveled around the room and came to rest on Tiffy Rose, surprising her. For some reason, she hadn't expected him to be looking for her. Randolph turned toward her with a smile on his square, clean-shaven face. His focus on her was so intense that he failed to see J.P. Morgan standing to the left of him. As Randolph Patterson advanced, Mr. Rawlins bumped into Randolph Patterson, jostling him. A collision became inevitable.

As Tiffy Rose watched the accident unfold in what seemed like slow motion, she wanted nothing more than to disappear. She should have agreed to her mother's suggestion to go lie down. A good lie down would be just the thing to stop her head from spinning. She began to think that her presence here on Jekyll Island was cursed.

Randolph Patterson struck J.P. Morgan with enough force to knock the banker off balance. As the two men collided, their bodies clipped the edge of a table, flipping plates, cutlery, and crystal glasses into the air. Both men clutched at each other trying to keep from falling. Instead, they fell to the floor accompanied by the noisy clatter of broken china and glass. There was a moment of complete and utter silence in the dining room. Tiffy Rose wished she could hide beneath the pristine white tablecloth or perhaps behind one of the columns that graced the elegant room.

The silence was broken by J.P. Morgan who snarled, "Unhand me you fool!" Morgan, mortified by his loss of dignity in a public setting, brushed bits of food from his otherwise pristine lapels. He swatted away Randolph Patterson's abject apologies.

Compelled by some sort of feeling of responsibility, Mr. and Mrs. Baldwin went to Morgan's aid. The social disaster had been their future son-in-law's fault and they felt it necessary to bear the consequences.

Embarrassed by the events unfolding before her, Tiffy Rose stood up abruptly only to become entangled in the train of her yellow satin gown. She heard the delicate fabric tear. She stumbled and began to fall. Her cry of alarm was cut short when she found herself safely caught in the arms of the stranger.

"Miss, I don't believe that your presence at this moment will serve any reasonable purpose. Why don't we go outside so that you may have time to recover your wits?"

Tiffy Rose wondered why she felt so protected—so safe in this man's arms. She wondered why she didn't fight to break free of his grip like any woman of her social standing should. She wondered about many things—except why she shouldn't go with him.

Before she realized what was happening, the stranger had whisked her out onto the quiet of the adjacent porch.

"Relax," he said as he gently placed her in a rocking chair on the veranda. "Take a moment to recover. That young man's less than graceful appearance tonight must have been upsetting to you." He smiled when he said those words, taking the sting out of them.

He stood behind her chair and gently rocked it. Tiffy Rose leaned her head back hoping to feel his presence. She wished she could stay like this—in the dark, being rocked gently, safe from the world with all of its expectations—forever. Slowly her sense of equilibrium returned. Even so, she couldn't think of a word to say. What was it about this stranger that caused her to turn shy and tongue-tied whenever she was in his presence? Tiffy Rose merely stared out at the moonlit marsh. The darkness on the veranda served to emphasize the brightly twinkling stars. After admiring them for several minutes, it occurred to Tiffy Rose that she had placed herself in a compromising situation yet again.

She leapt up out of the rocking chair, very nearly upsetting all three of them: the stranger, the chair, and herself. Once again, the stranger came to her aid. He put out a steadying hand and held onto her until she got her feet under herself. Standing straighter, she came to a very pleasant realization. That morning, with both of them on horseback, she hadn't realized how tall he was. Here was a man who more than matched her height of five feet, seven inches. Tiffy Rose sighed happily. Finally, she had found a man taller than she was. Next to him, she didn't feel like the Amazon the other girls at school had teased her about being. She smiled at the thought.

"There, that's better," he said, smiling back at her.

Tiffy Rose felt warmth rising from her toes. She could get used to his sudden smiles, his gentleness with her, and the way his eyes warmed whenever he looked at her. Her thoughts stopped rambling and she focused on his face. In the dim light, she could barely make out any details. Disturbed by his presence, she couldn't think of a single clever response. Fortunately, she was saved from having to reply by the arrival of the three Rawlins sisters.

"There you are, Tifton," exclaimed Alice. She wore her thick dark hair coiled tightly at the base of her head. The weight of it caused her head to tilt backward, giving her a condescending air.

Focused on Tifton, the sisters failed to notice the stranger standing in the deep shadows.

"Are you alright? We couldn't help but notice your swift departure after Mr. Chatsworth crashed into J.P. Morgan. Imagine knocking over someone that important!" Grace giggled with mock concern. "Clumsy of Randolph Patterson, wasn't it?"

"He's not clumsy. It was an accident," cried Alice coming to Randolph Patterson's defense.

"Oh, Alice, you are always standing up for Chatsworth. One would think that you would grow tired of defending him. Personally, I think he is a frightful bore. I am sorry Tifton. I know he is supposed to be your fiancé, but I do find Randolph Patterson to be a bore. He is so nice all the time. Who wants to live with someone who is nice all the time?" asked May, showing her youth. "How uninteresting."

"I know someone who wouldn't mind," began Grace gleefully.

"Be quiet, both of you," snapped Alice. She rapped her fan on her sister's arm with a sharp snap.

"Ouch!" Grace rubbed the spot where the fan had landed. Despite her long white gloves providing some protection, she would have a bruise tomorrow.

"Tifton, why did you come out on the porch alone? You never know who might be out here," cautioned May. "Just think about the man on the beach this morning! Father has been talking about him all day! No one knows anything about him! Not one single thing!"

"River pirates! Anarchists! Kidnappers! All sorts of unsavory characters surround us!" shivered Grace, the youngest of the three sisters.

"Hush, Grace. We're safe here on the island. There are guards both on land and at sea," countered her oldest sister, Alice. Not one to leave well enough alone, she admonished, "But, what Grace says is true, for the sake of your reputation, Tifton Rose, you shouldn't be out here alone!"

"I'm not alone," protested Tiffy Rose. The Rawlins sisters looked at her strangely. She spun around and realized that the stranger was nowhere to be seen.

Chapter 8
Burke

Burke returned to the dining room after leaving Miss Baldwin on the veranda with her friends. That morning on the beach, he had found her refreshing when he compared her with women closer to his own age of thirty-five. Tonight however, she was a distraction he didn't need. He searched the crowd for J.P. Morgan and his entourage but didn't find them. Unsure of the protocol for dining alone at this members-only club, uncharacteristically, Burke hesitated.

"Good evening, Captain Thayer. You missed quite a show. Randolph Chatsworth ran right into J.P. Morgan. Knocked him down. Upset a table at the same time. You can't imagine the mess. I thought our illustrious financier was going to blow his top. He gave Chatsworth a tongue-lashing that he isn't likely to forget. About time too. I never have liked that pompous youngster. He may come from money, but he hasn't got the business sense of his father and grandfather. Too bad."

Burke faced the talkative speaker. The man stood nearly as tall as Burke's own six feet. He had a pleasant face with rather small, narrow eyes. His graying hair was carefully brushed to hide a bald spot. The man wore a dinner jacket that failed to conceal the extra weight, the result of years of living and eating well. Burke had met Charles Rawlins that morning when they both confronted the specter of an anarchist who had invaded this special island. Despite his argumentative nature and his tendency to talk too much, Burke liked Rawlins. "Good evening, Mr. Rawlins." He shook the man's hand.

"Are you here to dine?"

"Yes, I was to have dinner with Mr. Morgan, however you know how that turned out. I am not sure what the protocol is for a guest dining alone. Would you be so kind as to assist me?"

"I'll do better than that. Why don't you join me and my family at our table? There is certainly room for one more. Come this way." Rawlins gestured to where a woman sat waving her white handkerchief in the air in front of her. "I see my wife signaling me."

"Captain Thayer, I would like you to meet my wife, Millicent Rawlins. And, these are my daughters; Alice, May, and Grace. Ladies, may I present Captain Burke Thayer, late of the battleship Maine."

"How do you do?" asked Burke politely. He wished that Rawlins had not mentioned the Maine. Any reference to the ship tended to bring about conversation that was truly unpleasant for him.

Mr. Rawlins continued with his introductions. "I've asked Captain Thayer to join us for dinner. He is J.P. Morgan's guest and, as you know, Mr. Morgan has chosen to return to his suite in *Sans Souci* after the unfortunate incident this evening."

"Won't you please sit down, Captain Thayer?" Millicent Rawlins asked politely. A socially adept woman, unexpected guests rarely flustered her.

"Thank you for allowing me to join you this evening,' responded Burke.

"Are you familiar with *San Souci*, Captain Thayer?" asked Mrs. Rawlins, when he was seated. "It is the elegant apartment building located across from the clubhouse proper."

"No, ma'am, I am not." Burke could tell that Mrs. Rawlins was a skilled hostess. It was as if she had practiced every motion and gesture. Every inflection of her pleasant voice was controlled and deliberate.

She continued Burke's initiation to the island. "Built in 1896, *Sans Souci* contains six separate, and if I may say so, very elegant apartments. They are owned by Joseph Pulitzer, Henry Hyde, John Rockefeller, Joseph Stickney, William Anderson, and James Scrymser. J.P. Morgan recently purchased one of the units. I am not sure which one he bought."

The mention of the great financier reminded Mrs. Rawlins of the evening's excitement. She sniffed. "What was Chatsworth thinking or perhaps he wasn't thinking? He's always been a clumsy boy. I can see that adulthood hasn't changed that about him."

"Now, Mama, don't be so hard on Mr. Chatsworth. He's just shy and nervous in public," said Charles Rawlins' oldest daughter, Alice.

"You're always defending Mr. Chatsworth," teased her sister, Grace. "If I didn't know better, I'd think you were sweet on him."

"Alice, now that Mr. Chatsworth's parents have arranged for him to marry Miss Tifton Rose Baldwin, you will have to find a new puppy to defend," added May, a dark-haired beauty of nineteen.

"Hush, all of you. Captain Thayer will think you have all lost your manners."

"But, it's true, Mama!" protested Grace, a pretty teenager dressed in a frothy mint green concoction of ribbons and lace.

"I said hush!" said Mrs. Rawlins sharply.

Actually, Burke was pleased to have their attention focused on someone else besides himself. He also found it interesting that Miss Baldwin was betrothed to Randolph Patterson Chatsworth III. Though he knew very little about either party to this engagement, he wondered what the attraction was. On the surface, Miss Baldwin was composed and solemn. Chatsworth on the other hand, didn't know a stranger. He gave the impression of being an overly friendly and excitable puppy.

"Captain Thayer, don't you think arranged marriages should be a thing of the past?" asked Alice boldly.

"Alice, mind your tongue. Captain Thayer will think you ill-bred!" snapped Mrs. Rawlins. She gave her errant daughter a hard stare before she turned and spoke to Burke. "Are you by any chance related to the New York Thayers?"

"It's possible," he responded evenly. He added in his thickest Southern drawl, "My people on both sides of my family have been in Georgia for a long while, but Thayer isn't all that common a name. One or two may have drifted up to New York."

"Oh, I see." The look on Millicent Rawlins' face revealed her disappointment in Captain Thayer's lack of connections.

Though he rarely shared personal information, seeing her dismay, Burke decided to cheer her up a bit. "My brother, William Thayer, is a successful financier on Wall Street."

Mrs. Rawlins brightened perceptibly. "Really? That is interesting. It must be from Mr. Morgan that I heard the name."

"My brother and Mr. Morgan have more than a passing acquaintance." That much was very true. Despite his stellar military career, Burke wouldn't have gotten his current job unless his brother had vouched for his character to the great man.

"Please, tell me more about your family," encouraged Mrs. Rawlins as the soup was served.

The evening progressed accordingly, with Mrs. Rawlins and her daughters probing Burke's past, each seeking to determine his eligibility in the marriage market. Burke entertained himself by giving the women just enough information to tickle their interest but not enough to tie himself down.

After dinner, the men strolled over to the bar for brandy and cigars, leaving the women to make their way back to their rooms.

"I hope you didn't mind my wife's persistent questions," said Mr. Rawlins when they were alone. "Though I have warned her time and time again that any man worth his stripes likes to do his own courting, she continues to interview candidates for my daughters' hands."

"I am certain that she has their best interests at heart," answered Burke smoothly before he took leave of his host.

Chapter 9
Tiffy Rose

"Tifton, this morning we are breakfasting with the Mrs. Barnes and her twin daughters. I, for one, certainly hope that you will conduct yourself in a manner befitting a young woman of quality." Her mother stared at Tiffy Rose with mute appeal. "Please do try, Tifton. Becoming members of this club means so very much to your father and I. Mr. Barnes is on the membership committee. The approval of Mrs. Barnes is paramount to our successful application. Please, Tifton."

Tiffy Rose could hear the longing in her mother's voice. She could see the pleading in her mother's eyes. Suddenly, her formidable mother seemed uncertain and perhaps a little bit scared. Tiffy Rose had never considered that her mother was vulnerable. Overcome with emotion, she embraced her mother gently. The action caught both women off-guard. They sniffled in unison.

Her mother's smile was tremulous as she said, "It's been a long time since you've hugged me, Tifton Rose. I hadn't realized how much I missed my little girl."

They embraced again, longer this time.

Her little girl. How long had it been since her mother had called her 'her little girl'? Months? Years? Guilt flooded Tiffy Rose. How often had she made sport of teasing and tormenting her mother? How often had she chosen the opposing viewpoint just to irritate her mother? Tiffy Rose realized how unkind she had been. Her mother was only trying to do her best to see her daughter securely settled in a world that was filled with uncertainty. Could her mother help it if the world offered so few choices for women beyond marriage and raising a family? Her mother loved her and only wanted the best for her. Tiffy Rose silently swore she would be better behaved and kinder to her mother in the future.

Drawing apart, her mother patted her eyes delicately with her lace handkerchief. "Come along now. We mustn't be late for breakfast with Mrs. Barnes."

Tiffy Rose and her mother made it to the dining room in good time. There they found Mrs. Barnes and her twin daughters, Becca and Beverly, had also just arrived. The brown-haired, brown-eyed twins wore matching outfits consisting of flowing powder blue skirts and lacy white blouses. The feathers in their hats had been dyed blue to match their skirts. Besides dressing alike, the twins were virtually identical in coloring, manner, and disposition. Even their smallest expressions and gestures were alike. Tiffy Rose wondered how she would possibly tell them apart.

"I hope you don't mind," began Mrs. Barnes after the introductions were made. "I have invited Miss Pendergrass to breakfast with us this morning. Were you aware that women are allowed to join the Jekyll Island Club?"

"I had no idea," said Mrs. Baldwin, very impressed with this news.

"Yes. Miss Pendergrass is a member in her own right."

"How interesting."

"She is quite an unusual woman. I think you'll find her most stimulating, especially if you keep an open mind. She has traveled all over the world to places like Outer Mongolia, Jerusalem, darkest Africa, and Peru. I must warn you, though unmarried, Miss Pendergrass has some rather radical ideas about how young ladies should be raised." Mrs. Barnes lowered her voice to a whisper. "She might even be a suffragette."

Wiping away the frown that those words put on her face, Mrs. Barnes looked around the dining room and spotted her friend. "There she is."

Miss Pendergrass made an excellent first impression on Tiffy Rose. In her late twenties, she was dressed simply in a brown skirt with a linen shirt. She possessed an aristocratic face with an aquiline nose that gave it character. She held her head proudly, seemingly unaware that the other diners were staring at her and gossiping behind their hands. As Mrs. Barnes introduced Tiffy Rose, Miss Pendergrass studied her with eyes that were both kind and assessing.

"How very nice to meet you," gushed Tiffy Rose and she meant every word. She took an instant liking to this self-contained woman. Miss

Pendergrass had a way of looking directly at you, as if your opinion truly mattered to her.

After discussing their choices for breakfast for what seemed to Tiffy Rose an endlessly long time, the women placed their orders.

Miss Pendergrass, who up until this time had tasted her tea and sat looking like a dignified, yet rather willful duchess, shot off her opening salvo. "Miss Baldwin, what do you think of our practice of discussing food ad nauseum?"

Becca and Beverly Barnes tittered behind their hands, happy that Miss Pendergrass had not singled them out.

Caught between her pledge to be kinder to her mother and her desire to impress this magnetic woman, Tiffy Rose hesitated before answering. Finally, she settled on a mild response that would satisfy neither woman completely. "I believe that food is important. Dining together is what binds us together."

Mrs. Baldwin smiled encouragingly to her daughter.

"But must food be discussed and dissected at every meal?" asked Miss Pendergrass more forcefully. "I find it rather tedious to discuss the merits of each and every dish, don't you?"

Tiffy Rose demurred. "I have not had the opportunity to dine out frequently. Discussing food is a relatively new experience for me. I have not yet grown tired of it."

Miss Pendergrass laughed heartily. "Well said, my dear." She turned to Tiffy's mother and said, "Mrs. Baldwin, you are raising your daughter to be a fine diplomat."

Mrs. Baldwin beamed with pride. The Barnes twins shared a disgruntled look. Tiffy Rose felt as if she had passed some sort of test with flying colors.

"Tifton has had the benefit of two years at Bryn Mawr." Mrs. Baldwin proudly referred to the prestigious women's college founded in 1885.

Mrs. Barnes shot her offspring a look of disappointment before venturing another topic. "This past October—October 2 to be exact—Jekyll Island experienced a hurricane. If you look closely, you can still see the effects of its passing. It was said to have been the most severe storm ever known to strike the island."

Eager to add to the conversation, Mrs. Baldwin interjected, "I was told that a tidal wave covered the island with five feet of water!"

"It was only four feet," sniped Beverly, still miffed by Tiffy Rose's success with Miss Pendergrass. "You can measure the watermarks on several of the buildings, if you don't believe me."

Mrs. Baldwin looked disappointed and a little hurt. Miss Pendergrass patted her hand which brought a small smile to her mother's face. Tiffy Rose wished that she, too, could do something that would comfort her mother.

"The new golf course was absolutely ruined," pouted Becca. "The wharf was completely destroyed. Only Hollybourne Cottage and the Fairbank Cottage escaped damage."

Mrs. Barnes added, "High winds blew the windmill away. The flooding washed away the terrapin pens. Of course, none of us were on the island at the time. Naturally, the caretakers had everything cleaned up by the time we arrived for the winter."

Miss Pendergrass topped them all in the conversation game when she said mildly, "In 1883, I lived through a volcanic eruption followed by a tsunami in Krakatoa in the Dutch East Indies. The house where I was staying was destroyed by a forty-foot-high tidal wave. Fortunately, we were able to use boards to cross over to a neighboring rooftop before our building crumbled beneath us. The experience was rather like tightrope walking." She smiled at the women at the table who regarded her with open mouths.

Beaten but still game, Mrs. Barnes tried a new topic. "President McKinley will be arriving on the twentieth of this month. It's only a few days away. Won't it be interesting to meet him?"

"He is our most popular president," said Becca.

"He is wonderfully devoted to his wife. Everyone admires him for how he takes care of her. From what I understand, she suffers from a nervous condition," said Mrs. Baldwin somewhat timidly.

"He has done so much for our country. He rescued us from the depression of 1893," added Mrs. Barnes.

"Yes, he kept us on the gold standard and that stabilized our economy and brought a return of national prosperity," commented Tiffy's mother more confidently.

"With a little help from J.P. Morgan and his cronies," added Mrs. Barnes cryptically.

"I overheard Papa saying that President McKinley wouldn't have gotten elected if not for the financial backing and support of J.P. Morgan," giggled Becca Barnes.

"Hush, Becca. Ladies do not discuss money or politics in polite company," admonished her mother.

"But you were discussing money!" snapped Becca, never one to be thwarted.

"No, dear, we were discussing the president," stated Mrs. Barnes firmly. She picked up the teapot and offered a fresh cup to each of the ladies. Once she had taken care of her guests, she returned to the topic at hand. "I am impressed by the way that President McKinley handled the situation in Cuba. Imagine—sinking the Maine! What were the Spanish thinking?"

"At least he brought the Spanish-American War to a quick end," offered Mrs. Baldwin.

"I have yet to hear from any of the young ladies present on this topic," announced Miss Pendergrass abruptly. "I assume you have taught your daughters that a woman should be able to speak on any subject in an interesting and amusing manner."

"Yes, of course," murmured both Mrs. Barnes and Mrs. Baldwin.

Tiffy Rose squirmed uncomfortably. She had wondered when Miss Pendergrass would enter the conversation, but she hadn't expected to be put on notice. She had been perfectly content to listen to her mother and Mrs. Barnes converse. Certain that she would say something wrong, Tiffy Rose was not looking forward to yet another lecture about decorous behavior. From the looks on their faces, she didn't think that Becca and Beverly were either.

Taking up the banner of women's rights, Miss Pendergrass continued. "Needlework! Bridge! Fashions! It would be better for everyone if women's brains were put to a higher purpose. A woman doesn't have to be passive. She can work with the talents she has been given and use them to make her life worthwhile. Personally, I prefer a purpose-filled life to any other."

Mrs. Barnes stood up abruptly. "Oh! Look at the time! We simply must leave. So sorry. Lovely to have breakfasted with you." She gathered up her daughters, clucking at them like a mother hen.

Clearly Miss Pendergrass had definite opinions about the roles of women in society. Tiffy Rose was enthralled. Never had she met such an interesting woman. How she wished she could spend more time with her. However, it appeared that Mrs. Barnes had decided that her daughters had heard enough radical talk for the day.

Chapter 10
Burke

Following an early breakfast in the dining room, Burke was in his room at the clubhouse when a message arrived from the dock. The Glynn County sheriff had arrived on the morning boat from Brunswick. Would it be possible for Captain Thayer to join him at the dock to speak with the *Howland*'s Captain Clark?

Burke hurried to the dock to meet the boat used to transport members and their guests to the island. He was keen to begin his investigations into the victim's identity.

"Sheriff Higgins, thank you for making an effort to arrive so promptly today," began Burke. "We are eager to solve the mystery surrounding the victim."

"Rest assured that the Glynn County sheriff's office is interested in solving this crime, too. So, tell me, Captain, have you learned anything new since I was here yesterday?"

"Unfortunately, not a thing. We have so little to go on." Burke shrugged apologetically.

"Never-the-less, we must start somewhere. May I suggest that we interview Captain Clark? He is sure to have a few moments to spare while he waits for passengers for the return boat."

"After you, Sheriff."

They found Captain Clark in the wheelhouse of the boat.

"Hello Sheriff Higgins. Come back already?" asked Captain Clark.

"Good morning, Captain Clark. Have you met Captain Thayer? He is here investigating yesterday's unfortunate death."

The two captains nodded their greetings to each other.

Burke began the questioning. "You are undoubtably familiar with many of your passengers, by face if not by name, aren't you?"

"If you're asking me if I ever met the dead man, I have no idea. From what I understand his face was damaged beyond recognition. I see a lot of people on the *Howland* this time of year. I can't see how I can be of much help to you."

"Let's try this from a different angle," suggested Burke. "In the past two days, have you noticed a man traveling alone. He'd be about five feet eight inches tall, somewhat portly, well-dressed in a business suit."

"Well, now that you put it that way, let me think on it." Captain Clark stared out the window of the wheelhouse and carefully thought back over the past two days. Finally, he snapped his fingers. "Come to think of it, there was such a man. I brought him in the afternoon before the storm. Nice looking gentleman. Very polite. Looked a bit bookish to me. He spent much of the ride over staring at seabirds through his binoculars and writing in a little notebook. Do you think that might have been him?"

Burke suppressed his excitement. This was the first he had heard of a notebook. "It could have been. Did you happen to speak with him?"

"Not as I can remember."

"Do you keep a passenger manifest?" asked Burke hopefully.

"No, only a count of the number of passengers."

"Did you happen to see where he went when he got off the boat? Did anyone meet him?" asked Burke.

Captain Clark gave Burke's questions careful consideration. He shook his head and admitted that he hadn't noticed anything else about his passenger. Realizing that Captain Clark could tell them nothing more, they thanked him for his time and went to the clubhouse to continue their questioning there.

Burke and Sheriff Higgins began with the manager and worked their way down to the clerks and baggage carriers. Unfortunately, no one remembered seeing a middle-aged, portly man with graying hair. Due to the president's approaching visit, the hotel was at full capacity. This kept everyone from the manager to the bellboy busy. A review of the hotel register revealed that there were no single men travelling alone unaccounted for.

"Where did he go? We know he got off the boat. Where did he go?" repeated Burke in frustration. "He can't just have disappeared. He had to have spent the night somewhere. His clothing, though damaged by the action of the waves did not look like he had spent the night outdoors. Someone must have seen him somewhere!"

"Don't worry. We'll find out who he is sooner or later," said Sheriff Higgins confidently.

"It's going to have to be sooner. President McKinley is due here the day after tomorrow." Burke kicked at the shell gravel on the roadway in undisguised anger.

Optimistically, the sheriff said, "There are still a number of people to interview; guards, clerks, Superintendent Grob, and others. We should also revisit where he was found. Perhaps something will turn up."

"Yes, that was my plan."

"Have you had time to visit Mr. Horst, the clockmaker?"

"No, not yet. It's on my list of things to do."

"He is the man to see when you want a timepiece repaired. That is why he is on Jekyll Island this week. It seems that the clocks are going on strike and refusing to run." The sheriff laughed at his own joke.

"I will be interested in what he has to say about the watch we found on the victim."

Burke spent an unsatisfying morning in search of information. As it turned out, no one knew anything about the man. His search revealed no new clues. The sheriff decided to return to Brunswick on the next boat so the two men parted company.

Having spent the better part of the morning walking around without a hat on, Burke decided to remedy the situation with a visit to the commissary.

"Good morning, sir. How can I help you?" asked the clerk when Burke entered the store.

"I am hoping to acquire a hat. I lost mine yesterday at the beach."

"Blew away, didn't it? Quite a wind we had yesterday following the storm. Not surprised you lost your hat. Got to wear one with a string on it to hold it onto your head when it's windy. I don't know how women do it. They must use a lot of those hatpins. Wicked looking things, hat pins." The clerk finally ran down.

"Would you happen to have a hat?" repeated Burke.

"Oh, yes, sir. Right over here, sir." The clerk led the way over to a small but adequate selection of hats. After trying on several and looking at his reflection in the mirror, Burke found one that suited him.

"I believe this one will do," Burke said.

"Very good, sir. Looked well on you. I suppose there is no need to wrap it up. That is, you will be wearing it, won't you?" asked the talkative clerk.

"Yes, I will wear it." Burke paid for the hat. As he was about to leave, he decided it wouldn't hurt to ask the man a few questions. "By the way, I happen to be looking for a friend of a friend. I've lost the man's name which puts me at a great disadvantage. You haven't by any chance seen a middle-aged, slightly portly man with graying dark hair in the past couple of days, have you?"

"Haven't you got more to go on than that? Nearly every man on the island, at least your types, is a middle-aged, portly man with graying hair. Best of luck to you in your search." Laughing harshly, the clerk turned away to help another customer.

Feeling a bit foolish, Burke left the commissary. Once outside, he noticed Tifton Rose Baldwin walking toward the clockmaker's shop with Randolph Patterson Chatsworth. Seeing them reminded him of the silver pocket watch he was carrying in his pocket. It was time to discover its secrets.

Chapter 11
Tiffy Rose

After breakfast, Tiffy Rose promised her mother that she would behave herself. "Randolph Patterson Chatsworth III has asked me to take a stroll around the grounds with him." She waved his note in the air in front of her mother's nose.

Her mother drew a breath to say something. In keeping with her promise to be nicer to her mother, Tiffy Rose beat her to it.

"I plan on taking Miss Goodwin along as our chaperone, if you can spare her today."

Mrs. Baldwin glowed with pleasure. Tifton rarely agreed to a chaperone without an argument. "Certainly. I think it is a marvelous idea for you to venture out with Mr. Chatsworth. It's high time you got to know him better. Just remember to return in time to rest before dinner. We are dining with the Chatsworths at eight. Wear your green gown. I want you to look your best."

"Must we always dress in our best for dinner?" asked Tiffy Rose.

"Yes, Tifton. Dressing well shows your host and hostess how much you appreciate their invitation. It is important to honor your guests also by looking your best. Can you understand that?"

"Yes, Mama. It's really all about being kind and respecting others."

"I am very pleased that you agreed to take a little tour around the club with me this morning, Miss Baldwin," said Randolph Patterson Chatsworth III jovially as they strolled down Pier Road.

Tiffy Rose smiled up at the large, clumsy man at her side. He really was rather a nice man, very polite and well-schooled in social etiquette. Even his clumsiness was part of his charm. She supposed that she liked him, but as to whether or not she could come to love him—well—that was for the future to tell. She glanced over her shoulder at her chaperone, Flora Goodwin, who followed at a short distance behind them as was fitting. "I appreciate the opportunity to learn more about the club," she said demurely, trying very hard to emulate her mother's good manners.

"I must say, our little stroll this morning will have none of yesterday's excitement."

"I certainly hope not." Tiffy Rose shivered despite the warmth of the day. Yesterday had turned out to be a nightmare from morning to evening. All in all, it was a day she would rather forget. She particularly planned to make an effort to banish thoughts of the dashing and enigmatic stranger from her mind.

Completely unaware of the effect his words were having on Tiffy Rose, Randolph Patterson continued to prattle on. "One dead body is enough. God rest his soul. Still, one can't help but wonder who the fellow was. I am also very curious about what he was doing on the island in the first place. Last night, over brandy and cigars after dinner, my companions made some interesting comments about who he might be. I can't say that I agree with them, but one has to keep an open mind, doesn't one?"

In an effort to shift the focus away from yesterday's tragedy, Tiffy Rose broke into his monologue and asked, "Mr. Chatsworth, would you please tell me more about the Jekyll Island Club?"

"Of course, Miss Baldwin. I would be happy to do so." Randolph Patterson tucked her arm in his protectively.

Tiffy Rose chaffed against his proprietary manner. Gritting her teeth and vowing to remain calm and pleasant, she smiled serenely at her companion.

"Ah, yes. Jekyll Island. Did you know that it is called a 'millionaire's paradise' by the press?"

"No, I hadn't heard that, but it seems appropriate."

"The Jekyll Island Club is the most exclusive, most inaccessible club in the world," boasted Randolph Patterson. "We do live an isolated, leisurely life here. It is rather nice to have acres of marsh and water separating us from the riff-raff that usually attends us in New York or Chicago or even Atlanta. I suppose it is the bane of the wealthy to be pestered for money. Here on the island, we are left alone. Reporters and hangers-on can be so tedious. Don't you agree?"

Having had no experience with either reporters, riff-raff, or hangers-on, Tiffy Rose refrained from comment. She had the impression that Randolph Patterson Chatsworth III hadn't had too much experience with hangers-on either. Rather it seemed to her that he wanted to include himself and his family in the same class as the unimaginably wealthy Rockefellers, Morgans, and Vanderbilts of the world. Despite having no idea of his personal wealth, she wondered whether or not Randolph Patterson was reaching above his station in an attempt to impress her.

"You are, of course, aware of the guards that patrol the island and the waters surrounding it," Randolph Patterson said a bit pompously. "At sea, they turn away any boats coming closer than ten miles to the island."

"I had no idea!" exclaimed Tiffy Rose. And she didn't. A question popped into her mind and she voiced it before she could stop herself. "Why didn't the patrols find the man on the beach?"

Randolph Patterson patted her hand in a manner meant to be reassuring but wasn't. "Don't you worry your pretty little head about it. That's man's business. We will take care of you."

Tiffy Rose snorted with annoyance. Realizing that her unladylike reaction to Randolph's comment would be taken badly, she swiftly covered it with a tiny sneeze. "Please excuse me. There must be something in the air."

Gallantly, Randolph Patterson whipped out a spotlessly clean and well-starched handkerchief. He handed it to her. She made a fuss over using it delicately.

They followed the crushed shell road away from the Jekyll River and the pier and toward a group of buildings located to the east of the clubhouse.

"Over there is the infirmary. In previous years, it was staffed by Dr. Merrill, however, this year, I have been given to understand that Dr. Martin is our attending physician. Apparently, Dr. Merrill ran into a bit of difficulty due to a misunderstanding about Rhode Island physician licensing laws. We expect him back next year."

"Club members must feel very secure indeed. An attending physician would be a great comfort."

"You are right, my dear. Despite its bracing sea air, illnesses like typhoid, yellow fever, and smallpox can plague our island. The last yellow fever epidemic ruined the 1893-94 season."

"Oh my, yellow fever. That is bad."

"Now we come to the working part of the Jekyll Island Club," Randolph Patterson announced grandly. "I hope you don't mind that I must run a short errand while we are in this area of the club. My timepiece is losing time. It won't take but a minute."

Tiffy Rose lifted her eyes to his to see if he was making a play on words. He wasn't, of course. Randolph Patterson Chatsworth III had little skill at making jokes.

Tiffy Rose looked around her and saw that small establishments lined either side of the wide crushed-shell roadway. In quick succession, she identified a bicycle shop, a small general store or commissary as a discrete sign announced, a blacksmith shop, a laundry, a coal house, and servants' quarters. She also noted a small cluster of unlabeled buildings, one of which Randolph Patterson led her toward.

"Here we are," he said once they had reached the smallest of these buildings. "Mr. Horst's clock repair shop."

"A clock repair shop? Surely there aren't that many clocks on the island that need attention to warrant a clock repair shop!"

"No, silly." Randolph Patterson smiled indulgently at her naivety. "The clock repairman is here for a short while specially to repair several of the floor clocks on the island that seem to have decided to go out on strike all at once." He laughed loudly at his little joke. "Did you hear what they are calling floor clocks? Grandfather clocks! Imagine that! Grandfather clocks! Personally, I don't think the name will catch on, do you, Miss Baldwin?" He chuckled again, a grin covering his entire face.

Tiffy Rose didn't know what she found more annoying—Randolph's condescending manner or his braying laughter. Miss Baldwin? Such a formal name for such an informal young woman. Weren't they supposed to be engaged? Would he ever call her Tiffy Rose like her friends did?

She opened her mouth to ask him and then shut it. Remembering her promise to behave, Tiffy Rose stifled her irritation. Out of the corner of her eye, she caught movement. Casting a glance behind herself, she felt the eyes of the stranger upon her. He looked at her with something akin to sympathy. She blushed furiously.

The stranger was positively insufferable, appearing in her life in such a willy-nilly fashion. Tiffy Rose hated to be caught at a disadvantage. Putting aside all of her new-found resolve to behave herself, she reacted. Abruptly, she turned and tucked her hand in Randolph Patterson's arm. The young man's face showed his consternation over her unexpected gesture.

A small gasp escaped Miss Goodwin. Tiffy Rose had forgotten all about her chaperone. The unmistakable sound of disapproval reminded Tiffy Rose that her chaperone had a way of moving unnoticed into the background. She even dressed consistently in sober gray outfits. From this vantage point, Miss Goodwin watched everyone and everything with her quiet, yet very observant, gray eyes.

"If you don't mind, I would like to speak to the man about my pocket watch," Randolph Patterson managed to blurt out nervously.

"Certainly, my dear Mr. Chatsworth," Tiffy Rose said in a daringly intimate manner. She smiled sweetly and batted her eyelashes. "Anything you would like."

Taken aback by her surprising warmth, Randolph Patterson smiled nervously and bowed slightly before leading the way into the small shop. Filled with curiosity about this new development, Miss Goodwin followed them into the building.

The stranger chose this exact same moment to enter the tiny shop, disconcerting Tiffy Rose. Randolph Patterson didn't seem to notice. Her face flushed, she tried to concentrate on what Randolph Patterson was saying to the clockmaker.

"Good morning, sir." The clockmaker, a tiny gnome of a man, greeted them distractedly. His wispy hair floated around his round, wrinkled face like a halo. His skin was chalk white, as if he hadn't been out in the sun for a long time.

Tiffy Rose was perturbed when she observed that the man had one blue eye and one brown.

"Good morning, Mr. Horst. I have brought with me a watch which I would like you to take a look at. It has become quite unreliable of late."

"When did the trouble begin?" asked the clockmaker.

"I'd say about a month ago."

"Did something occur that might have damaged the watch, sir?" asked the clockmaker. A flicker of annoyance crossed his face.

Tiffy Rose got the impression that the clockmaker preferred to deal with watches and clocks rather than people.

"How on earth should I know. I only know that it doesn't work!" said Randolph Patterson impatiently. Randolph Patterson's manner became increasingly pompous, as it always did whenever he was uncomfortable. "Perhaps I should just confine it to the trash heap. It's never been particularly good at keeping time." Randolph Patterson's face took on a disgruntled expression.

"Now, sir, don't be hasty. I am certain that I will be able to ascertain what the trouble is. If you'll just leave it with me. I can work on it tomorrow."

"Tomorrow? Can't you get to it today?" snapped Randolph Patterson.

Between Tiffy Rose hanging on his arm and the confrontational demeanor of the clockmaker, Randolph Patterson became increasingly uncomfortable. This discomfort manifested itself in abrupt words and actions. Tiffy Rose actually felt sorry for him.

"If you absolutely must have it, I might be able to. As you can see, I am very busy at the moment." Exasperated, the small man gestured around his shop which had clocks of all kinds stacked here and there in jumbled heaps on every available shelf and countertop.

With five people, the single-room shop was becoming overly warm and Tiffy Rose began to feel a bit overcome with the heat. She touched Randolph Patterson's sleeve lightly. "Excuse me, Mr. Chatsworth?"

"Just a moment, Miss Baldwin. We shall depart shortly." Randolph Patterson turned his attention back to the clockmaker and observed sarcastically, "All of these clocks and no time."

Trying to distract herself from her own lightheadedness, Tiffy Rose picked up a small mantle clock and lifted it to the light. "It seems as if a lot of timepieces are in need of repair here on the island. Do any of these clocks work?"

Roughly, the clockmaker snatched the clock from her hands held it to his bony chest. "I'll take that," he snapped. "It must be the salt air."

Tiffy Rose, Miss Goodwin, Randolph Patterson, and even the stranger, looked aghast at the clockmaker's social *faux pas*. It was decidedly impolite to speak roughly to a woman in public.

Tiffy Rose pulled herself up to her full height and announced with exaggerated politeness, "I feel in need of some air. Mr. Chatsworth, Miss Goodwin and I will wait for you outside. Good day, gentlemen."

More than a little embarrassed by his sharp words, the clockmaker looked chagrined but did not apologize.

Taking matters into his own capable hands, the stranger politely held the door for Tiffy Rose. He helped her out the shop and down the steps to a nearby bench. Miss Goodwin, a chaperone who took her charge seriously, also exited the shop and stood nearby.

"It appears that my duty while I am on this island is to assist you whenever you feel faint." The stranger smiled briefly into Tiffy Rose's eyes.

Again, Tiffy Rose felt the strange light-headedness that seemed to plague her recently. She touched her forehead. Perhaps she was coming down with something. Perhaps it was the heat. Perhaps—just perhaps—it was the handsome stranger standing so nearby.

She drew in a deep breath, grateful that she was not wearing a corset. She turned her face to the stranger and said severely, "While I appreciate your attentiveness, I swear to you that I do not feel faint. I never faint." Tiffy Rose turned her face away and tried to recover her *sang froid*.

"That is a good thing indeed. Dealing with young ladies in distress is not my *forte*," the stranger shot back just as stiffly.

A small smile crept onto Tiffy's lips. Here was a man who would not be easily intimidated. She dared a glance at his face and liked what she saw there. His smile seemed to penetrate the deepest corners of her heart.

"Regardless of the protocol involved, I believe it is time we introduced ourselves properly. It seems necessary if we are going to be constantly thrown together."

Tiffy Rose stifled a strange desire to run away while she still had a chance. Things were happening very quickly. She squirmed in her seat, excited at the prospect of learning the stranger's name.

Seemingly unaware of her interest in him, the stranger looked at her with a bland expression on his face.

Unable to bear his examination any longer, Tiffy Rose blurted out, "You first."

The stranger ducked his head and bit his lip to stifle a laugh that escaped as a short bark. "As you wish. May I present myself, I am Captain Burke Thayer, late of the battleship Maine." Captain Thayer bowed respectfully.

Tiffy turned his name over and over in her mind. Burke Thayer. It was a good, strong name. A nice masculine name. A name full of possibilities. She smiled up at the man who with one small sentence was no longer a stranger.

"Tifton Rose Baldwin. Tiffy Rose to my friends. I am pleased to meet you, Captain Thayer." Her eyes twinkled with delight. She held out her slender hand to him. "Very pleased indeed."

Chapter 12
Burke

"Miss Baldwin? Where have you gotten off to? I hadn't expected you to go beyond the porch." Randolph Patterson sounded more worried about her speaking with a stranger than angry over losing her. He planted himself firmly between Burke and Tiffy Rose. "Miss Baldwin, I must ask if speaking to strangers is becoming a habit with you?"

Her face, white with anger over his implied accusation, Tifton Rose Baldwin, in her finest imitation of her mother, rose from the bench and faced Randolph Patterson as if he were a bug to squash. "I did not expect you to be so inattentive or inconsiderate."

"I am sorry, Miss Baldwin. I had business to attend to. That man deserved a dressing down for the way he treated you and he got one. From me," responded Randolph Patterson shortly. He shot an intolerant glare at Burke, then focused on Tiffy Rose. "Imagine my surprise to find you yet again in the company of a complete stranger."

Furious, Tiffy Rose went on the attack. What she said surprised Burke as much as it did Randolph Patterson Chatsworth III. "For your information, Captain Burke and I are *not* strangers. As a matter of fact, our acquaintance is quite long-standing. Is it not, Captain Burke?"

Caught off-guard, Burke scurried to catch up with the conversation. He wondered where Miss Baldwin was going with this. While it was true that he had learned her name before their introduction just now, he had never met her before yesterday on the beach—at least not that he recalled. He quickly decided it was safest to say very little. "Yes, Miss Baldwin, that is certainly true. We are not strangers." Not a lie exactly, more like a slightly exaggerated truth.

Burke's efforts were rewarded when Tiffy Rose favored him with a dazzling smile. The gentle breeze stirred the Spanish moss in the live oak trees. It brought a hint of the scent of rose water to his senses. Burke had to admit that Miss Baldwin really was quite an attractive young woman.

"Captain Thayer is of the Georgia Thayers," she said, obviously adlibbing.

"With ties to the New York Thayers," added Burke as he began to enjoy himself. The entire scene had a feeling of unreality attached to it.

"Mr. Chatsworth, as I am sure you are aware, my great-great granddaddy, Abraham Baldwin, was one of the founding fathers of our nation. He signed the United States Constitution back in 1787." Tiffy Rose assumed a dramatic pose and placed her hand on Burke's arm. "Captain Thayer's great-great granddaddy fought in the Revolutionary War!"

"Right beside Abraham," Burke intoned solemnly. He placed his hand over his heart for emphasis.

"Our families have been intertwined ever since. Captain Thayer is my third cousin—twice removed," said Tiffy Rose, her eyes twinkling merrily.

Her audacity amazed Burke. Never had he met such a daring girl—a darling girl. Then came a sobering thought. Tiffy Rose was just a girl of twenty. At thirty-five, he was closer in age to her father than to her own. When the initial interest in each other waned, what would they have in common? The fifteen-year gap in their ages was, to him, insurmountable. Burke realized that Chatsworth was speaking.

"Oh. I see. Then I suppose it is all right for you to be together unchaperoned," Randolph Patterson conceded.

"All right? All right? How dare you question the morals of this young woman—a woman who I may be so bold as to call—my sister!" Burke gazed upon her tenderly.

Tiffy Rose held his gaze for a brief moment and then turned her full attention on Randolph Patterson.

Burke actually felt sorry for the man.

Eyes snapping, Tiffy Rose continued to take Randolph Patterson to task. "As for my lack of chaperonage, I will have you notice that Miss Goodwin stands less than ten feet away." She nodded in the older woman's direction, a tight smile on her face.

At the mention of her name, Miss Goodwin, who appeared to be enjoying herself immensely, acknowledged them with a small smile and a wave of her hand.

"I do apologize, Miss Baldwin. Really, I do." Randolph Patterson choked out the words.

Tifton Rose gathered her skirts and shook them out. "I do believe that I have had enough of a walk today. If you don't mind, I will rest a while longer on this bench in the company of my dear cousin." Gracefully, she sat down again. Patting the seat next to her on the bench, Tiffy Rose clearly indicated that she expected Burke to join her.

Tentatively, he did so.

She nodded crisply to Randolph Patterson who stood hovering above her. "I am sure that I will have the pleasure of your company this evening. We are dining with your parents in the grand dining room at eight. Good day, Mr. Chatsworth."

Summarily dismissed, Randolph Patterson Chatsworth III drifted off down the crushed shell lane, his dejection clearly visible in the slope of his shoulders.

"He looks lost, doesn't he?" asked Tiffy Rose softly.

Once again, Burke almost felt sorry for the young man.

Tiffy Rose continued in a whisper, "Will I never stop hurting people with my sharp tongue? Am I doomed to a life of misbehavior? I have been raised to know better." Tiffy Rose sighed. A tear rolled down her cheek. She dashed it away with the back of her hand.

Captain Thayer handed her his handkerchief to wipe the tears that now rolled uninhibited down her cheeks.

"Thank you, Captain Thayer," she sniffed. "This is the second handkerchief that I have ruined today."

"Are you really descended from Abraham Baldwin?" asked Burke in order to distract her from whatever had brought on her tears. He had limited experience with young women, especially those who cried so easily.

Smiling weakly, Tiffy Rose rallied. "Of course, I am. You didn't think that I would lie about such a thing, did you?"

Her response caused them both to laugh.

"Third cousin, twice removed?" he asked, reminding her that she had lied about their kinship.

"It was the first thing that came to mind," Tiffy Rose said primly. She grew very still. She bowed her head and said seriously. "Captain Thayer, I must apologize for my unseemly behavior. I have no excuses for it. I have involved you in a deception and I have no idea who it will affect. I am very sorry and will understand if you snub me in public in the future."

When Burke made protesting noises, Tiffy Rose held up her hand to stop him from speaking.

"No, no. Your behavior was very supportive and gallant. Mine however was not. I should never had made fun of Mr. Chatsworth at his expense. I must make amends to him. Truly, he is a good man." Instead of stopping there, Tiffy Rose committed another social error by admitting to a complete stranger the position she was in. "I am not worthy of his affections. We are terribly unsuited for each other. It is our parents who seek the alliance."

Burke sat quietly, absorbing what she had said. Instead of being put off by her inappropriate behavior, he found that he admired her all the more. He had never met a woman who threw caution to the wind quite so creatively. Nor had he met one that apologized.

Wanting to distract her from her distressing thoughts, Burke stood up. Taking her hand, he helped her up. "May I suggest that you accompany me into the clock shop?"

"But—I," she began to protest.

"I know that you shouldn't, but since you are the one who has kept me from my errand, then it is you that I depend upon to help me accomplish it."

"That is very prettily said, however, I think I have transgressed the boundaries set by polite society enough for one day. I must go, Captain Thayer. Really, I must."

"Please, not yet." Burke stood staring at Tiffy Rose for a full minute wondering what he could say that would convince this lively and interesting young woman to stay with him a little while longer. He dangled the pocket watch in front of her. The sun glinted off of its bright surface. "Can't I persuade you to help me unlock the secrets of this pocket watch?"

Tifton Rose Baldwin stared back at him. Suddenly, she gave in. A hint of a smile played on her face as she said, "Why not? You are my brother in spirit after all."

They returned to the shop. The clockmaker looked up in surprise.

"Good day, Mr. Horst."

"Good day, sir. I see that the lady has recovered from her faint."

"I don't—" Tiffy Rose halted mid-protest and struck a modest pose. She feigned interest in the dismantled clocks covering every flat surface imaginable. She stopped in front of a chamois cloth unrolled to expose a variety of sharp tools, small hammers, pliers, and tiny screw drivers. Burke joined her.

"I see that you have an interest in a clockmaker's tools," said the little man when he noticed them inspecting the tools on the counter.

"I have always found clocks fascinating," admitted Burke. "I never realized that so many tools are necessary to repair clocks and watches."

"Timepieces are very delicate devices that must be carefully taken care of so that they may always keep time."

"Yet not a single clock in your shop is ticking away the minutes and hours," said Burke.

The clockmaker froze for an instant, his face angry, and then he recovered. "That is why I am here."

"I am afraid that I have been rather careless with my own watch." Burke removed the silver watch from his pocket and dangled it from its chain. "I am afraid I dropped it in the sea."

"Oh my. That is bad news. The salt water is very corrosive. Tell me, how long was it in the water?"

"Not long, perhaps an hour at most."

"An hour!" cried the clockmaker in dismay. "My dear sir, that is catastrophic to a fine watch. May I see the watch, please?"

Burke handed the watch to the little man.

"Ah, this is a lovely piece. Sterling silver with gold work on the casing. That it is in your possession shows that you are a man of discriminating taste," said Mr. Horst as he studied the case, running his finger over the raised gold-work pattern.

"It was a gift."

"From me, his dear cousin," smiled Tiffy Rose. She took Burke by the arm and lead him over to where a large ormolu clock sat on a countertop. It positively glowed golden in the light from the window. "Isn't this a lovely piece?"

"Very unusual." Burke fingered the ornate ormolu mercury fire gilded mantle clock.

"It is from the French Empire period, of course," said Tiffy Rose, parroting her mother without realizing it.

A work of art in gilded bronze atop a polished walnut base, the clock stood approximately twenty inches high. Fifteen inches wide and eight inches deep, the polished wooden base was adorned with gilded bronze roping. A very refined and elegant gilded statue of Psyche, modestly draped with a flowing cloth, reclined against the clock. The clock face was white enamel on copper with gilt brass hands covered by a glass bezel.

"Psyche, the symbol of rebirth or awakening." Surprising even himself, Burke took Tiffy's chin gently in his fingertips and tilted her face toward the sunlight.

Miss Goodwin gasped. He ignored her. Instead, he compared Tiffy's profile with that of Psyche. "Lovely. I do believe that you could have posed for the sculpture. The artist has finely wrought your face in gold, my dear cousin."

Burke felt a shiver run through Tiffy Rose. He hesitated only a moment before releasing her chin.

The clockmaker broke the spell by bustling over and throwing a large cloth over the clock. He ushered them firmly back over to the other side of the small room.

"I believe I've seen this clock before, but I don't recall where," said Burke as he stared thoughtfully at the mound under the cloth.

"I rather doubt that, sir," said Mr. Horst, cutting into his thoughts. "The piece is exceptional. A one-of-a-kind creation. It belongs to one of the club members. They wish to have it repaired. For all its beauty, it doesn't keep time very well." The clockmaker stood between them and the clock, nervously wringing his hands.

"We can't have that, now, can we?" asked Burke to lighten the atmosphere.

"Most definitely not," answered the little man emphatically. "Now, Mr. eh...I apologize. I don't know your name, sir."

"Thayer, Captain Burke Thayer."

"Well, then, Captain Thayer, about your pocket watch."

"Yes, what can you tell me about its condition? Is it repairable? I can't even get the case open."

The clockmaker stroked the case gently. "Unfortunately, it has suffered greatly from its swim in the Atlantic Ocean. As you can see, the sterling silver case with its lovely gold embellishments has been scuffed by the tide as it rolls on the beach sand. The engraving on the front has been damaged as if by sandpaper. I fear you have not told me the truth about how long your pocket watch was in the water." He tested the winding mechanism at the top of the pocket watch. "Fortunately, we Swiss make things to last. The winding mechanism feels sound. I will know more after I open it up and clean it. If, of course, that is what you wish."

"I haven't been able to open it. Would you mind opening it now?" asked Burke. "I am very curious to learn whether or not it can be salvaged."

"Certainly, I can try." The clockmaker went over to where his tools lay spread out on the chamois cloth.

Fascinated, Burke, Tiffy Rose, and Miss Goodwin watched as the man picked up a small pointed tool, not unlike an oyster pry stick. He gently worked the sharp tool around the edge of the casing, slowly persuading the lid to come free. It gave way with a small click.

"Ah, we have success. I see that the engraving has been unharmed. *'To my beloved Percy, Your sweetheart Milly'*. You told me that your name was Burke Thayer." The clockmaker tilted his head, making his statement into a question.

Burke found himself to be tongue-tied. He hadn't expected the watch to be engraved. He was a fool—a fool with no quick response at the ready.

"That is easily explained," said Tiffy Rose smoothly.

Miss Goodwin, the clockmaker, and Burke leaned forward to hear what she would say next.

Unfazed by all the attention, Tiffy Rose said calmly, "Percy is my nickname for my dear cousin. It has been since we were small children. It is a long story. And, of course, I am his Milly." She smiled graciously at her audience.

"Ah, I understand," said the clockmaker, clearly unamused by the idiosyncrasies of the wealthy. He glared at Burke as if he was the cause of all his problems. He began to usher them all out the door. "I will take a look at your watch later today and have news for you tomorrow, Captain Thayer." The clockmaker barely suppressed an unexplained angry note in his voice.

Burke said as graciously as possible, "Thank you for your time. I will return tomorrow to learn more about my watch."

Chapter 13
Tiffy Rose

Captain Thayer walked Tiffy Rose back to the entrance to the clubhouse. She thanked him profusely, and received only a slight nod of his head in response. Dissatisfied by Captain Thayer's abrupt departure, she dismissed Miss Goodwin, thanking the quiet woman for her services. Left to her own devices, Tiffy Rose walked slowly along the shell path to the veranda, uncertain of what to do next. It was too early to return to her room. She didn't feel like walking any further. For once, the sound of the wind in the live oak trees failed to lift her spirits.

Her mind was in turmoil over recent events. What had she been thinking? Pretending a relationship with a man she hadn't been properly introduced to? Third cousin twice removed? What had possessed her to say such a thing? And to make matters worse, she had enjoyed herself enormously. Given the chance, she would do it all over again. Surely Captain Thayer must have been appalled by her behavior. As he should be, she thought morosely. What had she been thinking? It didn't help that Miss Goodwin had witnessed the entire episode. And she had promised her mother that today she would turn over a new leaf—that she would behave with good sense and decorum. Instead, Tiffy Rose had trumped any other misdeed she had ever committed. She would have to deal with the fallout from her escapade.

It had all begun as a lark. She had grown very tired of Randolph Patterson's condescending attitude toward her and others. Captain Thayer's presence had provided a convenient way of irritating Randolph Patterson. She knew she had been unfair to involve Captain Thayer in her deception. She knew she had been unkind to Randolph Patterson, who, given his over-bearing parents, couldn't really be blamed for turning out as he had.

And now, she had only to make it right. Make it right. The phrase stopped her runaway thoughts momentarily. Did she really want to turn back the clock and erase what had happened that afternoon? How could she? Why would she? How could she forget how Captain Thayer held her chin so gently and compared her to the beautiful statue of

Psyche? It was enough to make her swoon. What was happening to her? Normally, she was a most sensible young woman.

Tiffy Rose didn't want to ponder that particular question. She shifted her attention to two questions that had bothered her ever since the clockmaker had opened the pocket watch: Who was Percy and why did Captain Thayer have his watch?

"Tiffy Rose!" called a familiar voice.

"Over here," said another.

Tiffy Rose looked up at the broad veranda that fronted the clubhouse. Seated side-by-side in two wicker rocking chairs were the Barnes twins. They had changed for the afternoon into rose-colored dresses embellished with deep mauve ribbons.

"Come up and sit with us."

Having no desire to remain alone with her thoughts, Tiffy Rose willingly walked up the few stairs and joined the sisters.

The covered veranda of the Jekyll Island Club provided the women with an unobstructed view of the stunning expanse of salt-water marsh that separates Jekyll Island from the mainland. Not a single tree broke the level sweep of green marsh grass that undulated for miles in all directions before them.

"Isn't it a lovely view of the salt-water marsh?" asked Beverly.

"We are fortunate that it is still early in the day. This veranda faces west so the setting sun can be very warm in the late afternoon." Becca fanned herself in a desultory manner.

For a little while the young women stuck to safe topics like the weather and the view. Eventually they exhausted those avenues of small talk that lead nowhere and sat silently rocking in their chairs.

"You ladies look very comfortable," said Miss Pendergrass as she approached the veranda. "May I join you for a few minutes? I have a little time before I meet Miss Goodwin for some birdwatching."

Tiffy Rose noted that Miss Pendergrass wore a new style of skirt, more streamlined and shorter than the current fashion. She could see the tips of her shoes peeking out from beneath the skirt. No trailing hem to get dirty in the streets. It looked far more comfortable and practical than the lacy, ribbon-bedecked confection she was wearing.

Becca Barnes greeted the new arrival warmly. "Miss Pendergrass! How lovely of you to appear at such a fortuitous time. We were beginning to grow bored of our own company. Come and sit with us." She beckoned for the older woman to join them on the veranda.

"Always keep a good book with you and you will never be bored. Books can teach us much about the world around us." As she sat down in one of the comfortable rocking chairs, Miss Pendergrass held up a small volume of poetry that she was currently reading. "Please allow me to read a small section of a lovely poem about the salt marshes of Glynn whose magnificence we are enjoying right in front of us. In 1878, Sidney Lanier wrote a poem which he titled, '*The Marshes of Glynn*'. She opened the book, found the passage she sought and read it aloud.

"'The world lies east: how ample, the marsh and the sea and the sky!
A league and a league of marsh-grass, waist-high, broad in the blade,
Green, and all of a height, and unflecked with a light or a shade,
Stretch leisurely off, in a pleasant plain,
To the terminal blue of the main.
Oh, what is abroad in the marsh and the terminal sea?
Somehow my soul seems suddenly free
From the weighing of fate and the sad discussion of sin,
By the length and the breadth and the sweep of the marshes of Glynn.'"

Tiffy Rose found Lanier's words soothing. She made a mental note to locate a copy of Sidney Lanier's complete poem. Perhaps, Miss Pendergrass would loan her her copy.

The Barnes twins stirred restlessly.

Miss Pendergrass was determined to educate them whether they desired it or not. "Do you realize that a salt marsh is a veritable nursery for aquatic life? The *Spartina patens* grass grows in the dryer portions of the salt marsh. The *Spartina alterniflora* grows along the edges of the marsh creeks. The common name for *Spartina alterniflora* is cordgrass."

In unison, Becca and Beverly rolled their eyes. Tiffy Rose thought their behavior was in bad taste. The twins made no effort to disguise their boredom with the topic. After her earlier transgressions, Tiffy Rose felt compelled to support Miss Pendergrass.

"Please, tell us more, Miss Pendergrass."

Miss Pendergrass smiled at Tiffy Rose. "You are an apt pupil, Miss Baldwin. Let us return to the topic of the marsh. Were you aware that Periwinkle snails hide in the cordgrass? Not only does this small creature keep the cordgrass from taking over, they are also a source of food for a variety of birds. Did you know that the oysters you ate last night came from the marsh? Oysters keep the marsh clean by controlling erosion and filtering the water. Naturally, we enjoy eating them too!"

"What about the shrimp we eat? Do they come from the marsh?" asked Tiffy Rose despite the groans coming from the Barnes twins.

"Wild Georgia shrimp are born and grow up in the marsh. They feed on the *Spartina alterniflora*. These sweet grasses are related to the sugar cane plant. This diet is what makes Georgia shrimp so sweet."

"I will remember that the next time I eat Georgia shrimp," promised Tiffy Rose.

"Please allow me to tell you one last thing about an occupant of the marsh. I am sure that you will find it amusing," said Miss Pendergrass. She seemed blissfully unaware of the Barnes twins lack of interest. "The Clapper Rail, a type of marsh hen, lives in the salt marshes. I am sure that you have heard the expression 'thin as a rail'. It derives from how the Clapper Rail compresses its body so it can move through the thick cordgrass."

"How very interesting," exclaimed Tiffy Rose with more enthusiasm than necessary.

Becca Barnes yawned and changed the subject. "This veranda is perfect for people watching, isn't it?"

"Tifton, I've noticed that you are studying the faces of the men passing by. Who are you looking for?" asked Beverly meaningfully.

"Her beau," giggled Becca Barnes.

Beverly Barnes was far too observant and Becca far too giggly, thought Tiffy Rose uncharitably. She had come to the realization that though the twins were gay and charming, they loved to gossip and giggled at the slightest provocation. The sisters were indifferent to or unaware of anything other than their own desires and wishes. She also realized that the well-educated and well-traveled Miss Pendergrass couldn't be more different from them.

Beverly Barnes whispered to her sister in her best and loudest stage whisper, "I believe she is comparing Randolph Patterson Chatsworth III with every other wealthy and single man she has met during her stay on the island."

At that comment, Miss Pendergrass voiced her opinion loudly. "I will never understand why an unattached man possessing a reasonable fortune becomes prey for every female."

"Why not? It's not as if any young woman of quality would want a poor man. Take for instance, Captain Thayer. He is reasonably good looking and has presentable manners but he is not worth pursuing," said Beverly Barnes dismissively.

"For heaven's sake, why not?" asked Miss Pendergrass abruptly. "The family one is born into is not one's choice. Therefore, a person has no reason for familial pride. It is only what one accomplishes in life that matters." She went on to challenge them. "How will you change the world for good?"

Missing the point completely, Beverly answered simply, "Captain Thayer has no fortune."

"How do you know he has no fortune?" Tiffy Rose was curious how one could tell such things about other people.

"By his clothing, naturally," explained Beverly. "Everyone knows that clothing enables viewers to identify a person's gender, class, and social standing. So, while Captain Thayer conducts himself well in society, his clothing is dated and unsuitable for life here on the island."

"Yes, I know what you mean," echoed her sister. "One only has to look at his stiffly tailored jacket to know that Captain Thayer is rather self-contained and rigid in his personality."

Tiffy Rose thought back on her brief time with Captain Thayer. "I didn't find Captain Thayer to be self-contained or rigid in the least," admitted Tiffy Rose before she realized she should have kept her mouth shut.

Becca and Beverly's heads snapped up. They stared at Tiffy Rose as if she had grown two heads.

"How is it that you know Captain Thayer?" asked Beverly with avid curiosity.

Blushing furiously, Tiffy Rose had never considered Captain Thayer's financial position nor his standing in society. She stammered, "I encountered him briefly when I found that man on the beach." She faced her new friends and said in a no-nonsense voice, "You are correct in your assessment of his personality. Captain Thayer conducted himself as a gentleman."

Becca and Beverly eyed her speculatively.

"Regardless of how he dresses, Captain Thayer seems impervious to a woman's charms. Is that what is really bothering you?" asked a very astute Miss Pendergrass.

Beverly neatly avoided Miss Pendergrass's question by changing the topic of conversation. "Tell me, Tiffy Rose, are you aware that Miss Alice Rawlins has a crush on Randolph Patterson?"

"Randolph Patterson Chatsworth?" asked Tiffy Rose, shocked. "Alice Rawlins has a crush on Randolph Patterson Chatsworth?

"The very same," responded Becca smugly.

"I had no idea," exclaimed Tiffy Rose. She really had had no indication that her new friend, Alice, had any interest in Randolph Patterson. She shook her head in disbelief. "Are you certain?"

"Oh, yes! Look at the way she looks at him the next time you see them together," said Beverly.

"Why, Tiffy Rose, if you hadn't come along and dangled your fortune in front of him and his parents, he'd surely be Alice's beau by now!" announced Becca with glee.

"It's true. Alice and Randolph usually spend all their time together when they are both on Jekyll Island at the same time," added Beverly. "It's his parents who have pushed him your way. So sad, especially since he has feelings for Alice Rawlins."

Confused and upset that her fiancé had feelings for another younger and prettier woman, Tiffy Rose stood and gathered up her shawl and reticule. "Excuse me, ladies, I must return to my room. My parents are expecting me."

Chapter 14
Burke

Burke whistled as he strolled away from the clubhouse. He had enjoyed his time with Miss Baldwin; however, he had work to do.

His visit to the clockmaker had not revealed as much as he would have liked. The clockmaker managed to open the casing, something that Burke had not been able to do. Then came the uncomfortable moment when the man read the inscription on the inside of the case. What would have happened if Miss Baldwin hadn't cleverly made up that bit of nonsense about his being Percy? Remembering how her marvelous improvisation saved the day, Burke shook his head, a half-smile on his face. That girl could certainly think fast on her feet.

Captain Clark had pinpointed when Percy had arrived on the island. Now, Burke could check the guestbook at the registration desk for a man with the first name of Percy who had arrived the afternoon before he had been found on the beach. He also had a first-class train ticket to New York, although a first name and a city were not much to go on. He would pull in a few favors and have his friends investigate. He wasn't hopeful that they would discover much.

Burke spent the remainder of the day asking questions around the island. Except for creating a list of where Percy had not been seen, he had uncovered nothing particularly useful. He wondered whether or not he should tell the Jekyll Island Club board about his findings, meager as they were. Instead, he decided to return to the clubhouse and check the registration guestbook again.

As he strolled by the *San Souci* apartments, a steward approached him. After handing Burke a folded piece of paper, the man waited patiently for a response. Burke read the note. It was from Joseph Pulitzer, the well-known publisher, asking him to come up to his rooms for a meeting later that day. Knowing that the publisher did not like noise, light, or people, Burke was rather surprised that the man would have requested a meeting. He consulted his pocket watch and decided that he had time to send a few telegrams, inspect the registration guestbook, and return to his room to change before going over to *San Souci.*

"Captain Thayer, what do you know of the anarchist movement?" asked Mr. Pulitzer, the editor and publisher of the **New York World** newspaper, after the two men had exchanged greetings.

Burke was surprised when the publisher asked him to meet with him in his apartment in *Sans Souci.* He had arrived early and allowed himself some time to study the building's architecture. Six apartments, three on each side, were serviced by a central staircase. The dark wood wainscoting gave a kind of dignity to the simple design. Big rooms with high ceilings and thick walls added to the overall comfort of the apartments. Large windows provided ample light, though Pulitzer had the shades drawn. Burke doubted that the man enjoyed the west facing balconies that overlooked the salt marsh.

Burke knew not to be drawn into a political discussion with the well-informed man. "I probably know as much as any U.S. citizen who reads your papers, Mr. Pulitzer."

"Well said, young man. Well said." The older gentleman smiled slightly before commanding, "Please, tell me what you know. I am curious about the viewpoint of the common man."

Only slightly annoyed at being called a 'common man', Burke rose to the publisher's implied challenge. "All right. I know that anarchists could also be called terrorists. They believe in 'Propaganda by the deed', which is just another way of saying that they are willing to take violent action to make a point."

"That's true," nodded Pulitzer. "Continue." He made a swirling motion with his hand. He gave the impression that he was used to ordering subordinates around with a wave of his hand.

"Though they meet regularly with other anarchists, in general, anarchists tend to act alone—a single gunman, for instance."

"I believe that is true enough," intoned the publisher, an original Jekyll Island Club member. "Anarchists are secret enemies of everything the United States stands for including freedom and justice."

"Well said. Anarchists believe that there should be no government."

"Once again, Captain Thayer, you are correct. However, anarchists go much further in their beliefs. They believe that there should be no accumulation of property or wealth. Many believe it should be illegal to be successful and acquire the trappings of success." The publisher smiled a tight smile. "We, here on this island, will need to watch out, won't we? We stand for everything anarchists hate."

"Yes, sir, there is a very real risk that your lives may be in danger," said Burke seriously.

"I assure you, we are well aware of that," snapped the publisher, suddenly unfriendly. "Haven't you noticed the design similarity of the homes built along the Jekyll River? They are narrower on the side facing the water and large and accommodating to the rear. They are designed like this in order to make them appear less pretentious—and less interesting—to the casual observer on the river."

"I hadn't realized that, sir. Thank you for enlightening me. What other precautions have you and the other club members taken?"

"The island's location is one of our biggest safety features. You are likely aware that Jekyll Island is several miles from the nearest solid land."

"Yes, sir. Yet a man was murdered yesterday," challenged Burke. He knew he was stating the obvious, but he was annoyed that virtually no one seemed to care about the dead man.

"I am well aware of that, too, Captain Thayer." A hint of anger came into the publisher's voice.

"I have no doubt that you are, sir."

Both men sat silently for a few moments, each attending to his own thoughts.

Burke broke the silence with a question. "Didn't one of your writers coin the phrase 'The Golden Age of Assassinations'?"

"Yes. Do you realize that more monarchs, presidents, and prime ministers than ever before in the history of the modern world have been assassinated since 1892?" As if to answer his own question, Pulitzer went on to list them. "The French President, Marie Francois Carnot in 1894. The Prime Minister of Spain, Antonio Caravan de Castillo, in 1897. The empress of Austria-Hungary, Elizabeth Hapsburg, in September 1898. We mustn't forget that on our own shores Andrew Carnegie's second in command, Henry Frick, was attacked and nearly killed by an anarchist in 1892. The implications are that we can expect more high-profile assassinations in the future."

"You must protect yourselves from anarchists, sir. There is much anxiety about President McKinley's rather lax concern for his own safety," stated Burke succinctly.

"I can understand everyone's concern. President McKinley's practice of shaking hands with everyone leaves him open to assassins. So far, most of the past attacks on public officials have come from anarchists wielding guns. But what about our now widely available weapon of mass destruction: dynamite? What will happen when anarchists increase their use of bombs?" The publisher suddenly looked bleak.

Burke gave a heartfelt sigh. "The future looks grim, doesn't it?"

"Yes, it certainly does," agreed Pulitzer. He turned to face Burke. "What are your plans for protecting McKinley?"

"Shouldn't that discussion take place with the members of the Jekyll Island Club board in attendance?"

"I couldn't agree more. That is why I have invited the board over here for a meeting. They should be arriving shortly. You can also tell them about the progress that you have made in the investigation of the dead man. You do, of course, realize how important it is to solve this mystery very soon? There has never been a death on Jekyll Island, at least not of this nature."

Burke realized that he should have been prepared for a surprise meeting. The trouble was that he didn't really have anything to tell the board about the dead man. He understood how crucial it was to solve the mystery—both for his future and for the peace of mind of the residents of Jekyll Island. Unfortunately, beyond the contents of the man's pockets, he didn't have any new clues to go by. He awaited news from New York, but was not hopeful.

A few moments later, the board members began to arrive. Charles Lanier, the club president, arrived first, followed by Charles Maurice, Cornelius Bliss, Charles Rawlins, Marcus Barnes, Gordon McKay, Dr. Martin, and Frederic Baker. J.P. Morgan and Ernest Grob came together. Burke noticed the comradery between the superintendent and Joseph Pulitzer. Though welcomed by all the men present, the superintendent received a particularly warm greeting from the publisher.

Once the men were all settled in the large and comfortable sitting room, the questions began to come at Burke from all sides.

"Please, tell me, Captain Thayer, how do you plan to protect President McKinley when you haven't solved the mystery surrounding the dead man? We don't even know who he is, for heaven's sake. He could be an anarchist for all we know!" Charles Rawlins had already worked up a head of steam.

"My esteemed colleague brings up an important matter. Is the dead man in any way connected to an anarchist plot?" asked Mr. Baker. His anxiety over President McKinley's stay at Solterra was evident.

"That's what I want to know!" exclaimed Charles Lanier.

"Gentlemen, gentlemen, let's deal with this logically," said J.P. Morgan. He motioned for quiet with his hands. "I, for one, would like to hear Captain Thayer's plans to protect the president. I believe that would be a good place to begin this afternoon's meeting."

Others nodded with agreement, willing to follow the financier's lead.

Burke stepped to the front of the room. He cleared his throat. "Plans are in place for President McKinley to arrive in Brunswick aboard a special train. He may, however, decide to come by boat. We won't know until tomorrow which he will choose. If he arrives by train, after a brief welcoming speech at the platform, he and his wife will transfer to a carriage to be transported to the Brunswick dock. Once there, the president will board the *Howland* and make for Jekyll Island. It is at this point that the president becomes our responsibility." Burke took a sip of his ice tea. The drink was well-chilled and a welcome refreshment. He marveled at the availability of ice in the deep south. Burke could see the benefits to being rich.

"You have yet to tell us how you plan to protect the president," said Mr. Barnes accusingly.

"The first thing that you all must realize is that we are all responsible for the president's well-being and safety while he is on Jekyll Island. It is no small thing to have the president here for a visit. It will be—it must be—*our* plan to protect the president." Burke paused and let the import of what he said sink into their minds.

"But, how can we be responsible?" asked the club president, Charles Lanier.

"Isn't that why you are here?" This question came from Mr. Rawlins.

"Leave it to the Navy to saddle us with a shirker," sneered Mr. Barnes.

"Sir, I take offense at those words," said Burke forcefully. "I am willing to give my life to protect the president. However, I cannot protect him without your help and cooperation. Who among you are willing to help me?" Burke studied each man's face in turn. He didn't like what he saw there. Cooperation did not appear to be their strong suit.

Hiding his disappointment, Burke persevered. "The first thing that I would do would be to search the *Howland* with zeal. One of the easiest access points to President McKinley is on the *Howland* as he rides over to the island. With the excitement of hearing the president speak, the boat will probably not be watched closely, leaving it open for anarchists to plant a bomb with a timer. If the blast does not kill the president outright, the sinking of the boat in the deep waters of the Brunswick River before it reaches Jekyll Island probably will."

Several of the men present drew in sharp breaths.

"Do you really think that an anarchist will attack President McKinley before he gets to Jekyll Island?"

Burke nodded his head. "It should be fairly obvious that a bomb is an easy way to dispatch the president. An anarchist could plant the bomb on the *Howland*, set the timer, and disappear on the mainland long before the president arrives. From the point of view of the anarchist, this is a much less risky plan."

"Why a bomb?" asked Ernest Grob.

"The development of dynamite is changing how people express their feelings about authority. Dynamite is much more stable than black powder or nitroglycerin, making it relatively safe to transport and work with," Burke explained. "Timers and detonators are simple to construct. All one needs is a timing mechanism, like a clock, for instance. Put it all together and you've made a bomb."

"Surely, it can't be easy to obtain dynamite," protested Mr. Rawlins.

"Actually, dynamite is relatively easy to acquire," responded Burke.

"What can we do?" asked Superintendent Grob.

"We need to out-think a possible anarchist," encouraged Burke. "We will need to make a list of all of the times and places that President McKinley will be vulnerable and shore up our defenses."

"That's what you meant earlier with your statement about your needing our help, isn't it, Captain?" asked Mr. Maurice respectfully. "We know the island and its people and you know the mind of an anarchist. We must work together to protect the president."

"I cannot say for sure that I understand how anarchists think. I am not certain anyone understands them," answered Burke with humility. "But I have had training in the planning and implementing of defenses against anarchist attacks."

"I, for one, believe we should all be more helpful to Captain Thayer," announced Mr. Rawlins, suddenly helpful instead of obstructive. "Why don't we begin by making a list of activities that are planned for the president? Will that help, Captain Thayer?"

"That is exactly what we need. Don't leave anything out. Even the smallest detail will be important to keep President McKinley safe." Burke breathed a sigh of relief when the other men in the room nodded their heads in agreement.

Cornelius Newton Bliss, the current United States Secretary of the Interior and an original Jekyll Island Club member, asked Pulitzer for writing paper. He extracted a fountain pen from his pocket and prepared to write. "First, I believe I will ask President McKinley to use the presidential cutter, the *Colfax*, to bring him directly to the Jekyll wharf on the afternoon of March 20. Since the *Colfax* is a more comfortable ship than the *Howland*, the arrangement should suit him better."

"Definitely," agreed J.P. Morgan. "Doing so will release us from the burden of protecting the president while he travels over water to reach us."

"We can be sure that the *Colfax* will be closely guarded by his own men during his visit here."

"Cornelius, can you tell us what the president plans to do while he is on the island?" asked J.P. Morgan.

"Certainly. Senator Mark Hanna and I went over the details of the president's stay before I left Washington." Bliss pulled a small note card from his pocket and began to read it aloud. "Besides President and Mrs. Ida McKinley, the party includes Vice President and Mrs. Garret A. Hobart and Senator Hanna."

"Where will the President and Mrs. McKinley be staying while on Jekyll?" asked Burke. He already knew, but he wanted confirmation.

"I will be housing the entire party at my cottage, Solterra," confirmed Frederic Baker.

"That is very accommodating of you. It will make guarding the president and his party much easier," said Burke. He didn't say that it also made it much easier to eliminate the men in the two highest offices of the nation at the same time. Solterra would need to be carefully guarded at all times.

Bliss continued, "Once the president's party disembarks from the *Colfax*, he will give a short speech. Following a brief greeting of the crowd, they will be taken by carriage to Solterra. There, they will spend the afternoon getting settled and resting."

"Is everyone aware that Thomas Reed, the Speaker of the House of Representatives, is on the island visiting John G. Moore? Mr. Reed is staying at *San Souci* as a guest of Mr. Moore."

Murmurs of discomfort rolled through the gathered men. Burke raised his eyebrows in question.

Having seen Thayer's confused look, J.P. Morgan clarified, "Captain Thayer, you may not be aware of the animosity between Mr. Reed and President McKinley."

"The two men had a falling out over the annexation of the Philippines," shared Mr. Bliss.

"Will the two men have to meet?" asked Burke. Wanting to avoid fireworks between the men and the confusion that might follow, he sincerely hoped not. Any unplanned event, regardless of how small, might give an anarchist a chance to attack.

"Jekyll Island is a small island. The two are bound to meet," protested Pulitzer.

"Hopefully, they will behave with decorum," said Burke. "Back to the task at hand, how will the president be occupying his time?"

"The president is here to rest. Very few activities are actually planned. He has turned down the opportunity to go hunting or golfing or boating. He does plan to ride around the island in a carriage. The president and his wife would like to visit Horton House." Bliss mentioned the ruins of the old tabby plantation house built by William Horton in the early 1700s during the British occupation of the area. "There is also an informal reception for club members at Solterra in the evening on March 21."

"Rest assured that the president will have many informal meetings during his stay," added Charles Lanier.

"What about reporters?" asked Burke.

"There will be no reporters permitted on the island," grumbled J.P. Morgan. He glared at Joseph Pulitzer.

Pulitzer harrumphed. "I don't see why not. The president's visit is news!"

"Can't be done, Pulitzer. We already discussed all the reasons why not," said J.P. Morgan sternly.

"Freedom of the press, J.P. Freedom of the press," taunted Pulitzer.

"Allowing reporters onto the island significantly increases the risk to the president and his party," agreed Burke.

"I agree," said Charles Lanier.

"Jekyll Island is currently patrolled by two boats that prevent outsiders' boats from coming too close to the island. During the president's stay we will double that number and provide extra men so the crews can stay vigilant," said Ernest Grob.

"We should never have dismantled the fortifications that were installed on the south end of the island in case the Spanish invaded last year. They could have provided much needed protection."

"I couldn't agree more," responded Superintendent Grob.

"What about the hired help? Shouldn't they be checked out?" asked Mr. Maurice.

"Yes! There may be an anarchist among them!" said an alarmed Mr. Baker.

"Do you have any idea how many of the servants and other workers on the island are new this season? How many have worked here before?" asked Burke.

"Do you mean servants and workers employed directly by the club?" asked Superintendent Grob.

"Or do you mean our personal servants that we have brought with us?" asked Mr. Lanier.

Burke tried another approach. "How many people are currently on the island? Who are they? How may they be classified? Members, guests, and employees?"

The men in the room looked at Burke, perplexed. Finally, Charles Lanier ventured, "I am sure that Superintendent Grob can provide you with that information."

Burke could tell by the look on Superintendent Grob's face that the man didn't know and didn't have time to find out. The president was coming the day after tomorrow. Burke had a dead man, a group of millionaires primarily interested in the upcoming opportunity to interact with the president, and too many people to keep track of. Why had he been given this particular nightmare of a job?

The men continued to discuss the president's visit until it was time to change for dinner. As he walked back to the clubhouse, Burke hoped he had all the information he needed.

Chapter 15
Tiffy Rose

Once back in the room she shared with Miss Goodwin, Tiffy Rose replayed her conversation with the Barnes twins as she stood in front of the mirror. In her reflection, she saw that her clothes and blonde hair were so proper and unexciting that she looked dowdy. She couldn't help but wonder what the Barnes sisters said about her after she left. Would either of those perfectly dressed and beautifully coifed young women look beyond her clothes and hair at the woman inside? Would the woman inside her ever escape from society's strict rules about comportment and behavior? What would become of the woman she saw inside if she never escaped? Suddenly, Tiffy Rose felt trapped.

The thought of smothering her inner self in order to comply with social norms was so strong, Tiffy Rose felt as if she couldn't breathe. Despite the breeze from the open window, the air in the room became suffocating. Tiffy Rose bolted from the room in a headlong rush to escape her thoughts. In her haste to reach the outside, at the top of the stairs, she ran squarely into Miss Pendergrass.

"My dear, what is wrong?" Miss Pendergrass took Tiffy Rose by the shoulders and steadied her. "I was just coming to see you when you came hurrying down the hallway. What has upset you so?"

Rather than answer, Tifton Rose Baldwin, a young woman who never fainted, collapsed in a graceful heap into Miss Pendergrass's arms.

Miss Pendergrass held onto Tiffy Rose as she looked around for help. She spied a man coming from the opposite corridor. A good-looking man with strong arms and back. "You there! Come and help me get Miss Baldwin back into her room. She has fainted." Miss Pendergrass's voice brooked no refusal.

Together, she and the stranger moved Tiffy Rose to the couch in her parents' suite. Thanking the man graciously, Miss Pendergrass showed him to the door.

She returned to where Tiffy Rose lay. Miss Pendergrass took her hand and patted it gently in an effort to bring her around. Even with the aid of smelling salts, it took several minutes for Tiffy Rose to fully revive. Her eyelids fluttered open.

"Oh! What happened? Why am I on the couch?" Tiffy Rose touched her hand to her forehead and found a damp washcloth on it. She touched her neck and found her blouse unbuttoned.

Miss Pendergrass smiled. "Welcome back, Tifton. I took the liberty of applying a cool compress to your forehead to help soothe you. I applaud your lack of a corset, by the way. They are nothing but evil things that can ruin a woman's health."

"Oh! I fainted?" asked Tiffy Rose weakly. "I never faint." She vaguely remembered being held and carried by someone.

"Yes, you did indeed. You fainted right into my arms." Miss Pendergrass smiled. "Not quite as romantic as it would have been if the arms were those of your intended."

Tiffy Rose burst into tears.

"What have I said to make you cry, Tifton?" Miss Pendergrass put her arm around Tiffy Rose's shoulders. "Young women shouldn't be allowed to faint. It is a sign of either a weak character or a too-tight corset. Tell me, my dear, what is wrong?" She looked around the well-appointed room with its chaise longue heaped with satin and lace pillows, the heavy damask curtains, the carved mahogany furniture. "What would a young woman like you have to cry about? You have jewels, gowns from famous dressmakers, furs—everything a girl could want."

"Everything except love!" cried Tiffy Rose.

Through her tears, Tiffy Rose explained about her mother's ambitions for her, Randolph Patterson Chatsworth III, Alice's desire for Mr. Chatsworth, her conversation with the Barnes sisters, and then in a final burst of candor, she told Miss Pendergrass about Captain Thayer without telling his name.

Miss Pendergrass listened carefully to Tiffy Rose's disjointed story. At the end of her tears and words, the older woman sighed. "The marriage market with its contracts and dowries disturbs me. Many a young girl has been sacrificed on the altar of marriage. I will never understand the exchange of a wealthy young woman for social standing or a title. Many a misalliance has been contracted in the name of ambition. I have cautioned several young women against buying a title that way. It does not buy happiness. Many marriages contracted under such circumstances are in name only and end in divorce. I would hate to see that happen to you—to any woman."

"No one will want me except for my money. I'm not at all well-mannered or compliant. It is against my nature. How am I supposed to turn myself into a cuddly, submissive creature? What about my spirit?" asked Tiffy Rose defiantly. She hiccupped and mopped her eyes with her damp handkerchief.

"Yes, you certainly have a lot of spirit. What you are struggling with is two conflicting desires. On the one hand, you would like to please your parents by conforming to society's expectations. On the other hand, you seek independence. In other words, you are a perfectly normal young woman standing on the brink of a new century. Mark my words, many things will change in the next decade, many things."

Tiffy Rose was caught off-guard by the forcefulness of Miss Pendergrass's voice. In her eyes, Tiffy Rose could see the conviction with which the older woman held her beliefs. Miss Pendergrass's radical attitude and ideas made Tiffy Rose uncomfortable. Was this woman one of those anarchists her parents had warned her about?

In response to this question, Tiffy Rose's rebellious nature took over. What did she care about this woman's political beliefs? She found Miss Pendergrass very interesting. She intended to spend as much time with her as possible.

"Why do parents feel that they need to select who their daughters are to marry? Why can we not be trusted to make that decision on our own? Why aren't we allowed to marry for love?"

"Parents only want what is best for their children," responded Miss Pendergrass in what seemed to Tiffy Rose to be a complete about-face.

"Parents base their choices only on social status and wealth," sniffed Tiffy Rose. "What's the sense in that?"

"If you had ever been poor, you would understand their reasoning. They are trying to protect you from the hardships of life."

Tiffy Rose sat still for a moment, remembering the women and children she had seen at the soup kitchen where her mother insisted she volunteer several times a month. Miss Pendergrass and her parents did have a point. Based on what she had witnessed at the shelter, being poor was a hard way to live.

"I see you understand my meaning," said Miss Pendergrass gently. "You'll understand better when you are older and perhaps, married."

"I shall never marry unless it is for love!" Tiffy Rose lifted her chin a little higher.

"Not for you to be trapped in a gilded cage, is it? Perhaps you will find true love. One never knows when Cupid will strike. Who knows? Your prince charming might be right before your eyes this very minute."

"He might," said Tiffy Rose, thinking of Captain Thayer. In a very short time and with very little knowledge of the man, she had built him up to the status of a knight-in-shining-armor ready to carry her away to his castle.

"Don't rush to a hasty decision, my dear." Miss Pendergrass embraced Tiffy Rose quickly.

"Thank you for listening to me, Miss Pendergrass. I feel so much better having shared my thoughts and feelings with you."

"Anytime, my dear, anytime. Now, I think it would be better if your parents did not find me here with you. They may not agree with my politics. Will you be all right if I leave you?"

"Yes, I am much better now. Thank you so much for listening to me. I truly appreciate the time that you have spent with me. Thank you. Will I see you around?" asked Tiffy Rose, suddenly feeling frantic.

"Of course, you will."

Suddenly, both women stiffened at a noise from the hallway.

"My parents!" exclaimed Tiffy Rose. Her eyes darted around the room in fright.

"Tifton, look me in the eye." Miss Pendergrass held Tiffy Rose firmly by her shoulders. "You strike me as an intelligent, self-contained young woman, yet I sense that you are hiding deep emotions. Whether you believe it or not, you do have some control over your life. You do not have to face a future that frightens you. We will talk more tomorrow. I promise. Do not lose heart."

Her parents entered the room just as Miss Pendergrass stood up and smoothed her skirts.

"Oh! Hello Miss Pendergrass. We didn't expect to find you here." Mrs. Baldwin looked confused. She noticed her daughter's red eyes.

"Hello, Mrs. Baldwin. I am so happy you have returned. I was just about to look for you," Miss Pendergrass smoothly improvised. "It seems that Tifton got something in her eyes, probably from a plant. It has irritated them. We came up to her room to wash her eyes out with warm water. She seems better now." She held up the damp wash cloth as evidence.

"My goodness! Tifton, are you all right?" Mrs. Baldwin hurried to her daughter's side. She took Tifton's face in her hands and turned her head from left to right, checking her eyes.

Tiffy Rose submitted to her mother's ministrations docilely enjoying the motherly attention. It had been a trying day—two trying days actually. "Yes, mother, I am much better thanks to Miss Pendergrass. She has been very kind." Tiffy Rose would never tell her mother just how kind.

"Thank you for watching over my precious daughter. You have our sincere appreciation." Franklin Baldwin helped Miss Pendergrass to the door. "Are you dining with anyone tonight? If not, we would enjoy your company at our table. We are dining with Mr. and Mrs. Randolph Patterson Chatsworth II and their son, Randolph Patterson."

"I would be delighted," responded Miss Pendergrass quickly. As she left the room, she added in parting to Tiffy Rose, "Keep your chin up, my dear, but don't lead with it."

Chapter 16
Burke

After concluding his meeting with Joseph Pulitzer and the board, Burke walked back toward the clubhouse. As he neared the croquet lawn, he saw the woman who had requested his assistance with Miss Baldwin walking toward him. She waved to him.

"Hello. I am so happy to have run into you just now," said the woman warmly. She possessed a very musical voice. "I want to thank you for your help today. You were so kind."

"Think nothing of it," said Burke graciously. "When I saw you struggling to prevent someone from falling down the stairs, how could I refuse to come to your aid?"

"Your arrival was quite fortuitous, sir. You prevented both of us from coming to harm. My young friend fainted so abruptly; I had no time to prepare. I was so afraid that we would both tumble down the stairs." She looked at his uniform, noting the insignias. "I do so appreciate your help, Captain—"

"Thayer. Captain Burke Thayer."

"I am Miss Pendergrass."

Confidently, she offered him her hand. Surprised and unsure of how to respond, Burke hesitated. Then, he took her hand and shook it firmly. Her fine expressive eyes met his and she smiled.

When she spoke again, it was to say, "I do not understand what brought about my young friend's faint, today. I do not know Miss Baldwin very well, but she doesn't strike me as the type to faint."

Burke smiled at the memory of the lovely Miss Baldwin in his arms. For just a brief second, he imagined he smelled the light scent of rose water. He returned his attention to Miss Pendergrass and said, "For someone who constantly tells me she never faints, Miss Baldwin did a very good imitation of a prostrated young woman today."

Miss Pendergrass halted in her tracks. She took ahold of his arm and stopped him. "You sound as if you are well-acquainted with Miss Baldwin."

Thinking that he would probably never see this woman again, Burke answered blithely, "We are third cousins, twice removed."

"Cousins?" gasped Miss Pendergrass. "Cousins," she said more slowly. She studied Burke for a long moment, taking his measure. She added cryptically, "It fits. You fit. Yes, yes."

"How is Miss Baldwin?" Burke asked, politely choosing to ignore Miss Pendergrass's unusual comments.

Miss Pendergrass assumed a well-mannered smile. "She has fully recovered from her fainting spell. She is with her parents now."

"I see. If you happen to see her, please give her my best."

"I will, Captain Thayer. I will. Thank you again for your help. It is much appreciated."

As he dressed for dinner, Burke turned possible connections over and over in his mind. It was feasible that a banker or a financier could be connected with anarchists. After all, anarchists needed money to support themselves and their activities. Could Percy have been tied into anarchists? If so, what brought him to the island? Why had he died in such a gruesome fashion? And if Percy wasn't connected to anarchists, then why had someone killed him on the island? Why had someone taken great pains to ensure that he wouldn't be recognized? Was the murderer still among them? Could it be one of the millionaires?

On his way to dinner, Burke returned to the front desk to ask about the dead man. He hadn't made much progress in the case. He had yet to decide whether or not the victim's death was connected with President McKinley's visit to Jekyll Island. Burke didn't want to revise his earlier opinion that Percy had a job in the city, probably working with numbers. Even his name—Percy—pointed to a man who spent his time in an office, somewhere, toting up columns of numbers. Yes, the man was definitely a prosperous, middle-aged, banker or financier. The first-class train ticket to New York narrowed down where to look for Percy's past. He needed to determine the man's last name. Frustrated, Burke stopped at the reception desk. As he expected, a different clerk was on duty.

"Excuse me."

"Yes, sir. How may I help you?

"My name is Captain Thayer. Have you received any telegrams for me?"

The man turned around and checked the contents of the room numbered letter box. "No sir, we have not received any messages for you today."

"I see. Well, thank you." Burke made to turn away and then thought of something. He hadn't spoken to this particular clerk about Percy. "Just a few more questions, if you don't mind."

"Certainly, sir," responded the clerk politely.

"I am looking for a man whose first name is Percy. Has anyone by that name checked in during the past three days?"

"Please allow me to check our records." The clerk spun the registration book around and perused the signatures of the guests. After a few frustrating minutes, he said, "No. No, sir. I don't see anyone with a first name of Percy. No 'P's' either."

"I see."

"Does Mr. Percy have a last name, sir?" asked the helpful clerk.

"No, not that I know of—yet."

The clerk gave Burke a strange look.

Feeling compelled to give the man some sort of explanation, Burke said, "I am trying to locate Mr. Percy for a friend of mine. Unfortunately, my friend's communication to me was somewhat garbled. I have only the first name to work with."

"I see," said the clerk, his tone indicating that he did not see.

Burke snapped his fingers as he thought of something else. "Is there any unclaimed luggage?"

The clerk squirmed uncomfortably. Clearly, he felt he had been helpful enough.

"Perhaps you could look," encouraged Burke.

The clerk's head swiveled back and forth as he searched for a manager. "I'm not sure," he began. Then he spotted a familiar face. "Mr. Chatsworth! How are you this evening?" the clerk asked with exaggerated warmth.

Surprised by the overly friendly greeting from the clerk, Randolph Patterson Chatsworth looked behind him, half-expecting to see his father. He turned back to the clerk and patted both hands flat against his chest and said, "Me? Do you mean me?"

"Yes, sir, Mr. Chatsworth. Lovely evening, isn't it?" The clerk moved to stand nearer to Randolph Patterson which only served to increase the young man's discomfort.

Randolph Patterson saw Burke and grasped at him like a lifeline. "Captain Thayer! How nice to see you again."

As soon as Chatsworth identified Burke by name, the desk clerk relaxed. The man slipped behind the desk and busied himself, keeping his eyes down, obviously grateful for the interruption Randolph Patterson Chatsworth provided.

Burke decided not to query the clerk anymore this evening. The matter of unclaimed luggage could wait until tomorrow when Superintendent Grob could make the request. Besides, Burke was very curious about Mr. Chatsworth.

"Mr. Chatsworth, how nice to see you. Are you on your way to dinner or do you have time for a drink?"

Randolph Patterson checked the time on the clock above the reception desk against that of his pocket watch. He tugged at the too-tight collar of his tuxedo shirt. "I am meeting Miss Baldwin and her family in a few minutes, but I do have time for a quick one."

Under his breath, Burke heard the young man murmur, "Heaven knows I need one."

Unexpectedly, Burke felt a wave of empathy toward the young man. Now he was even more curious to learn more about him.

"Shall we retire to the bar?"

"Yes, that would be nice," agreed Chatsworth.

They made their way to the small bar outside of the dining room. Chatsworth chose a chair which allowed him to see who was entering the dining room. Burke could tell that he intended to keep a weather eye out for his parents and Miss Baldwin.

They ordered whiskeys and waited to speak until the bartender had brought them their drinks.

"I see you were able to reclaim your pocket watch this afternoon," offered Burke to start the conversation.

Chatsworth pulled the watch from his pocket as if it offended him. "Yes, I was. It's a gift from an aunt and uncle. Never really has kept good time. Seems much better now. Perhaps the clockmaker does know what he is doing." Randolph Patterson abruptly ceased his ramblings and took a stiff drink.

Content to let him talk, Burke remained silent.

Eventually, Chatsworth began to speak again. "Queer fellow, that clockmaker. Name of Horst, by the way. When I returned this afternoon, he was all smiles. Had my watch fixed and everything. Don't understand the man. He was quite unlike the way he acted this morning. Remember, he was positively beastly to Miss Baldwin."

After slipping his watch back in his pocket, Chatsworth took another drink, nearly draining the glass. He held up his glass to the bartender, signaling for another.

"If you are dining with your parents and the Baldwins tonight, perhaps you should go easy on the booze," cautioned Burke. He regretted suggesting that they visit the bar. Chatsworth was obviously upset about something.

"Doesn't seem to make a bit of difference to my parents what I do. All they care about is that I make a match with the woman of their choice: Miss Tifton Rose Baldwin. Got to refill the family coffers. You know what it is like."

"Can't say that I do," said Burke, feeling out of his depth. He couldn't imagine a life where his parents thought so little of him and his desires in life. Burke didn't know what to say next. He had taken a liking to Chatsworth.

He ventured a question. "Don't you like Miss Baldwin?"

"Like her? Like her? I love her. The point is that she doesn't even know I exist. Don't get me wrong, she is nice enough to me, very polite and all that. She's rather wonderful actually—very charming, witty, and smart! Have you ever taken a good look at her? She's really quite beautiful. It's just that I don't know what to say or do when I am around her. I usually make a hash of things. She probably thinks of me as a complete idiot."

"Surely it's not that bad," exclaimed Burke.

"Yes, it is." Chatsworth looked Burke full in the face. Encouraged by the whiskey he had consumed, he spoke freely. "I saw you with Miss Baldwin today. The two of you were laughing together. You don't think that I knew that you were trying to pull the wool over my eyes with all this nonsense of your being cousins." Randolph Patterson took a sip of whiskey.

Ashamed at his participation in the deception of this unassuming young man, Burke bowed his head.

"You needn't apologize, Captain Thayer. I know you meant no harm. It's just that I am jealous of your ease with women. I have never been able to make Miss Baldwin laugh. Not once." Chatsworth stared at the contents of his whiskey glass but did not take a drink.

Burke made a quick decision to try and help Randolph Patterson. Unfortunately, he could think of nothing to say that wasn't trite or pompous sounding. Eventually, he settled on, "Perhaps you are trying too hard."

Randolph Patterson merely stared at him.

Burke tried again. "Look, what I mean to say is that Miss Baldwin strikes me as a nice young lady. Granted, she is not the typical pliant and soft young woman preferred by most men, but she has qualities that few women possess. She is intelligent, imaginative, and brave. Rare qualities in a woman." Burke realized that he was speaking far too eloquently about another man's fiancé. He had better be careful.

Chatsworth didn't seem to notice and merely nodded his head in agreement. "That is why I find her so appealing. Miss Baldwin surprises me at every turn with her unexpected views on life. Take this morning, for example. Rather than demurely apologizing for her inappropriate behavior, she brazened it out with her bold tale about you being her cousin. She made it all sound so much like a pleasing lark that I wanted to kiss her."

Burke considered the young man in front of him. After a moment, he said, "Why didn't you?"

"I don't know. Not brave enough, I imagine."

The young man's attitude angered Burke. "Chatsworth, it must be hard to be someone you are not all the time. Doing so makes it hard to have confidence in yourself. Why don't you try being yourself?"

"Be myself?" asked Randolph Patterson.

Burke looked into Randolph's eyes. "Look here, you've got a lot going for you. You're easy-going and pleasant to be around. You're a good man. You should act like one. Why don't you try being yourself for a change? I think Miss Baldwin would like that very much."

Sensing that they had reached some sort of accord, Randolph Patterson Chatsworth raised his glass to Burke's and touched rims. The crystal made a faint, sweet sound.

Chapter 17
Tiffy Rose

"Tifton! What are you doing to your ballgown?" asked a disconcerted Miss Goodwin.

Tiffy Rose lifted her chin defiantly. "In a fit of protest against the trappings a woman must wear, I am merely snipping off all of the trims and ribbons festooning my ballgown." Tiffy Rose held up the dress for Miss Goodwin to see, spilling yards of fancy trim and tulle and ribbons onto the floor at her feet.

Together, the two women contemplated what remained.

"To my eyes, it is a vision in simplicity," said Tiffy Rose proudly.

"Your mother is going to be furious!"

"Probably," admitted Tiffy Rose. Standing in front of the mirror, she held the dress in front of her. Liking what she saw, she stroked the apple green satin fabric of the gown. Now it was possible to admire the sheer lace overlay that softened the bright color.

Miss Goodwin studied the results of Tiffy Rose's scissor happy activity. "You know, I do believe that the lines of the dress will flatter your youthful figure very nicely."

"What about the off-the-shoulder style?" Do you think that I have revealed too much?" Tiffy Rose held the dress over her bust.

"You might as well try it on and see."

Miss Goodwin tightened the stays on her corset before pulling the dress on over Tiffy Rose's head. Together, they tugged the dress into position. Tiffy Rose's creamy white shoulders and bust were definitely visible above the low-cut bodice. Both women contemplated the dress in the mirror.

"I've made a mess of things again, haven't I?" wailed Tiffy Rose. Her confidence had vanished when she saw how much skin she exposed. Her mother would be furious. Her father would have apoplexy.

Miss Goodwin smiled reassuringly. "No, I don't believe that is the case. May I make a suggestion? I believe if I just tuck a bit of tulle across here and here, your gown will be lovely." She picked up a few bits of tulle off the floor and began pinning it into place along the bodice.

"There, I think that should do it," said Miss Goodwin as she pinned one last flower into place.

They stood back and admired Miss Goodwin's handiwork.

Tiffy Rose gasped with sheer delight. Instead of a dress shorn of ornamentation, the addition of the tulle framed Tiffy Rose's shoulders, neck, and face.

"Oh, Miss Goodwin! It's lovely! It's perfectly lovely. How can I ever thank you?"

"There is no need for thanks," answered Miss Goodwin humbly. "Oh, goodness! Look at the time! We must hurry!"

Miss Goodwin pulled Tiffy Rose's hair upward and away from her face as was fashionable. Next, she secured her hat, which probably weighed five pounds, on her head using long sharp pins.

They returned to the mirror and frowned.

"Oh, no! I look awful! I look like a cartoon character! The hat overwhelms the elegant simplicity of my dress! What am I going to do? I can't wear it, but I have to wear something."

"You are right. Quick, let's get it off of your head."

Tiffy Rose pulled the hat off of her head and together, she and Miss Goodwin removed most of the decoration. When just a few ribbons and feathers remained, Tiffy Rose tried on the hat again.

Miss Goodwin frowned. "No, definitely not."

"If anything, it is worse, isn't it?"

"Yes, I am afraid so. Hats are so difficult."

"Do you have any suggestions?" asked Tiffy Rose.

Miss Goodwin searched the rubble on the floor until she found what she wanted. She tucked a few feathers into Tiffy Rose's hair and attached a few silk flowers here and there. Stepping back, she allowed Tiffy Rose to see herself in the mirror.

"Now, you look like a princess."

Turning her head to the left and right, Tiffy rose studied her reflection. "I look beautiful. I've never looked this beautiful before. Thank you, Miss Goodwin. Thank you." Impulsively, she hugged her chaperone. The intimacy of the unexpected embrace embarrassed both of them. They pulled apart and looked away from each other until the tension had passed.

Before she left the debris-strewn room, Tiffy Rose made sure that no flaw, no wrinkle could be seen in her lace-covered green satin gown. No detail, down to her shoes, gloves, or jewelry had been overlooked.

Tiffy Rose finished dressing for dinner with her parents with trepidation. She was anxious because she had spent what seemed like hours dressing for the evening. She could only imagine what her mother would say when she saw the dress—or what remained of it.

A burst of impatience touched her. Tiffy Rose controlled it with sheer willpower. Tonight, she would be a success. She picked up her long white gloves and jeweled purse and went out to meet her fate. Anyone meeting her in the hallway would have taken in her bright eyes, erect posture, and deliberate movements and thought her poised and confident. Inside, Tiffy Rose knew she was acting a part. She hoped that her beautiful gown would give her confidence and courage. She was so nervous, she thought she would faint. And she never fainted.

Besides dining with the Chatsworths, she knew that both Miss Pendergrass and Miss Goodwin would be joining the party. How would Randolph Patterson treat her after this morning's little foray into the world of make-believe? Did he know she and Captain Thayer were merely pretending to know each other? Only Captain Thayer was needed to complete the trap she had so carefully constructed for herself. She only had a few more minutes of freedom before it would be neatly sprung. Tiffy Rose sighed. It was going to be a long evening.

Randolph Patterson met her at the door to the dining room. For once, Tiffy Rose was grateful for his solid, reassuring presence. Unexpectedly, she smiled at him.

"Now that is what I like to see," he whispered in her ear. "Your smile. You really do have a lovely smile, Miss Baldwin."

His words surprised her. Randolph Patterson was not normally so eloquent. At a loss of how to respond, Tiffy Rose relied upon a standard reply. "How very kind you are, Mr. Chatsworth." With sudden insight, she realized that he was kind, very kind indeed. All of Tiffy Rose's feelings of trepidation melted away, at least until her mother caught sight of her daughter's remodeled gown.

"Tifton Rose Baldwin! What have you done to your dress?" cried Etta Baldwin.

Randolph Patterson stepped between Tifton Rose and her mother. He said firmly, "Miss Baldwin, I must compliment you on your gown. It is quite becoming on you. You are a vision of simplicity in our highly over-decorated world."

Randolph Patterson sounded so sincere that Etta Baldwin's harsh words died on her lips.

Smiling graciously, Randolph Patterson offered his arm to Tiffy Rose. "Shall we go into the dining room?"

"How is your smoked salmon?" Eunice Chatsworth asked Franklin Baldwin politely.

"Quite nice. Quite nice indeed. What manner of sauce is this?" Mr. Baldwin pointed to the sauce in the small silver serving dish.

"I believe it contains cream, lemon, and dill." Eunice Chatsworth sampled some that she had already placed on her plate. "Yes, I can definitely taste the dill."

"The chef here is absolutely marvelous," commented Mr. Randolph Patterson Chatsworth II. "He is here for the season from New York."

"The chef likes to focus on native dishes," added Mrs. Chatsworth. "For instance, the lettuce for tonight's cream of lettuce soup was grown in the kitchen gardens here."

"You simply must try the cornbread. It is delicious. Best in the South," added Patterson Chatsworth.

"Tifton, you have hardly eaten a thing," noted Eunice Chatsworth. She turned to Etta Baldwin and asked, "Why do young women eat like birds these days?" She turned toward Franklin Baldwin and said confidingly, "Perhaps you ought to take Tifton to see Dr. Martin. He is taking Dr. Merrill's place this season. He came highly recommended."

Tiffy Rose, who was struggling to breathe in her tight corset, wanted to break with societal conventions and tell Mrs. Chatsworth that her corset was too tight thereby making it impossible for her to breathe let alone eat. It was useless to say so. The woman wouldn't understand, trussed like she was in a fashionable high-waisted, tightly-laced, and corseted gown.

Without waiting for a response from either Tiffy Rose or her mother, Eunice Chatsworth continued, "Tifton, you simply must bring your appetite with you to the Maurices' garden party tomorrow. There is to be quite a crowd, perhaps as many as thirty. We are expecting to dine on shrimp, sweet potatoes, fresh peas, corn bread, and a lettuce salad."

"My heavens that is a lot of food to prepare! Imagine, Tifton, a picnic for thirty people!" exclaimed Etta Baldwin. "Mrs. Maurice will be very busy cooking, won't she?"

Laughing politely, Eunice Chatsworth corrected Mrs. Baldwin's blatant misconception. "My dear Mrs. Baldwin, Charlotte Maurice won't make any of the food. It will all be prepared in the kitchens in the clubhouse. Even the wine will come from the club's cellars. When the food is ready, it will be brought to the picnic by waiters in black and white livery."

"It's all very civilized," commented Patterson Chatsworth, looking up from his smoked salmon.

"Of course, it is, dear. This is the Jekyll Island Club." Eunice Chatsworth tilted her nose a bit higher into the air.

Embarrassed at her lack of knowledge of island customs, Etta Baldwin flushed bright red.

Tiffy Rose wanted to say something that would bolster her mother's fragile ego. Her mother was kind and gentle, unaccustomed to the one-upmanship displayed by many of the people here. It was like a game to them, a very important game. And when they played it, they displayed a fierce determination to win at any cost. Tiffy Rose wanted to protect her mother from these people she didn't understand. She smiled encouragingly at her mother. Her mother smiled weakly in return.

The conversation remained firmly entrenched in the food. Tuning out the culinary discussion at her table, Tiffy Rose studied the other diners around her. She tried to listen to their conversations. She hoped they were not as banal as the one at her table. Listening to them talk about the chef, the food, and their accommodations, Tiffy Rose realized that these people must be very hard to please. She hoped that the other diners were not as snobbish as the Chatsworths had become. Funny, they hadn't seemed that way back home in Tifton. Perhaps they felt the need to impress the Baldwins with their posh manners in front of these truly wealthy people. She hoped that the Chatsworths would return to their normal pleasant selves following President McKinley's visit to Jekyll Island. As for the millionaires around her, they seemed to inhabit their own world which they shared with their own people. There wasn't room for anyone new in their pampered lives. Tiffy Rose doubted that her sensible parents would ever fit in. She knew she wouldn't.

"Were you aware that our cream and butter comes all the way from Franklin, Tennessee?" Patterson Chatsworth asked Franklin Baldwin.

"No, I wasn't. Why so far? Surely it must cost a fortune to transport it over such a great distance."

"Not when you own the railroads," laughed Patterson.

"There is talk of starting a creamery on the island," said Eunice Chatsworth. "I think it is a splendid idea."

Multiple times during dinner, Randolph Patterson's eyes met Tiffy Rose's. She understood that he was taunting her. She could tell that he did not believe her story about Captain Thayer at all. He knew it to be a frivolous concoction of lies. Tiffy Rose felt as if she was trapped in a spider web of her own making. Her world would soon fall apart. Her parents' greatest desire would soon be lost to them. All because of her inability to fit into the role that life had assigned to her.

Her behavior today would forever seal her parents' fate. They would never become members of the Jekyll Island Club, nor would Tiffy Rose ever marry well. She would be ruined. All because she couldn't stand the rigid social codes to which she must adhere to as a wealthy young woman. She sighed.

Miss Pendergrass, as if sensing Tiffy Rose's distress, squeezed her hand gently and smiled. Tiffy Rose nearly burst into tears of gratitude.

Buoyed unexpectedly by Miss Pendergrass's kind touch and sympathetic eyes, Tiffy Rose lifted her chin defiantly the next time she felt Randolph Patterson's eyes rest on her. She met his gaze unflinchingly. In for a penny. In for a pound. The truth might as well come out and it might as well be now.

Randolph Patterson reared back, surprised by her blatant defiance. He frowned.

This was the moment Tiffy Rose had dreaded. He waited only for a break in the conversation to begin his attack.

"Mr. Baldwin, Tifton introduced me to Captain Burke Thayer this morning. I understand he is a good friend of your family," announced Randolph Patterson his eyes fixed on Tiffy Rose.

Mr. and Mrs. Baldwin stared at each other, confusion showing on their faces. They asked in unison, "Captain Burke Thayer?"

Mr. and Mrs. Chatsworth stopped eating, confused by the change in the normal flow of polite dinner conversation. Why had their son diverted the conversation away from the safe topic of food?

In preparation to explain, Tiffy Rose took as deep a breath as her corset allowed.

Suddenly, the perpetually silent Miss Goodwin spoke up, startling everyone, including Tiffy Rose. "Captain Burke Thayer is of the Georgia Thayers, with connections to the New York Thayers. His brother, William Thayer is a successful financier on Wall Street and a friend of Mr. Morgan."

"He is?" murmured Etta Baldwin weakly.

Having found her voice, Miss Goodwin put it to good use. "Surely, Madam, you have only momentarily forgotten Captain Thayer. Despite their age differences, he and Tifton Rose used to play together whenever you attended a party at the Tifts."

Much to Tiffy's amazement, her mother, looking like a startled deer, agreed. "Why, yes, I remember now. It's been such a long while since we have seen him what with his being in the military and all."

The Chatsworths watched and listened to this exchange with grave interest. Tiffy Rose could see the wheels turning in their minds, each asking themselves: who is this Captain Burke Thayer?

Miss Goodwin began to praise Captain Thayer. "Yes, Captain Thayer is very brave. He was decorated for heroism for his actions during the sinking of the battleship Maine."

Tiffy Rose couldn't help but stare at her chaperone. How had she known all of that? Never had she ever dreamed that the woman would come to her defense so completely and with such unquestioning loyalty.

"I happened to meet Captain Thayer today, too," added Miss Pendergrass.

"Oh, really, in what capacity?" asked Franklin Baldwin, decidedly curious about this Captain Thayer that he never remembered meeting.

"The man has impeccable timing. A young lady acquaintance of mine fainted in the hallway of the clubhouse. I could barely support her. Fortunately, Captain Thayer came along and assisted us back to her room."

Taken by surprise, Tiffy Rose spit out the water she had sipped in a decidedly unladylike manner. Captain Thayer had been the one who had carried her to her room? Captain Thayer? The man she repeatedly told she did not faint had carried her to her room? What fresh horrors would this evening bring?

Spellbound by all this information so freely given, instead of rebuking Tiffy Rose, her mother merely handed her a napkin.

Tiffy accepted the napkin and blotted the water from her face. She dared a look at Randolph Patterson. He, too, seemed flabbergasted by the direction his attempt to catch Tifton in a lie had taken. There was nothing for him to do but gracefully withdraw his question, however, the conversation had taken on a life of its own.

"Tifton, why didn't you tell us that you had bumped into Captain Thayer while on the island?" asked her father.

"I meant to, Papa. Truly I did. Things have been so busy, there wasn't the right moment to do so." Tiffy Rose hung her head to hide her smile. She felt as if a great weight had been lifted off of her shoulders. She felt as if she could soar into the night sky. She would be forever grateful to Miss Goodwin and Miss Pendergrass. She would thank each of them profusely the next time she was alone with each of them.

Franklin Baldwin cleared his throat. "Thank you so very much, Randolph Patterson for alerting us to Captain Thayer's presence on the island. We shall need to reconnect with him very soon."

"Here is your opportunity now. Captain Thayer is walking into the dining room as we speak."

Chapter 18
Burke

Burke walked into the dining room just in time to see Tifton Rose Baldwin slip out of her chair and onto the floor. She had fainted again. He smiled. For a woman who never fainted, Miss Baldwin was beginning to make quite a habit of it.

Unexpectedly, the quick-witted Miss Pendergrass called his name. "Captain Thayer! It appears that we are in need of your assistance. Please help Miss Goodwin and I take Miss Baldwin up to her room so that we may attend to her."

"Certainly." Captain Thayer bowed to the people at the table before he scooped up Miss Baldwin into his arms.

Randolph Patterson came late to the realization that here was an opportunity to act in a chivalrous manner. He stood up and demanded, "Miss Baldwin happens to be my fiancée. I should be the one to carry her to her room."

"We can't have the girl tossed about like a sack of potatoes. I am certain that Captain Thayer will do quite nicely," stated Miss Pendergrass firmly.

"No, of course not! My daughter is not a sack of potatoes!" squeaked Etta Baldwin frantically, her mothering instincts aroused.

"No, of course not." Randolph Patterson backed down immediately in response to Mrs. Baldwin's disapproving glare.

Miss Goodwin sought to reassure the Baldwins that their daughter was in no danger. "Mrs. Baldwin, I am certain that Tifton, who is not accustomed to corsets, has fastened hers too tight. You needn't worry about her. She will be fine once it is loosened."

"No wonder she fainted. The poor girl can't breathe. What possessed her to wear a corset?" asked Miss Pendergrass, frowning. "I was under the impression that she never wore one."

Eunice Chatsworth, tightly laced into her corset, looked aghast at the idea of not wearing a corset much less discussing its absence in public.

Having no daughters and only two sons meant that she was unaccustomed to the new ideas being shared among the younger generation. She was sure to meet every new idea with suspicion and intolerance. With one simple question, Miss Pendergrass had become the enemy of good taste.

Miss Goodwin supplied the information concerning Miss Baldwin's choice of costuming. "Mrs. Baldwin had me lay out Tifton's most elegant gown. Unfortunately, in order to wear the gown, she needed to wear a corset. The gown requires an eighteen-inch waist in order to fit properly. Tifton wanted to please her mother so she agreed to a corset."

It was Miss Pendergrass's turn to look aghast. "An eighteen-inch waist! It is positively criminal the way women are held slaves to fashion! Quickly! Get her to her room! There is no time to lose!"

Miss Goodwin put an end to the talk about corsets. It wasn't done in polite society. She took command of the situation, something she had never done before. "Mr. and Mrs. Baldwin, you stay and finish your dinners. I'm sure that you have much to talk about with the Chatsworths. Miss Pendergrass and I will take care of Tifton."

"Thank you, Miss Goodwin. Captain Thayer, if you would be so kind," said Etta Baldwin meekly.

Burke looked down at the unconscious young woman in his arms. To him, she seemed like an angel, a sweet vulnerable angel. Her dark lashes fanned across her pale cheeks. "Certainly," repeated Burke.

With Miss Goodwin leading the way, Burke carried Miss Baldwin to her room. Miss Pendergrass followed in their wake.

"When you have deposited my daughter in her room, please return and join us for cigars and brandy, Captain Thayer. We have a lot to catch up on," Franklin Baldwin called after them.

As he left the dining room, Burke wondered what on earth they would have to talk about.

Chapter 19
Tiffy Rose

"Wake up, Tifton. We have a busy day ahead of us what with the president arriving tomorrow. Aren't we fortunate to be on Jekyll Island at the same time as President McKinley? Most fortunate indeed. The day after tomorrow, we will be at Solterra Cottage attending a reception given for President McKinley. Imagine—meeting the president. I am thrilled, just thrilled." Mrs. Baldwin puttered around Tiffy's room happily opening curtains, fluffing the lovely vase of flowers sent by Randolph Patterson, and picking up Tiffy's discarded corset.

Tiffy Rose groaned into her pillow.

Her mother continued as if she hadn't heard her daughter's unladylike sound. "Remember today is the day of the Maurices' picnic. I can hardly wait to see Hollybourne Cottage. I've been told that the woodwork is fabulous and that the public rooms are enormous. I wonder what the private family rooms are like?"

Tiffy Rose made a motion to pull the pillow over her head when her mother gently placed her hand on her daughter's shoulder. "Tiffy Rose?"

Tiffy Rose? Her mother hardly ever called her Tiffy Rose anymore. It was a term of endearment that was rarely used in their cantankerous relationship. She stopped moving about and focused on what her mother was saying.

"Tiffy Rose, I want to apologize for doubting you. You *are* a good girl and I know that. Last night was another indication of just how good a person you are. You remembered Captain Thayer when I had forgotten him. You stood up to Randolph Patterson when he acted inappropriately. You have earned the devotion and love of Miss Goodwin, a woman I highly respect. And you have made several new friends among the young women here on Jekyll Island. Thank you for that. Thank you for everything."

Tiffy Rose rolled over and sat up in bed. She hugged her mother tightly. Perhaps now they could be friends.

"Oh, and Tiffy Rose, I think we can dispense with corsets from now on."

Randolph Patterson had changed since the previous evening. He had become much more attentive to her, much less pompous. This morning, she had received a bouquet of Cherokee roses from him. The flowers had been accompanied by a friendly note inviting her to go on a buggy ride around the island. Tiffy Rose looked forward to seeing the tabby Horton House and Driftwood Beach. Having recently taken up birdwatching, she also hoped to see a bald eagle. From what she had been told, there were two nesting pairs on the island.

Since her mother had dispensed with corsets, Tiffy Rose wore her most comfortable white lawn dress. Its only adornment was sash of a lively spring green ribbon. Her wide-brimmed straw hat was much less cumbersome and heavy than the over-decorated styles preferred by fashionable women. It featured matching green ribbon ties and a decorative bunch of fabric daisies on one side. Looking at herself in the full-length mirror, Tiffy Rose was inordinately pleased. For once, she felt like herself: simple, cool, and cheerful. After one last look, she skipped down the stairs.

As Tiffy Rose reached the lobby, Mr. Horst, the clockmaker, rushed up to her. "Miss Baldwin? That is you, is it not?" The gnome-like man squinted at her.

"Yes, I am Miss Baldwin. How can I help you, Mr. Horst?"

"I wanted to return this watch to your cousin, Captain Thayer, however he is not in his room. Nor is he in the dining room. Would you mind if I left the watch with you? Otherwise, I will have made the trip for nothing."

Tiffy Rose stifled a laugh. The distance between his small shop and the clubhouse lobby was scarcely three hundred yards. Certainly, it was not a long walk by anyone's standards. He probably didn't want to leave his precious clocks for long.

"I am sure to be seeing him soon. In the meantime, leave the watch with me and I will see that he receives it." Tiffy Rose smiled graciously.

The clockmaker leaned closer to Tiffy Rose.

"Miss Baldwin, would you please tell him that there is a photograph, too? I found it inside the back of the watch. Naturally, I returned it to where it came from."

"In the back of the watch?" she asked, confused.

The clockmaker looked at her shrewdly. "You do not remember the watch very well, do you? Yet it was a gift for your cousin. You even had it engraved: *'To my beloved Percy, Your sweetheart Milly'*. But—" He paused for effect. "It is not your photograph that your cousin keeps in his watch." With his one blue eye, the man leered at her.

Tiffy Rose felt slightly nauseous. Her fingers trembled. She had thought that last night would be the end of it. Why hadn't she listened when her mother warned her about fabricating stories. Her mother often quoted Sir Walter Scott: *'Oh, what a tangled web we weave when first we practice to deceive.'*

With nimble fingers, the little man opened the protective front or top case covering the clock face. Spinning the watch around, he snapped open a second cover on the back of the watch. He held it up for her to see. His hands were so close to her face, she could smell the lubricating oil on them. Greatly disturbed, she recoiled.

"Oh!" said Tiffy Rose, quickly recovering. "Yes, of course. I remember now."

"It is a very nice watch, a very expensive watch," he said meaningfully. "I took great care to clean the crown and the interior works. It runs very well now."

Unable to remain calm any longer, Tiffy Rose snatched the watch from the clockmaker's hand.

"Thank you for bringing my cousin's watch back to me," she said in a more pleasing tone. "I will see that he gets it the very next time I see him. I will also make sure that you are paid for your work. Now if you will excuse me, I have an appointment."

Tiffy Rose turned on her heel and left the little man in a swirl of skirts.

On the veranda, she encountered the Rawlins sisters. She groaned. Out of the frying pan and into the fire.

"Good morning, Tifton Rose. My you do look a treat this morning," cooed Grace.

Her sister, Alice, commented, "How simple your outfit is. How quaint. If what you wore last night is any example of your sense of style, you certainly are no slave to fashion."

"I think she looked just smashing last night," said May in Tiffy Rose's defense. "Very elegant."

"You would think so," snapped Alice.

"You're just angry about Mr.—"

"That is quite enough, May!" Alice cut May off before she could complete her sentence.

May pouted briefly. "I think Tifton is very daring in her choice of clothing. You just wait and see. Very soon, all the other young women will emulate her." She turned to Tiffy Rose and added, "It is all around the club that your mother no longer requires that you wear a corset, Miss Baldwin. How fortunate that with your lovely figure you have no need of one."

"How do you know about my corsets?" asked Tiffy Rose, shocked by May's revelation.

"My maid heard it from your maid," answered May. "Servants do talk, you know." She giggled as if this was an everyday occurrence, which it probably was.

Tiffy Rose silently cursed the maid for listening at the door. She would need to remember to be more circumspect in the future, otherwise her entire life would be the subject of gossip. She blessed Miss Goodwin for her devotion and for being a soul of discretion. Tiffy Rose remembered how the newspapers got hold of intimate details about Consuelo Vanderbilt's trousseau. She couldn't imagine what it must have been like to have information about your private undergarments read by anyone who saw a copy of a newspaper. How horrible. Tiffy Rose shuddered.

"Are you planning on attending the Maurices' garden party?" asked Grace innocently.

"If you do, you will wish to wear something more suitable, that is, if you don't want to be a laughing stock," suggested Alice, a derisive smile on her face.

Tiffy Rose was tempted to stick out her tongue at Alice's pretense of friendship. Fortunately, Miss Goodwin appeared at her side and greeted the three Rawlins sisters coolly.

"Good morning, Miss Alice, Miss Grace, Miss May. We would love to stay and chat; however, Mr. Chatsworth is taking us for a carriage ride. Come along, Tifton, we mustn't keep Mr. Chatsworth waiting." Taking Tiffy Rose firmly by the elbow, Miss Goodwin steered her charge off the veranda and into the bright sunshine.

In their wake, they heard Alice complaining, "I would never agree to a ride in an open carriage. A clean gown is ruined in the space of fifteen minutes—covered with road dust and splashed by puddles—to say nothing of what the wind does to your hair."

"Alice is so desperate for a man that I wouldn't put it past her to jump into an open carriage despite the risks to her clothing," said Tiffy Rose under her breath.

"Hush Tifton! Someone might hear you," cautioned Miss Goodwin.

"I don't care who hears me," said Tiffy Rose defiantly.

"You will when it comes back around to haunt you."

Tiffy Rose remembered what her mother had told her about what goes around, comes around and remained silent. As soon as they were alone, Tiffy Rose said, "Oh, Miss Goodwin, thank heavens you arrived when you did. I couldn't have stood another moment with the Rawlins sisters. They are so artificial; they are positively brittle. And the look on Alice's face when you mentioned our ride with Mr. Chatsworth! Priceless!" She giggled happily.

Miss Goodwin took a different view. "Tifton, a lady never takes pleasure in the discomfort of others. Nor does one attack one's rival. It's not good sportsmanship, nor is it decent."

"But, just now, you mentioned Randolph Patterson and you know she has a crush on him," pointed out Tiffy Rose.

"I must admit that I gave into my emotions when I heard them taunting you. However, I expect better from you."

"How did you know just what to say? You handled the situation much more smoothly than I could have done."

"I've had a bit of practice with wealthy young girls and their sometimes-spiteful words and behaviors."

"How? When?"

"My dear Tifton, how naïve you are. I haven't always been a lady's companion. My reduced circumstances are due to poor investments made by my father."

"I do apologize for my inappropriate questions."

"Think nothing of it. Here comes Mr. Chatsworth, now. Are you ready to enjoy yourself?"

Chapter 20
Burke

Burke stood on the pier with his back to the Jekyll River. In the distance, to the far left, was Hollybourne Cottage. Much nearer, but also to the left, was Solterra Cottage. Straight ahead of him and slightly to his left was the Jekyll Island Club clubhouse. Directly across the green sweep of lawn from where he stood, sat *San Souci*, squat and solid. Between those two structures stood Fairbanks Cottage. On its way to the shops and dormitories, Pier Road traced a path between *San Souci* and the Fairbanks Cottage. Indian Mound Cottage, built by the McKays in 1892, was located to the right of the green lawn. He could see the infirmary behind the McKay cottage and further to the right.

Burke tried to put himself in the victim's shoes. Where would he have gone after disembarking from the boat? The clubhouse? *San Souci* or one of the cottages to visit a friend? The shops? The infirmary? Where? The man had to have come to the island for a reason. Not just anyone could visit Jekyll Island. Who had invited him? Why had he come? Why had someone killed him? Why had the murderer taken pains to destroy his identify?

Burke, in the company of J.P. Morgan and Charles Lanier, had interviewed many of the cottage owners the day before. None had expected or received any visitors during the previous forty-eight hours. Burke had no indication that any of them had lied to him, therefore he decided that Mr. Percy had not come to the island to visit any of these families. If not them, then who? That was the question.

Reasoning that the man would not have gone directly to someone's house for a visit unless he was staying there, Burke decided to try the clubhouse. Before doing so, he made a mental note to check again to see if anyone had expected a visitor who had not arrived. Burke had visited the clubhouse with the Glynn County sheriff the day before but hadn't discovered anything about the man from the employees they had spoken with. Perhaps today, different people would be manning the front desk. He hoped they could tell him something about the elusive Mr. Percy.

His discussion with the desk clerk was typical of all his interviews.

"A man, you say? Average height? Balding? Gray hair? That describes nearly every man here—except the young ones." The clerk laughed.

"Are all your guests accounted for?" asked Burke feeling a little desperate.

"It's not as if we take a head count every morning, sir. Our guests prefer their privacy."

Burke started to go back to his room but then changed his mind. Instead, he walked up and down the hallways in search of housekeeping staff. Whenever he encountered one, he asked the same questions: Are all of your rooms occupied? Did any of your guests leave their room and not return? By the end of his search, the only thing that he had discovered was that the housekeeping staff were to a person a tight-lipped group. While Burke commended their discretion concerning the people staying at the clubhouse, he learned nothing at all about his victim.

Since he had already questioned many of the shopkeepers and other employees the day before, Burke decided to turn his attention to the island itself.

Burke selected a horse from the stables and set off to explore the island. He intended to make a thorough search of the area where they had found the murder victim. Captain Clark had spoken of a notebook. It had not been found. It could hold the key to the man's identity. Burke felt he needed another piece of the puzzle before approaching the Jekyll Island Club board.

The morning air was bracing and cool. The sun shone brightly promising good weather for the day and perhaps well into the night. If nothing else, a ride would blow the cobwebs out of his mind.

On his way to the island the previous day, Burke had learned that Jekyll Island was one of a string of barrier islands located between Jacksonville, Florida and Savannah, Georgia. These barrier islands were commonly known as the Sea Islands or the Golden Isles. Situated in a north-south orientation, Jekyll Island measures approximately seven miles long. Only one and a half miles across at its widest point, its broad flat beaches featured sand packed hard enough to easily support the weight of a horse and rider.

Burke decided that while he was out for a ride, he might as well inspect the island for areas where security was lacking. He chose to first visit the Horton House, a two-story ruin from 1742. From there, he planned to work his way to the north end of the island. After checking on places where a boat could land a person, he would ride down the eight-mile beach from north to south. When he reached the south end of the island, he would turn north again and return along the Jekyll River to the Jekyll Island Club which stood near the middle of the island.

He urged the horse into a steady trot. The crushed shell road was so smooth and well-maintained that he didn't really need to pay attention to the horse. To the west, tidal marshlands made an approach from that direction nearly impossible. If anyone wanted to easily reach the island, their best landing sites would be on the north, east, and south parts of the island. Much of the beach was only exposed during low tide, making landings from the south and east fairly tricky.

As they trotted along, he put his mind to work sorting out what he knew about the victim. The lack of information bothered him. Despite his efforts, except for the man's first name, Burke hadn't been able to uncover any new information in the past twenty-four hours.

When he reached Horton House, Burke dismounted and tied his horse to a hitching post. Seeing a break in the trees to the west, he decided to survey the water and marsh from this point. Unexpectedly, he came across an old graveyard.

Chapter 21
Tiffy Rose

Tiffy Rose sat beside Randolph Patterson in the small open carriage thoroughly enjoying herself. Miss Goodwin rode in the back of the carriage and made a serious effort to do some bird watching from the moving vehicle.

Randolph Patterson guided the horses down the well-maintained roadway lined with tropical palms, pine trees, and mysterious live oak tress draped with Spanish moss. As they proceeded north toward Horton House, openings in the trees afforded Tiffy Rose views of the Jekyll River and the tidal marsh. She noted that the tide was up, filling the tributaries with sea water and making a mosaic with the bright green marsh grasses.

"What a wonderful idea you had, Mr. Chatsworth. Thank you so much for your kind invitation. I am enjoying myself very much." As she spoke them, Tiffy Rose found her words to be true. She was more relaxed than she had ever been in his presence. For once, he focused on driving the horses and didn't try to make inane small talk. She liked his new persona.

"I had hoped that you would enjoy our time together today." He smiled at her shyly as if he too recognized the difference in himself.

"It is a lovely day. The weather is quite fine," said Tiffy Rose, unable to suppress a tongue-in-cheek reference to the socially acceptable topics for young ladies. She giggled and much to her surprise, so did Randolph Patterson.

Then his face turned serious. "Miss Baldwin, if you don't mind, I would like to talk to you of more important matters than the weather."

Just when she was beginning to relax, Tiffy Rose felt her insides twist in apprehension. What did he want to talk to her about? She hoped he did not mean to propose today during their time together. Covertly, she looked at Randolph Patterson. He had a sappy grin on his face. Uh oh, thought Tiffy. She decided to put it off as long as possible. She smiled tightly and said, "Must we, Mr. Chatsworth? I would prefer to enjoy what the day brings. Besides, we are not alone."

Randolph Patterson smiled at her. "Don't look so worried, Miss Baldwin, I was just going to ask you if I may escort you to the Maurice's picnic this afternoon."

Tiffy Rose stared at Randolph Patterson, then a delighted laugh escaped her lips. Nervously at first, but then with more confidence, Randolph Patterson joined her laughter.

Smiling warmly at him, Tiffy Rose framed her answer carefully. "Mr. Patterson, unfortunately, as much as I would like to, I cannot. My mother will expect me to accompany her."

Randolph Patterson's face fell.

Tiffy Rose smiled impishly when a thought came to her. "I would like it very much if you would join me for a glass of punch sometime during the afternoon."

At the unexpected invitation, Randolph Patterson's face lit up with a smile.

From the backseat of the carriage, Miss Goodwin gave a cry of triumph. "I just saw my first pine warbler. I had a nice clear view of it, too. Tiny birds with soft yellow plumage, they are rarely seen away from pine trees."

"There are certainly a lot of pine trees on the island," added Tiffy Rose, grateful for the interruption. "What other birds have you seen, Miss Goodwin?"

"I have seen many of the more common birds here on the island. I have made a list of them in my book." She pulled her birder's notebook from her pocket and thumbed through it. Miss Goodwin began reading her list. "I've seen cardinals, phoebes, mockingbirds, blue jays."

Randolph Patterson rolled his eyes, but perhaps realizing that being in Miss Goodwin's good graces would help his cause, he gamely went along with the conversation.

"Surely, you have seen more exciting birds than those, Miss Goodwin," said Randolph Patterson with an easy smile.

"Oh, yes," she answered quickly. "Some of the rarer birds that I have seen include indigo buntings, yellow flickers, killdeer, and blue heron."

"Since I arrived on the island, I've seen quail, mourning doves, wild turkeys, Clapper Rails, and marsh hens." Randolph listed off more popular sporting birds.

"Are you a birder, Mr. Chatsworth?" asked Miss Goodwin politely.

"Yes, as a matter of fact I am. I enjoy watching our feathered friends in flight. Would that I could join them," Randolph Patterson said quietly. He pointed overhead. "Look, there is a Great Blue Heron."

"So graceful," commented Tiffy Rose, without taking her eyes off of Randolph Patterson.

"What about you, Miss Baldwin, are you interested in birds? What birds have you seen so far on Jekyll Island?" asked Randolph Patterson. He turned and their eyes met.

Under his watchful gaze, Tiffy Rose felt herself grow warm. When she answered. Her voice sounded a little breathless. "Yes, I do enjoy bird watching, though I am new to it. So far, I've seen Osprey, brown pelicans, and any number of seagulls."

"That's not a very imaginative list," said Randolph Patterson kindly. "We must improve upon it before you leave the island."

Tiffy Rose could detect no teasing or taunting in his voice, no hint of condescension. Truly, Randolph Patterson was a different man today.

"I hope to see a Belted Kingfisher, a hairy woodpecker, and a Wilson's snipe before I leave the island," said Miss Goodwin wistfully.

"I would like to see a bald eagle," said an equally wistful Tiffy Rose.

"I am sure to see a hooded Merganser, a greater Scaup, a gadwall, a black-crowned leper, and an American wigeon before I leave," said Randolph Patterson.

"I believe that except for the imaginary black-crowned leper, those are all types of ducks, are they not, Mr. Chatsworth?" asked Miss Goodwin.

"You are right, Miss Goodwin. You certainly know your ducks." Randolph Patterson laughed at his own cleverness. "I must admit, I made up the black-crowned leper to test your knowledge."

"Do you plan on bird watching or shooting?"

"In answer to your question, I expect a little of both, Miss Goodwin. I suspect a little of both."

As if he had timed it, a shot rang out nearby. The sound flushed the birds from the trees in alarm. All three passengers in the carriage ducked instinctively. The horses, startled by the noise, reared up and began to gallop off. Only Randolph Patterson's talented handling of the horses prevented catastrophe. He finally brought the horses to a halt just as they reached Horton House. Randolph Patterson swiftly climbed down from the carriage and took ahold of the horses by their bridles. He led the animals to a shaded spot and tied them to a solid hitching post. Once the horses were secured, he helped the frightened women out of the carriage.

Tiffy Rose was so unnerved by the experience that she used his first name for the first time in their acquaintance. "Oh Randolph! You handled the horses marvelously well! You saved our lives!" She clung to his arm, appreciating for the first time his strength and protectiveness.

"Mr. Chatsworth, we owe you our lives!" added Miss Goodwin with stars in her eyes.

"While this little demonstration of my prowess with horses was unplanned, Miss Goodwin, I do hope that you and Miss Baldwin will see me in a new light," said Randolph Patterson almost shyly. He offered his arm to Tiffy Rose and then when she took it, he offered his other arm to Miss Goodwin. Together, they strolled toward Horton House.

"I must apologize, ladies. It was probably a hunter, though I carefully checked the lists and no hunters were expected to be in this area today. That is why I suggested this destination. I would never knowingly put you at risk. I will definitely tell Superintendent Grob when we return. It is important that hunters alert the general public as to where they will be hunting at any particular hour of the day."

"I think that would be very wise," agreed Tiffy Rose.

"May I take your mind off of our recent excitement by telling you what little I know about Horton House?" he asked.

"That would be very nice, Randolph," said Tiffy Rose agreeably. They all needed a diversion to steady their nerves.

Randolph Patterson began. "Major William Horton built his home on Jekyll Island during the English colonization of America. It is constructed of tabby."

"What is tabby?" asked Miss Goodwin.

"Here in the coastal South, tabby often replaces concrete and other building materials. It is fairly simple to make tabby. The process begins by burning oyster shells to create lime. This lime is then mixed with water, sand, ash and broken oyster shells until it achieves the correct consistency for construction purposes."

"How interesting," said Miss Goodwin.

"In the early 1740s, this area was threatened by the Spanish. In 1742, following the Battle of Bloody Marsh on neighboring Saint Simons Island, the Spanish retreated through Jekyll Island. They destroyed Horton's plantation and his home. He never rebuilt."

"1742? It is in remarkably good condition for such an old building," commented Miss Goodwin.

Randolph Patterson laughed. "I'll let you in on a little secret. Last year, twenty-three club members invested twenty-seven dollars each to restore the building."

"Ah, I understand. They have done a beautiful job," commented Miss Goodwin.

Throughout his discussion of Horton House, Tiffy Rose remained silent as she studied this man next to her in a new light. He had prevented disaster, yet afterward his first thought was for his companions, not his ego. She looked at his hands and noticed his shredded gloves and the burns left by the reins as he struggled to control the horses. He hadn't said a word about his injuries, though he must be in pain. Tiffy Rose found herself wanting to hold his hands and dress his wounds. She turned toward him and began to reach for his hands.

Misunderstanding her reason for turning toward him, Randolph Patterson asked politely, "Would you like to hear more?"

His question caught Tiffy Rose off-guard, causing her to misstep. Randolph Patterson took ahold of her elbow and steadied her gently. She studied him. She was more accustomed to his pompous, lecturing tone than this much more pleasant version of his personality. Perhaps she had underestimated him.

Needing time to think, Tiffy Rose disentangled herself from Randolph Patterson's arm.

"Please excuse me, I would like to visit the cemetery." Tiffy Rose drifted a little way away toward the du Bignon cemetery.

Randolph Patterson called after her. "Please keep an eye out for rattlesnakes and alligators, Miss Baldwin. There are many hidden dangers on this island."

Tiffy Rose signaled that she had heard and understood him. Reaching the cemetery, she paused to read some of the epitaphs on the tombstones. The epitaphs were so charming, she wished she could have met these people. Her favorite was that of Marie Riffault.

Sacred
To the Memory
Of
MARIE FELICITE RIFFAULT
Born the 14th December 1776

In St. Domingo,
And died at Brunswick Ga.
The 6th April 1852.
"Not only good and kind,
But strong and Elevated was her mind,
Fond to Oblige, too feeling to Offend.
Belov'd by all, to all a good friend."
And faithful to her GOD.
REQUIESCAT IN PACE

Tiffy Rose heard a curious noise and turned toward it. It was then that she spied the boots protruding from behind the largest of the above ground burial tombs. She stepped forward to take a closer look and screamed.

There on the ground lay Captain Thayer, unconscious and bleeding.

Chapter 22
Burke

Burke felt the convulsing of the ship as it exploded. Flames erupted in front of his face. He sensed that he was trapped. He could hear screaming all around him—screams of the dying, cries of the badly wounded. His skin burned in agony as he was struck by red hot missiles of steel. The ship was sinking. He would soon drown. He cried out for help.

Then he smelled it. Roses. The scent of roses wafted over him, calming him.

"Captain Thayer, you mustn't fret so. You are safe now."

What angel of mercy tended him? The soft voice whispered in his ear causing his tense muscles to relax. The nightmare memories of his last moments on the Maine receded.

"Hush, now," said the quiet voice. A hand gently stroked his forehead. Burke regained consciousness in a rush.

Tifton Rose! Miss Baldwin was his angel. She had called him out of his nightmare. Burke tried to sit up. His shoulder protested against the effort. His head throbbed with pain. He felt nauseous.

"I say there, Captain," said a male voice out of his line of vision. "You might want to take it easy. You've had a nasty bump on the head and you've been shot. Of course, it's only a flesh wound, but one can't be too careful, can one?"

Burke recognized the slightly pompous voice as that belonging to Randolph Patterson. Gratefully, he sank back down on the pillows. Opening his eyes again, he saw that Miss Baldwin sat at the side of his bed, blotting his forehead with a damp cloth.

"It appears, Captain Thayer, that you have fainted," Miss Baldwin said in an attempt to lighten the gravity of the situation.

Burke smiled weakly. "What happened?"

A third person was in the room and stepped forward. Burke recognized Dr. Martin. "Captain Thayer, I hope that you realize that you are a lucky young man. Miss Baldwin, Miss Goodwin, and Mr.

Chatsworth found you in the du Bignon cemetery. Recognizing that you needed medical help immediately, they brought you to the club infirmary where I treated the flesh wound to your shoulder and bandaged the cut on your head. The blow to your head is the more serious of your two injuries." The doctor spoke with a slight accent that Burke did not recognize. "I am Dr. Martin. Do you remember me?"

"Yes, yes, I met you when we brought the body back to the club," said Burke.

"Good. Good. I am glad that your memory has not been affected by the blow to your head. It is very sad about the dead man." The doctor looked appropriately grave and respectful before continuing. "But, let us talk about you. From the way that your friends described the scene, apparently you were struck by a bullet and it spun you around. You must have lost your balance and struck your head on the corner of one of the above-ground tombs."

"We were able to deduce that scenario because we found blood on the corner of the tomb closest to where you lay," clarified Randolph Patterson.

"You gave us quite a scare, Captain Thayer," said Miss Goodwin. "Head wounds bleed so very much. I am afraid that your uniform might be ruined. I have taken the liberty of sending to the laundry. Hopefully, they will be able to do something with it. As to Miss Baldwin's dress, I will see to it personally."

It was then that Burke noticed that the front of Miss Baldwin's white dress was stained rather heavily with drying blood. "Miss Goodwin, it will take a miracle to clean Miss Baldwin's dress," said Burke. He smiled weakly. "I sincerely hope that you will convince her parents to allow me to pay for the dress."

"That won't be necessary, Captain Thayer," protested Miss Baldwin.

"She positively insisted that we place your head in her lap on the drive back to the Jekyll Island Club." Miss Goodwin sniffed with disapproval. "But seeing as how you are distant cousins and know each other well; we will overlook social improprieties this once."

"Thank you, Miss Goodwin." Despite his aching head, Burke suppressed a smile. So, they were distant cousins now. Even Miss Goodwin believed Miss Baldwin's tall tale.

"What happened, Captain Thayer?" asked Miss Baldwin hesitantly.

Burke got the impression that she didn't really want to know.

"He may not remember very much," cautioned Dr. Martin. "Many people who experience a blow to the head don't remember much about the actual incident. His memory may return in time."

Burke searched his memory for the events leading up to his blacking out.

"I remember borrowing a horse from the stables this morning. It is still morning, isn't it?" he asked.

"It is nearly noon," Chatsworth replied. "I sent a boy over to check on the horse. It returned to the stable without you a short while ago. It had broken its reins in a manner which suggests that you had tied it to a hitching post."

"Very smart of you, Mr. Chatsworth," Burke congratulated him. "I distinctly remember tying the horse to a hitching post when I arrived at Horton House."

"What were you doing there?" asked Mr. Chatsworth.

"I suppose what everyone else does when they visit Horton House. I was looking around at the ruins. You say I was shot?"

"Yes, a flesh wound on your left shoulder."

Burke touched the bandage on his shoulder and winced. "Funny, I don't remember that. I definitely don't remember any part of being brought back to the clubhouse." But he did remember some things. Not a lot, but he did remember some key things from before he got shot. He chose not to share this knowledge with anyone, not even these people.

"As I said earlier, head wounds have a funny was of blocking our memories of traumatic events," reiterated the doctor.

The occupants of the room heard a commotion out in the hallway. A loud male voice said, "One minute we are enjoying a rousing game of croquet and the next we are being told that our daughter was seen going into the infirmary covered in blood. What on earth could have happened?" The door burst open and two figures dressed in white croquet outfits entered the room.

Finding her daughter whole and sound, Mrs. Baldwin immediately forgot her new-found respect for her daughter and nearly shouted, "Tifton! What are you doing in a man's room? Next to his bed, no less! It makes no difference to me that we are in an infirmary."

Tiffy Rose stood up abruptly, revealing the bloody front of her dress.

"Are you bleeding, child?" asked her mother, suddenly concerned for her daughter's welfare.

"No, Mama. It is Captain Thayer's blood."

Mrs. Baldwin instantly shifted her attention to the man in the bed. "Captain Thayer! What is the meaning of this? Why have you bled all over my daughter's gown?"

"Now, now, my dear," soothed Mr. Baldwin. "Can't you see that Captain Thayer has been injured? It would behoove us to determine what happened before we jump to conclusions." Mr. Baldwin surveyed the room, taking in the presence of Randolph Patterson, Miss Goodwin, and Dr. Martin.

"Good day, Miss Goodwin. I am pleased to see that you are fulfilling your duties as chaperone for my daughter." Mr. Baldwin turned his attention to Randolph Patterson. "Mr. Chatsworth, I take it that your presence here is related to the carriage ride that you and my daughter embarked upon this morning."

Miss Goodwin broke in to say, "It was really quite exciting. We did a bit of bird watching and then there was a gunshot and the horses bolted." Seeing the aghast look on the Baldwins' faces, Miss Goodwin quickly added, "Don't worry. Mr. Chatsworth handled the team of horses masterfully." She ducked her head shyly and cast an adoring glance at Randolph Patterson.

Randolph Patterson spoke up, his face flushed with well-deserved pride. "Yes, sir, it was exactly as Miss Goodwin said. After I got the horses stopped, we disembarked at Horton House. It was there that your daughter, Miss Baldwin, encountered Captain Thayer unconscious in the du Bignon cemetery."

"I see that my daughter continues to find bodies on Jekyll Island," snapped Mrs. Baldwin angrily.

"But Mama, Captain Thayer isn't dead," protested Tiffy Rose.

"Thank heavens for that," sighed her indulgent father. "Etta, why don't you and Miss Goodwin take Tifton back to our rooms? It will soon be time for the Maurices' picnic. Despite this morning's events, we must keep up appearances. I will stay here for a few minutes and ascertain this morning's events from Captain Thayer and Mr. Chatsworth."

"Yes, dear."

"Yes, Father."

"Here, Tifton. Put on this jacket of mine to cover your dress." Mrs. Baldwin, a stickler for appropriate clothing, handed her white jacket to her daughter. Dutifully, Tiffy Rose put it on.

"Oh! There is my birding journal!" Miss Goodwin picked up a small leather-bound notebook from the nightstand next to Captain Thayer's infirmary bed. "I thought I had lost it. Somehow someone must have carried it up to this room. I distinctly remember leaving it on the back seat of the carriage when we got out to visit Horton House. Then, with all of the excitement, I forgot all about it. Fortunately, here it is," gushed Miss Goodwin.

"Dear lady, I hate to disappoint you, however, this particular birding journal was left here by another visitor to the infirmary." Dr. Martin firmly took the book from Miss Goodwin's grasp. "I will see that it will be returned to its rightful owner." Dr. Martin smiled a tight smile at a disappointed Miss Goodwin. He slid the notebook into a drawer out of her reach and locked it. He placed the key in his pocket. With his other hand, he ushered the ladies out the door.

"As soon as I am done here, I will find your precious journal, Miss Goodwin," Randolph Patterson offered graciously.

Miss Goodwin's smile of gratitude was positively brilliant.

Chapter 23
Tiffy Rose

Tiffy Rose slipped her ruined dress over her head. She felt a heavy weight in her pocket. Percy's watch! She had placed it in the pocket of her dress earlier that morning and what with the events of the day, forgotten all about it. Frustrated, she curled her fingers around the watch. Silently, without arousing their attention, she put it behind the clock on the mantel to hide it from her mother and Miss Goodwin. For the moment, it would be safe there. When would she be able to return it to Captain Thayer? He would certainly want it back. And she certainly wanted to ask him the significance of the watch.

Leaving her bloody dress in a pile on the floor, Tiffy Rose, wearing only her undergarments, went over to stand before the full-length cheval mirror. She looked at herself. The image reflected there was unreal. Blood had seeped through her dress and stained her undergarments and skin. Captain Thayer's blood. She touched the dried blood on her chemise and shivered.

"Tifton! Are you hurt? The blood?" cried her mother.

"Captain Thayer's blood," answered Tiffy Rose in a voice that did not sound real to her. She couldn't seem to stop shaking.

"Quickly, Miss Goodwin, Tiffy Rose is in shock! Draw a hot bath!"

"Yes, ma'am." Miss Goodwin dashed into the bathroom. Tiffy Rose heard her adjusting the taps as the water splashed into the big white tub.

Mrs. Baldwin wrapped her arms protectively around her shivering daughter. "Tiffy, you'll be all right. You've had a dreadful shock. You will be fine."

Her mother gently guided Tiffy Rose into the commodious bathroom. Captain Thayer's blood on her clothing contrasted sharply with the bright white penny tiles that covered the floor and walls.

"I'm sorry I ruined my clothes, Mama," apologized Tiffy Rose sincerely.

"You didn't ruin them. Captain Thayer did." Her mother explained away the damage with the wave of her hand.

Tiffy Rose slid gratefully into the warm water. Knowing that her mother had spared no expense when she added the scented bath salts, Tiffy Rose even made an effort to swish the bubbles that perfumed the bathwater around on the surface of the water. She sunk deeper in the tub. If only she could stay in this warm cocoon for the rest of their time on Jekyll Island. It had become very difficult to behave appropriately. At every turn, she confronted a new situation demanding her complete concentration to master. She felt exhausted by all the challenges she had already faced and did not relish another.

Tiffy Rose sighed and allowed her aching muscles to relax. She hadn't really realized how tense she had become. When she thought about it, she realized that she had every right to be tense and anxious. An impending engagement announcement—to a man she wasn't sure she could love. A dead body on the beach. A handsome Captain. Percy's pocket watch. Runaway carriages. A gun-shot wound. Bloody clothing. It was enough to give a person a nervous breakdown.

While she tried to relax, her mother idled about the room fluffing towels, straightening toiletries, picking up Tiffy Rose's discarded and bloody clothing. Tiffy Rose knew her mother wanted to speak to her about what had happened at the du Bignon cemetery. She hoped her mother would wait. She needed time to think through what she had seen and heard since arriving on the island four days ago.

Things had started out normally enough. Tiffy Rose and her mother had had their usual disagreements about what to wear, when to be accompanied by a chaperone, who would be appropriate company for a young woman of her wealth and social status. Just another typical day in the life of Tiffy Rose Baldwin.

Then, beginning with the discovery of a dead man on the beach, everything changed. Shrouded in mystery, the victim whose last name had yet to be determined, caused her to wonder who was Percy? Where did he fit in? Why was he on the island? Why had he been killed in such a gruesome fashion? And, what of Captain Thayer? How did he fit into the puzzle? Had his arrival on the island precipitated the death of the man without a face? Why did Captain Thayer pay so much attention to a pocket watch? Who shot Captain Thayer? Why? Was it deliberate? And, if it wasn't deliberate, why didn't the gunman step forward and apologize? Hunting accidents were just that—accidents.

It was all too much. Tiffy Rose willed the questions in her head to go away. It didn't seem to matter what she said or did, the questions remained. She wondered why people couldn't make their minds stop thinking about something that they didn't want to think about. Tiffy Rose was actually grateful when her mother decided to question her about the morning's events.

"Tifton, did anything untoward happen today while you were—while you were out with Mr. Chatsworth?" asked her mother as she selected an afternoon dress for Tiffy.

At least this was one question that Tiffy Rose could answer and answer truthfully. A small giggle of relief bubbled to the surface. She smiled sweetly at her mother. "Nothing at all happened. Mr. Chatsworth was a perfect gentleman. Miss Goodwin can vouch for his impeccable behavior. And of course, Captain Thayer was unconscious."

Her mother, seemingly satisfied with Tiffy's response, left the bathroom, taking Miss Goodwin with her. Alone, Tiffy Rose contemplated the brevity of life. Having read several epitaphs at du Bignon's cemetery, one in particular struck Tiffy Rose as the way she wanted to be remembered.

"Not only good and kind,
But strong and Elevated was her mind,
Fond to Oblige, too feeling to Offend.
Belov'd by all, to all a good friend."

Tiffy Rose really did want to be remembered as good and kind and a good friend to all. As things currently stood, she knew that she stood only a slim chance. It would be more likely that she would be remembered as someone who was strong-willed and likely to think for herself. She might as well admit that she would never conform—at least not without losing herself in the process.

Losing herself. The very words caused Tiffy Rose's heart to clench in pain.

Tears slowly ran down her face. Once they started, she couldn't stop them. In reality, Tiffy Rose had been frightened half out of her mind when she realized that Captain Thayer had been seriously hurt. Her heart hadn't stopped its erratic beating until he regained consciousness. She could have lost him.

Tiffy sniffed loudly. At least she had Randolph Patterson Chatsworth III. Or did she? She considered her relationship with Randolph

Patterson. She supposed that they formed a sensible, if passionless, alliance. What they lacked in devotion, they could replace with mutual respect. Did he care for her at all? Or was it her money and position in society that attracted him?

She had no romantic ideas about Randolph Patterson. Though they had known each other for over a year, Chatsworth had made no great effort to make love to her. His rare kisses were cool and brief upon her cheek. He hardly ever held her hand or touched her cheek. As a matter of fact, it was seldom that he touched her at all. Tiffy laughed bleakly. Despite their time together, Randolph Patterson still called her Miss Baldwin. Would he ever call her 'Tiffy' or any other term of endearment?

Randolph Patterson was a good man. There was never any doubt about that. He was pleasant, friendly, and attentive in his behavior toward her. But behind all his kindness, there was no fire, no passion.

Tiffy Rose swished the cooling water around in the tub. If her parents had their way, soon she would be marrying Randolph Patterson. Would their married life together be as tepid as the water she now soaked in? She and Randolph Patterson didn't even have the advantage of heated passion before it cooled. At least they could have remembered that with a sort of nostalgia. Would mutual respect be enough to keep them together or would their relationship wreck on the rocky shores of indifference?

And what about her needs? Would she never be kissed with passion? Would she never experience true love? Could she live that kind of empty life? And conversely, what about Randolph's needs? Would it be fair to Randolph Patterson? Could she ever come to love him?

And what of Captain Thayer? What type of man was he? She made a face. Tiffy Rose acknowledged that she didn't know anything about the man. Instead, she had firmly planted the myth of him in her mind. Look at her, wondering how she could possibly live without a man who she had barely spoken to. What type of romantic images had she created in her mind? Would they never be real?

Fresh tears rolled down her face. She tried to wipe them away, but more came in their wake.

Chapter 24
Burke

After the women left the room, Mr. Baldwin dropped his friendly, tolerant manner and became serious. He pulled a chair over next to Burke's bed. He sat down, folded his arms over his chest and got down to business.

"Gentlemen, it is time that we have a serious conversation," he began. "While many people believe that I indulge my daughter's whims and fancies, I do not. Because she is intelligent, I have sent her to the finest schools available. I have encouraged her to think for herself without relying on others to think for her. She has grown into a capable young woman. I am also aware that, while Tifton is somewhat impulsive, she would never knowingly enter a dangerous situation. Therefore, I would like to know in detail what occurred today and why my daughter was involved. I want the truth and I want it now." He glared sternly at both Burke and Randolph Patterson.

In response to Mr. Baldwin's firm words, Randolph Patterson moved closer to where Burke lay on the bed. Burke sensed the beginning of an unspoken alliance between the two of them. He gestured at the doctor, who showed no signs of leaving the room.

The doctor stepped forward. "I insist that I be allowed to remain in this room. Since your wound was caused by a gunshot, I will need to know more about what happened. I am required to report all gunshot injuries or deaths to the Glynn County Sheriff's office."

After a few moments of consideration on the part of Mr. Baldwin, who was concerned about his daughter's reputation, and Burke, who was concerned about who he could trust with the information, both men decided it would be best to speak as openly as possible.

"Chatsworth, let's hear your side of the story first," said Mr. Baldwin.

"It was as Miss Goodwin said earlier. After leaving the clubhouse, we enjoyed a quiet ramble through the woods. We did some bird watching. It was when I made a rather inappropriate reference to duck hunting that we heard a single shot—very nearby. The horses, which up until that point had been docile, bolted. It took some effort, but I managed to bring them under control. Thank goodness the shell road on which we traveled was smooth and in good repair. By the time I got the horses stopped, we were close to Horton House. We decided to break our journey there."

"Did you hear any more gunshots?" asked Mr. Baldwin sternly.

"No, sir. We did not," answered Chatsworth briskly. "Not before. Not after. There was just one single shot."

Mr. Baldwin was a man on a mission. His questioning became relentless. "Why didn't you turn around and return to the Jekyll Island Club after the shot was fired? Why did you go on to Horton House? Weren't you putting my daughter in more danger by doing so?"

Randolph Patterson squared his shoulders and drew himself upright. The change in him was immediate and impressive. Burke got the sense that he would no longer bow under pressure.

Instead of the expected excuses, Randolph Patterson declared, for the first time, his love for Tifton Rose Baldwin.

"Mr. Baldwin, I love Tifton Rose with all my heart. She is everything to me. I would never knowingly put her in danger."

Silenced by the young man's sincere proclamation, Mr. Baldwin signaled for Randolph Patterson to continue.

"I had to use my judgement, sir. First and foremost was the safety of Miss Baldwin and Miss Goodwin. Both women were frightened by the shot and the runaway horses. I think they would have chosen to walk back to the club if they could have. As they were in their finery and lacked stout walking shoes, I felt that the hike of several miles would be too much for them."

Mr. Baldwin nodded for Chatsworth to continue.

"As I said, the horses and the women were upset. Having brought the horses to a halt, I helped the women to the ground. We strolled around Horton House while everyone, including the horses, regained their equilibrium. Had we heard further gun shots, my course of action would have been quite different. I assure you that at all times, I had your daughter's welfare foremost in my mind."

Randolph Patterson Chatsworth III spoke with maturity and consideration. His answers impressed both Mr. Baldwin and Burke. When Mr. Baldwin continued his questioning, it was with greater respect.

"How is it that my daughter found Captain Thayer on her own?" queried Mr. Baldwin.

"Miss Baldwin left us for only a moment. She wanted to see the graveyard. We were never more than ten feet away from her. I could see her clearly at all times. She was in no danger."

"For your sake, I certainly hope not. What happened next?"

"After your daughter screamed and alerted us to her predicament, we all crowded around Captain Thayer. I felt for his pulse and determined that he was alive. Since we could not bring him around, we loaded him into the rear seat of the carriage and made our way back to the Jekyll Island Club as quickly as possible. I assure you, sir, that Miss Goodwin and I were with your daughter at all times. Proprieties were maintained."

"Thank you, Chatsworth, for your concise summary of events. Captain Thayer, do you have anything to add to Mr. Chatsworth's statement?"

"No, sir. I only recently recovered consciousness here in the infirmary."

"Ah, I see. Let's start earlier. What took you out in the woods?"

"I wanted to see more of the island."

Dissatisfied with his short answer, Mr. Baldwin continued questioning Burke. "What reason would anyone have to shoot you while you were out 'seeing the island'?"

Burke began to feel like he was facing a military tribunal. Knowing that Mr. Baldwin would not be satisfied with simple or evasive answers, he answered the first question in more detail. "As to what took me out into the woods—I am solitary by nature and often enjoy rides alone, especially on an island as beautiful as Jekyll. I wanted to visit Horton House, having heard everyone speak so highly of the preservation work done last year. This morning, I had some free time and borrowed a horse. After riding out to Horton House, I dismounted and tied off my horse to a hitching post. I spent some time exploring the house and then, moved over to the du Bignon cemetery. I do not remember being shot or striking my head when I fell."

There was little more to tell. Burke turned to Chatsworth. "I am eternally grateful to you, Miss Baldwin, and Miss Goodwin for rescuing me."

Chapter 25
Tiffy Rose

"Welcome to Hollybourne Cottage," said Margaret Maurice. The four Maurice sisters met Tiffy Rose, her mother, and Miss Goodwin on the south-facing porch where everyone gathered to greet their hostesses.

"Good afternoon, Miss Maurice," responded Mrs. Baldwin. She nodded to acknowledge Margaret's sisters. "I am Mrs. Baldwin. You have met my daughter, Tifton Rose, haven't you? And this is Miss Goodwin, her chaperone."

"Of course, we remember both Tifton Rose and Miss Goodwin," said Margaret warmly, speaking for her sisters.

"Thank you so much for inviting us." Tiffy Rose gestured toward Miss Goodwin to include her in the invitation. "We have truly been looking forward to your party." What Tiffy Rose did not say was that she hoped that the event would help distract her from thoughts of Randolph Patterson, Captain Thayer, the dead man, and the shooting.

"It is lovely to meet you, Margaret. I see your mother across the porch. I believe I will go and say hello to her," Mrs. Baldwin said, excusing herself.

"Wonderful, I am sure mother would enjoy that," said Marian, joining the conversation. "We hope that you enjoy yourselves at our party today."

Mrs. Baldwin departed leaving Tiffy Rose and Miss Goodwin alone with the Maurice sisters.

Silently, Tiffy Rose repeated their names. Margaret, known as Peg; Cornelia, known as Nina; Emily, who was called Emmy; and Marian or Mamie as the family called her. Having met them on a previous outing, Tiffy Rose found herself charmed by the four young women. All were intelligent as well as cordial. They all also tended to be taller than an average woman. At five feet, seven inches, Tiffy Rose often towered over other women. Naturally, she felt more at ease around the tall, slender sisters.

"May I say that your dresses are lovely," said Tiffy Rose.

The four sisters preened happily at her compliment. Tiffy Rose was pleased that the Maurice sisters had not chosen to dress in their most formal finery for their garden party. Instead, they wore comfortable clothing suitable for lounging on pillows and blankets on the ground. To cope with the warm day, all four sisters wore thin white lawn dresses. What made these dresses stand out among the outfits worn by other women was their simplicity of form and line. The dress fronts and three-quarter-length sleeves featured splendidly intricate white embroidery and lace.

Tiffy Rose ventured another compliment. "You have a lovely home. During my brief time on the island, I have walked past Hollybourne on several occasions. It is very pleasing to the eye."

"Would you like to see it?" offered Margaret. "I always enjoy giving visitors a tour of our home."

"Please say yes, Miss Baldwin," encouraged Margaret's sister, Cornelia. "Margaret finds being a tour guide so much more entertaining than dealing with the other aspects of hosting a party."

Marian added, "She is sure to avoid mundane matters like correspondence, answering invitations, working out seating arrangements for dinner, or giving instructions to the cook and maids."

"She leaves all of that for us to sort out," commented Emily with an exaggerated frown.

The sisters laughed together, obviously enjoying teasing each other. For the first time in a long time, Tiffy Rose missed having a sister or even a brother with whom she could share family stories and experiences. She had been lonely as a small child in her parents' comfortable home. Growing up, she had longed for a playmate. Tiffy Rose pushed her memories away. No sense dwelling on what couldn't be changed.

Tiffy Rose focused on the present as she responded, "A tour would be wonderful! We would enjoy seeing your home very much." Tiffy Rose emphasized the word 'we' in order to make sure that the sisters included Miss Goodwin in the invitation.

"I will put on my tour guide hat and take you around," laughed Margaret. She linked arms with both women and stepped toward an open French door.

As Margaret stepped aside, Tiffy Rose noticed that the porch featured a fireplace. Seeing the surprised look on Tiffy Rose's face, Margaret said, "The temperatures during the winter months can sometimes turn cold. Despite the chill in the air, we like to enjoy the porch and the views of the marsh. The fireplace is perfect for taking the chill out of the air."

"What a marvelous idea!" exclaimed Tiffy Rose. She wondered what other interesting features she would see in this house.

"Please come this way." Margaret gestured toward the door.

Mocking her sister with a bold smile, Marian bowed as she held open the wide French door that led from the porch to the house. She gestured for Tiffy Rose and Miss Goodwin to enter the parlor.

Once inside, Margaret began to tell them about the cottage. "Did you know Hollybourne Cottage was one of the first cottages to be built on the island? It was ready when we came here for the season in 1890. My father decided early on that our large family would never be comfortable in the clubhouse for long visits. He had Hollybourne built in the Jacobethan-style. You probably noticed that it is constructed of tabby, a local building material known for its strength and ability to stand up against the humid salt air. My father insisted that local materials be used as much as possible." The smile on Margaret's face showed that she enjoyed taking guests on tours of her splendid home.

The size of the grand parlor impressed Tiffy Rose. To say it was immense didn't do it justice. The high-ceilinged room was so large that the wicker furniture, tables, and plant stands filled with ferns seemed diminutive in comparison. Tasteful landscape oil paintings hung from the picture rail that encircled the room. One corner featured built-in benches and bookcases. Oriental rugs were scattered around randomly on the highly polished red oak floor. A huge fireplace, centered between two sets of French doors, dominated the room.

Emily came over to stand by Tiffy Rose. She eagerly added to her sister's commentary. She whispered, "In case you are curious, the parlor measures at least twenty-five feet wide by twenty-eight feet deep." She pointed to a door next to the windows. "Behind that door is the gun room. It's a very small room, only about eight feet deep by eleven feet wide. In case you haven't guessed, it is where Daddy keeps his guns."

Just then, Mr. Maurice stepped out of the gun room. His face lined with concern, he spoke to Margaret quietly while Tiffy Rose and Miss Goodwin looked around the parlor. Though she wasn't eavesdropping, Tiffy Rose overheard the words "missing", "sheriff", and "this morning".

Breaking away from her father, Margaret returned to her guests. She led the way through the broad archway separating the entrance hall from the parlor.

Tiffy Rose was completely enchanted by the beautiful entrance hall. The afternoon sun streamed through the leaded glass doors and windows causing the room to glow warmly. The effect was lovely.

Across from the front door was a wide staircase. A fireplace sat nestled to the left of the staircase. Over the mantel, it featured an intricately patterned design in wood. Built-in seating on each wall provided ample room for guests to relax upon arrival. This room was furnished too. There was even a bearskin rug on the floor by the fireplace.

"The entrance hall measures twenty feet wide by twenty-nine feet deep." Emily did a such a good imitation of Margaret's voice that Tiffy Rose wanted to laugh. Emily pointed to a door to the left of the fireplace. "That door there leads back to a small kitchen, a butler's pantry, and a storage area for dishes and things like that."

From where she stood, through an archway, Tiffy Rose could see the dining room, a mirror image of the grand parlor in size. An enormous mahogany table graced the center of the room.

Emily, at Tiffy Rose's elbow said, "It seats twenty-four."

Margaret shushed her sister with a glare. Then she smiled at her guests. "Please allow me to show you a very special feature of this house."

She walked over to the front door. "Did you happen to notice the design of the front stairs off of the porch?"

"Yes, I noticed," admitted Tiffy Rose. "I couldn't help but wonder about the break in the balustrade."

"Actually, the arrangement is another one of my father's ideas. It's really quite clever. Here, I will show you." Margaret Maurice led the way across the entrance hall. Once again, Marian met them at the door and bowed with a smile when she held it open.

Margaret smiled at Tiffy Rose. "I hope I don't sound as if I am teasing you, but it is much more fun to see if a visitor to our home can figure out why my father built the front porch this way."

Just then, a carriage containing two ladies and the coachman, Charlie Hill, drove up. Margaret waved happily at her arriving guests.

"Hello, Mrs. Baker. Hello, Mrs. Lanier." Margaret turned to Tiffy Rose and Miss Goodwin and said, "Now you will see first-hand how the carriage step works."

Tiffy Rose watched as the carriage swept up the smoothly raked gravel drive and halted at the break in the balustrade. She watched in amazement as the women simply stepped gracefully out of the carriage and directly onto the porch.

Tiffy Rose clapped her hands with delight. "Oh my! How very clever your father is! The coachman pulls the carriage up to the carriage step and stops. Since the carriage step is the same height as the carriage floor, a woman only has to step out of the carriage and onto the porch. No big step to get out of the carriage. How convenient! What a wonderful idea."

Margaret showed Tiffy Rose, Miss Goodwin, and her newly arrived guests into the house.

Mrs. Baker inclined her head toward Tiffy Rose and said softly, "The size of the rooms does rather take your breath away, doesn't it?"

"I don't believe I've ever seen rooms of this size without supporting pillars," commented Tiffy Rose, rendered nearly speechless by the enormous rooms. "How is it that it doesn't collapse?"

Margaret overhead Tiffy's question and explained. "Our father is a civil engineer. His career as a bridge builder influenced the innovative design and construction of Hollybourne Cottage."

"It is a beautiful house—so very interesting."

"Sometime, if you would like, I will take you downstairs and show you the nineteen pillars on which this house is constructed. A truss system distributes the weight and supports the living and dining room ceilings without the use of beams. This design eliminates load bearing walls on the ground floor which enables great spans of open space."

"Your father sounds like a very intelligent man. He certainly has built a strong house," agreed Tiffy Rose.

Margaret continued proudly, "I firmly believe it will last more than a hundred years and a dozen hurricanes. Last October, during the hurricane, only Hollybourne Cottage and the Fairbank Cottage escaped damage."

"Yes, I heard about the hurricane yesterday. How frightening! I am so happy that your lovely home wasn't damaged," Tiffy Rose answered.

Miss Goodwin hovered in the background, clearly enjoying being included in the house tour. She did not find it necessary or desirable to make her presence known by asking questions or making comments. That was for Tiffy Rose to do.

Margaret turned to Mrs. Baker and said, "Tomorrow is the big day. Are you and Solterra ready for your distinguished guests?"

"I suppose so. There are lots of things to see to. I've made so many lists, my lists have lists. I can't seem to check tasks off as quickly as I add new tasks to the lists. I hope I haven't forgotten anything truly important." Mrs. Baker smiled anxiously.

"You are so well organized that I am sure that you haven't. We are very happy that you have found the time and the energy to spend a few hours at our garden party."

"You, your mother, and your sisters host such lovely parties. I wouldn't want to miss one."

Just then a small, gnome-like man scuttled out of the back hallway, across the entrance hall, and into the dining room.

"Good day, ladies." He tipped his hat as he passed.

"Who is that?" asked Margaret, obviously concerned.

"That was Mr. Horst, the clockmaker," answered Mrs. Baker. "He is known for his ability to repair any clock."

Margaret thought for a moment and then said, "He must be here to work on our floor clock. It hasn't been keeping very good time lately."

Tiffy Rose could hear the tall floor clock ticking faithfully in the dining room.

"When I visited his shop yesterday, Mr. Horst told me that many of the clocks are not working well on Jekyll Island just now. He thinks it has to do with the humidity," Tiffy Rose said.

Mrs. Baker shared her experience. "Our French ormolu mantle clock is in the repair shop. I hope Mr. Horst completes his work this afternoon or tomorrow morning, otherwise my mantelpiece will be bare."

"I believe I saw your clock when I visited the shop," said Tiffy Rose. "Is it gilded? Does it sit upon a polished wooden base adorned with gilded bronze roping? Did it feature a very refined and elegant statue of Psyche?" asked Tiffy Rose. She flushed suddenly, remembering the pressure of Captain Thayer's fingertips on her chin. Fortunately, her small shiver of delight went unnoticed by the other women.

"Yes, that is my clock. Pray tell me, what condition was it in?" asked Mrs. Baker.

"I only saw it for a moment before the clockmaker covered it up with a soft cloth. He had the statue separated from the base and the glass bezel was off of the clock face. Other than that, I do not know how far along in his repair he is. He was quite circumspect and wouldn't talk about it." Tiffy Rose nodded in approval.

"You say our clock was in pieces?" asked Mrs. Baker, her face worried.

"From what I could see before he covered it, yes," answered Tiffy Rose.

"Oh, dear. He won't get it repaired in time. I shall need to find something else to display on the mantelpiece." Mrs. Baker sighed. "As much as I am looking forward to meeting President McKinley, I will be glad when his visit is over. The mantel clock is just one of the many things to do."

"Perhaps I can help," suggested Margaret. "I shall go and tell the clockmaker not to worry about our floor clock for the time being. I will insist Mr. Horst use his time to work on your mantel clock. That should improve the odds that it will be completed on time."

"You are too kind. Thank you." Mrs. Baker's face showed her relief.

"Shall we go outside and sit with the others?" proposed Margaret. She turned to Tiffy Rose and said, "There are several people I would like you to meet."

The cottage, if a 12,270 square-foot building with nine bedrooms and four bathrooms could be called a cottage, faced west providing a breathtaking view of the marsh. Tiffy Rose paused on the porch in an effort to take it all in.

"It is lovely here on Jekyll Island, isn't it?" asked Margaret Maurice with a catch in her voice. "You should see the marsh at sunset after a soft rain. It's all green and fresh and alive. We do so enjoy our time here. I never want to leave."

After staring at the marsh a little longer, her hostess went off in search of the clockmaker, leaving Tiffy Rose and Miss Goodwin to fend for themselves. Tiffy Rose spotted Randolph Patterson speaking with Alice Rawlins. Petite and fragile in appearance, her very chic and very expensive dress flattered her corseted figure. Tiffy Rose had enough feminine vanity to want to outshine her rival. Alice, attired in a dazzlingly white dress of cotton lawn and a feather-covered hat the size of a serving platter, made quite a formidable opponent. Alluring and appealing, Alice certainly presented a pleasing picture of a woman in every sense. She made Tiffy Rose feel tall and strong in comparison. Tiffy knew she was capable of taking care of herself in most situations. She also knew that she certainly would never be described as small or delicate.

Tiffy Rose looked about the lawn in search of her mother. Scattered around the grass were a number of wrought iron tables flanked by small chairs. Blankets, spread out on the grass, were made more comfortable by strategically placed pillows. Both the tables and blankets featured large umbrellas to block the warm rays of the afternoon sun.

As soon as Randolph Patterson saw Tiffy Rose, he trotted over to join them with such speed that she knew he had been waiting for her to appear. Taking her by her elbow, he guided her to comfortable seats on a blanket under a large umbrella. Then, just as quickly, he offered to help Miss Goodwin.

Randolph Patterson said, "I hope you don't mind that I took the liberty of procuring seats for us."

"How wonderfully thoughtful of you, Mr. Chatsworth. Of course, you have always been such a thoughtful man," responded Tiffy Rose. She felt quite decadent leaning back against a big fluffy cushion. She hadn't pictured Randolph Patterson relaxing on the ground. She thought of him sitting primly at one of the tables drinking tea. She gave him a considering look. Sometimes it seemed that she didn't really know him at all.

Randolph Patterson reddened slightly at her compliment.

"I'll be back in a moment with plates for you both. Would you prefer pink lemonade or champagne?"

"I would like pink lemonade. I've never had pink lemonade before," announced Tiffy Rose.

"Champagne is better suited for celebrations, don't you think?" asked Miss Goodwin, speaking for the first time.

"Perhaps we will soon have something to celebrate," said Randolph Patterson, a look of hope gracing his square, clean-shaven face.

Not wanting to meet his eyes, Tiffy Rose turned her face away. Looking downcast, Randolph Patterson bowed his head and departed in the direction of the food table.

"Mr. Chatsworth really is such a nice man. You are a lucky girl. He only has eyes for you," whispered Miss Goodwin confidentially to Tiffy Rose.

Tiffy Rose stared at her chaperone, wondering what possessed her to speak out in such a manner about a man. Normally the most reticent of women, Miss Goodwin seemed to come alive here on Jekyll Island.

While they waited for Randolph Patterson to return, the Barnes twins joined them. Their discussion centered on President McKinley's visit the next day. The conversation ebbed and flowed around Tiffy Rose, but she paid little attention to it. She was too busy watching Alice Rawlins flirt with Randolph Patterson while he prepared plates of food.

When Randolph Patterson brought back plates filled with treats, Tiffy Rose thanked him warmly, hoping to erase any lingering thoughts of Alice Rawlins. He returned her thanks with a shy smile.

"Miss Baldwin, I plan on being at the dock to greet the president, will you accompany me?" Randolph Patterson asked after they had sampled the excellent fare that included chilled shrimp, candied sweet potatoes, and fresh fruit salad.

"Yes, I would like that very much." Tiffy Rose smiled up at him.

"I will come and collect you when we know his arrival is imminent."

Beverly Barnes jumped into the conversation. "Everyone on the island will be at the welcoming reception at the dock tomorrow. We are going to be early in order to get a good seat. We have even given the servants time off to attend."

Becca Barnes commented, "Superintendent Grob is seeing to every detail personally. Don't the red, white, and blue banners look positively vibrant hanging from the clubhouse?"

"Very patriotic," agreed her sister. "With Superintendent Grob in charge, everything will be just perfect for the president's visit."

"From what I understand, after a brief speech at the dock, the President and Mrs. McKinley will be resting at Solterra for the remainder of the afternoon," added Randolph Patterson.

As usual, the Barnes sisters were up-to-date on the details. Becca answered, "Yes, there is a small, intimate dinner planned at Solterra for his first evening. It's by invitation only. I am not sure who will attending. We are all, of course, invited to Solterra for a reception on the evening of the twenty-first."

"Tifton Rose, what are you planning on wearing?"

"To the dock or to the reception on the twenty-first?" she asked.

"Both!" laughed Becca.

"I wonder how many people will attend the reception on the twenty-first?" asked Beverly before Tiffy Rose could reply to her sister's question. "Imagine, shaking hands with the president!"

"Our parents met him once at his home in Canton, Ohio," announced Becca proudly. "They said he was such a nice man. He shook hands with anyone who wanted to meet him."

"It must be difficult for the Secret Service to guard such a gregarious man," commented Randolph Patterson.

Beverly Barnes shrugged her shoulders. "He'll be safe on the island. Nothing bad happens here."

When she finished that particular sentence, silence drifted over the group. Something bad had happened on Jekyll Island. Someone had died. Tiffy Rose gripped the sterling silver watch in her pocket. Percy, whoever he was, had died. Tiffy Rose thought about what Randolph Patterson had said to her at Horton House. *There are many hidden dangers on this island.*

Chapter 26
Burke

Word spread quickly that Burke had been shot. A steady stream of visitors stopped by to see him despite Dr. Martin's best efforts to keep them away. J.P. Morgan, Charles Lanier, Marcus Barnes, Charles Rawlins, Frederic Baker, and Superintendent Grob, who had much to discuss, stayed the longest.

"Captain Thayer, do you have any idea who shot you?" asked Mr. Barnes.

Burke inclined his head almost imperceptibly toward Dr. Martin as a warning. The man had managed to hover nearby whenever a visitor entered the room. It was anyone's guess whether or not he would share what he had overheard and with whom.

Dr. Martin noticed Burke's gesture and said, "You may speak freely in front of me, gentlemen. I am merely present to ensure that my patient does not become over-tired in any way."

J.P. Morgan shrugged. He saw nothing unusual in the doctor's presence. Dr. Merrill, who Dr. Martin was currently standing in for, had always been treated more like a club member than an employee. There was no reason to treat Dr. Martin any differently.

"The attempt on your life, if that is what it was, must be connected with the dead man you found on the beach," observed Charles Lanier. The club president paced the room nervously. "J.P., should we cancel President McKinley's visit? What do you think?"

"Personally, I think that the death and the shooting are unrelated," said J.P. Morgan with his usual forcefulness. "I firmly believe that some hunter strayed from the rules of the club and failed to sign the list announcing where he would be hunting this morning. He was shooting at game when he accidentally shot Captain Thayer. He probably didn't even know he had struck Captain Thayer until he returned to the club and heard the news. Now, he is probably too ashamed to speak up and admit he was the shooter."

"Or he is fearful of repercussions," said Dr. Martin sagely.

"With all due respect, sir, I hesitate to agree with you," added Burke despite a raging headache.

"And why is that?" asked J.P. Morgan, affronted.

"First and foremost, I heard no other shots before the one that struck me. Second, when questioned, Randolph Patterson Chatsworth and the two ladies present heard no shots before or after that single shot. There was only that one single shot."

"I see. How many shots were fired? How many shots were heard? Those were questions that I had not thought to ask," admitted the great financier. "Please continue Captain Thayer. What do you think?"

"I think that I have accidently struck a nerve. Somehow, somewhere, I said something that has put our murderer on notice. "Perhaps I know something that I don't realize I know. Unfortunately, the blow to my head has scrambled my thought processes."

"All this conjecture is very interesting, but it isn't helping us answer the most important question of all: is it safe for President McKinley and his guests to visit the island tomorrow?" exclaimed Charles Lanier. For emphasis, he rapped his knuckles on a nearby tabletop.

"We will come to that, Charles. I have a few more questions for Captain Thayer," said J.P. Morgan. "Captain Thayer, have you been able to turn up any new clues?"

"No, sir. At least none that I can remember. I really don't remember why I went out to Horton House this morning."

The doctor's head snapped up. "You have just contradicted a statement you made earlier to your friends. You told Mr. Baldwin and Mr. Chatsworth that you 'wanted to visit Horton House, having heard everyone speak so highly of the preservation work done last year'."

"Unlike yours, my memory is faulty," answered Burke, mildly annoyed by both his aching head and his inability to solve this murder. "I am not sure why I said that. I do not remember why I went to Horton House."

"What clues have you followed up on, Captain Thayer?" asked Charles Rawlins.

"Not very many clues exist in this case. Normally, one would expect there to be lots of clues and several suspects with a variety of motives, but in this particular instance, there are very few clues, and even fewer suspects. We know very little about the victim. The man's clothing tells us he was comfortably well off. His hands tell us he worked indoors with pen and ink. His general muscular condition tells us that he did not exercise regularly. His clothing, his silver pocket watch, his shoes were all of high quality. All of this points to a modestly wealthy man of business. As to the binoculars and the small box compass, I don't know why he carried them on his person."

"Was the pocket watch engraved?" asked the doctor.

Instinct cautioned Burke about how much he should reveal at this juncture. He hedged. "I don't know whether or not it is engraved. I couldn't get it open. It had been badly damaged by its time in the water. I left it with Mr. Horst, the clockmaker, who is here on the island repairing clocks belonging to club members. He promised to open it and tell me what he has found today. If I can get out of this bed, I will go see him. If not, I will ask him to bring the watch here to me."

"Is that all you have done, Captain Thayer?" asked Mr. Rawlins.

"No, sir. I have interviewed and questioned literally dozens of employees of the Jekyll Island Club in search of answers."

Marcus Barnes could keep still no longer. "Gentlemen, we are wasting time chasing after an unknown dead man. You have already claimed that he is not an anarchist, so what does his death matter? Anyway, no man is an island. Someone will miss him and come to claim him eventually."

In response, Burke nearly shouted, "The man was somebody! We can't just ignore him and the fact that he died on Jekyll Island!"

"Who? Who is he?" asked Mr. Barnes.

"Mr. Barnes has a point. We don't even know whether or not the victim has anything to do with President McKinley's visit!" Superintendent Grob pounded his fist against his hand in anger. "Who is he? Why was he killed here?"

"We don't know the answer to those questions," admitted Burke.

"We are facing a serious dilemma. Do any of you understand that?" asked Frederic Baker forcefully. "President McKinley is staying at my cottage! Nothing must happen to him!"

"Of course, we do," said J.P. Morgan gruffly. "Before this meeting turns into a shouting match, does anyone have any suggestions about our course of action?"

Superintendent Grob looked distinctly uncomfortable as he stepped forward to speak. "Excuse me, sir. I have taken the liberty of investigating several people currently on the island."

"You have investigated club members?" roared J.P. Morgan. "Mr. Grob! That simply is not done!"

Burke could tell that Grob regretted his actions.

"Only one member, sir. The others are either visitors or employees," answered Grob apologetically.

Slightly mollified, J.P. Morgan said grudgingly, "You might as well tell us what you have learned. Nothing else is getting us anywhere."

The other men nodded in agreement.

Burke felt helpless and, more seriously, useless. He didn't see a way out or an answer to the questions that had plagued him since his arrival on Jekyll Island. Who murdered the dead man and why? And, would President McKinley be safe on the island?

"Who have you been investigating?" asked Charles Lanier.

Superintendent Grob answered quickly. "I will start with the staff. As you know, it is virtually impossible to interview or investigate any of the servants brought to the island by our club members or by their guests. Some of the club members bring with them imposing retinues of servants: valets, maids, and even private detectives to safeguard their jewels. Therefore, I have concentrated on the new members of the staff that are employed directly by the club: the dining room and kitchen staff, housekeeping, gardeners, and the stable hands. Preliminary investigations revealed that nearly all of the housekeeping and stable hands are seasonal employees of long-standing association with the club. The kitchen staff is another matter. New employees include three Hungarians and two Serbians. I strongly suggest removing them from the island as soon as possible."

"That might be a good idea," said Rawlins. He rubbed his face with his hands and looked tired.

"Do we know anything about them? What are their names?" asked Mr. Baker.

"How long have they been on the island?" asked Mr. Lanier.

"What does their supervisor think of them?" asked Mr. Barnes.

Superintendent Grob fielded the men's questions with alacrity. Burke turned his face away. He couldn't stomach the witch hunt this exercise in presidential protection had turned into due to his failure to find the murderer.

"We will put it before the board tonight," announced J.P. Morgan.

"If their decision is to remove the undesirables from the island, I will have a boat standing by to take them to Brunswick immediately," responded Superintendent Grob.

"What else have you discovered, Mr. Grob?" asked Morgan with a tired sigh.

"A Miss Flora Goodwin. She is a chaperone in the employ of a Mr. and Mrs. Franklin Baldwin. The Baldwins are not under suspicion nor are they under investigation. They are a well-established Southern family distantly connected with the TIfts of Tifton, Georgia. Mr. Baldwin made his fortune by establishing a chain of hardware stores across Georgia. They have been proposed for club membership by Mr. and Mrs. Chatsworth. Miss Goodwin has been in the Baldwins' employ as a governess and chaperone for their only daughter, Tifton Rose Baldwin, for the past two years. Miss Baldwin is expected to announce her engagement to Randolph Patterson Chatsworth III very soon."

"Ah, yes. The clumsy young man who crashed into me last night." J.P. Morgan made an expression of distaste.

"Don't underestimate Chatsworth," cautioned Frederic Baker. "When he wants to, he can throw quite a punch and knock a man down. Champion boxer at his university. I saw it happen once. It was rather unexpected. Normally, Chatsworth is so quiet and unassuming. Somehow the man provoked him—over a lady's honor, I believe. Chatsworth walked over and punched the man in the nose. Then, he calmly apologized to those present and left. Trust me. There is more to Randolph Patterson Chatsworth than meets the eye."

Burke kept his mouth tightly shut as he listened to them discuss a man that he had come to know and like in the past few days.

"What is it about this chaperone that disturbs you, Mr. Grob?" asked Charles Lanier.

"Her mother, who is from Lithuania, was a circus performer before her father married her. She rode liberty horses, the circus horses that perform without reins or saddles."

"Yes, we know what liberty horses are," said J.P. Morgan, his tone clearly indicating his disinterest.

"Miss Goodwin's parents met in Europe while the circus was on tour there."

"And? What other information do you have to share about the Goodwins?" asked J.P. Morgan.

"Miss Goodwin's father lost a substantial fortune in the financial panic of 1893," said Grob somewhat smugly.

"Being poor is not a crime," intoned Frederic Baker, effectively censoring Superintendent Grob.

"The family is now wholly dependent on Miss Goodwin's wages to survive."

Burke could stand it no longer. He raised up in his bed and said hotly, "Since when is it a crime to be from Lithuania, from a circus background, and be poor? The woman should be congratulated for supporting her family. I've met Miss Goodwin. She is as pleasant and well-mannered as any of your wives." He glared at the men and dared them to challenge him.

J.P. Morgan decided to sidestep the challenge with a question. "Is this all that Miss Goodwin is guilty of? A mother who rides horses? A father who suffered business reversals?"

"She spends an inordinate amount of time bird-watching," said Grob.

"That is interesting but hardly indicative of a tendency toward anarchy," countered Burke.

Superintendent Grob went on the attack. "Captain Thayer, whether you are willing to admit it or not, Miss Goodwin is a mere adventuress. On the surface she may appear to be docile and agreeable, however, underneath she is a very shrewd operator who intends to refill the family coffers."

"How is it that you know this?" asked Burke angrily.

Under Burke's hawklike stare, Superintendent Grob was forced to admit that he had no firm evidence of any sort that Miss Goodwin was a fortune-hunter.

"Grob, who else are you investigating?" asked J.P. Morgan, his dislike of the whole sordid business showing in his face.

Noting the lack of either a Mr. or Superintendent in front of his name and feeling less confident, Ernest Grob ventured, "Captain Thayer, have you had the opportunity to meet Miss Pendergrass?"

"Yes, sir. I had the pleasure of meeting her briefly yesterday."

"Miss Pendergrass is a member of the Jekyll Island Club in her own right. We accept women as members here," explained J.P. Morgan.

"As Superintendent, many people come to me with their concerns. It has come to my attention that Miss Pendergrass has been expressing some very suspect opinions. Very loudly, I might add." Superintendent Grob's confidence increased.

"Opinions? What type of opinions? Surely the second amendment promises freedom of speech," said Burke, angry that a woman would be insulted in such a way.

"Not seditious speech," snapped J.P. Morgan.

"Seditious?" asked Burke, very curious indeed about this Miss Pendergrass.

"Perhaps, Captain Thayer, it would be helpful if we provide you with more background on Miss Pendergrass," offered Charles Lanier.

"That would be helpful," agreed Burke.

"Miss Adelia Pendergrass is a well-known artist with certain artistic sensibilities." Superintendent Grob gave Burke a pointed look.

"Meaning that she doesn't see things the same way as you do?" Burke couldn't resist this small jab at the social norms of the day.

Instead of responding, Superintendent Grob withdrew a small notecard from the inside pocket of his jacket. From it, he read, "Miss Adelia Pendergrass is a talented artist who works with clay."

"Specifically, she makes pottery figurines," explained Mr. Baker. "She is actually quite well-known. I own a piece of her work."

Grob continued as if he had not been interrupted. "At an early age, Miss Pendergrass began her career painting facial features on bisque and china dolls. She studied at the Cincinnati Art School and spent some time working at Rookwood Pottery, also in Cincinnati, Ohio. It is there that she fell in love with glazes and the many different glazing techniques. To learn more, she attended the *Academic Julian* in Paris. There she was known to spend time meeting with artists and known socialists. After her three-year sojourn on the continent, Miss Pendergrass traveled all over the world to learn different glazing techniques." He consulted his card before adding, "According to her reviews, Miss Pendergrass is noted for creating glazes that are deep and velvety. Her pieces are considered to be simple yet evocative. One reviewer went so far as to say that her finished pieces are 'hypnotically alluring'." Superintendent Grob frowned as if the words left a bad taste in his mouth. He placed the card back in his pocket.

"Evocative. Hypnotically alluring. Absolute obscene nonsense," pronounced a disgusted Charles Rawlins.

Superintendent Grob went on. "This is what we know for certain about Miss Pendergrass. What we suspicion is that beneath her well-educated and well-financed exterior hides a subversive individual. Just look at her bohemian ways, her revolutionary speeches, and her loose morals." The tone of Grob's voice left no doubt in Burke's mind that the man had little liking for or tolerance of Miss Pendergrass.

"So, you consider Miss Pendergrass to be an anarchist?" asked Burke. The comments made about Miss Pendergrass angered him. He found her to be neat, intelligent, and full of spirit.

"There is that possibility. Once you have had the opportunity to speak with her, you will agree with us. Much of what she has to say is inflammatory and subversive at best and seditious and insurrectionary at worst."

"I see. I will definitely investigate Miss Pendergrass further." Burke's head throbbed so painfully, he would have said or agreed to anything at this point.

J.P. Morgan swore angrily. For a man noted for getting things done, this entire affair was very frustrating to the financier. "We are taxed with protecting President McKinley. I certainly hope that very soon you are able to raise more enthusiasm and energy to tackle this project. McKinley is due here tomorrow afternoon and yet nothing has been done about the murder."

The tension in the room mounted. Tempers flared. To a man, the board members preferred the theory that the murder victim was involved in an anarchist plot. Since Burke had not been able to tie the victim to any sort of plot, the safety of the president remained at risk. Considering the captain as derelict in his duties, everyone was in favor of releasing Burke from his obligations to the club.

Superintendent Grob voiced his concerns the loudest. "J.P., perhaps we need to dismiss Captain Thayer from his responsibilities. It might be better for us to handle this matter ourselves."

"I couldn't agree more," said J.P. Morgan. "Unfortunately, the Navy has sent him to us and with us, Captain Thayer will stay. At least until the president leaves."

In the end, no conclusions were drawn. No plans were made. No new accusations or ideas were put forward. The question remained: Should President McKinley and his party be allowed to visit Jekyll Island?

"I don't know. I just don't know," admitted Burke to himself, when the others had left the room. He shook his head miserably. He stopped the motion as the pain increased. He turned to Dr. Martin who remained in the room after the others had departed and asked, "Could I possibly have something for my headache?"

Chapter 27
Tiffy Rose

Tiffy Rose fingered the silver watch in her pocket. She grew restless as the conversation around her began to repeat itself. She suddenly felt an urgent need to speak with Captain Thayer. It was as if he was calling to her. Her heart began to beat faster. She turned to Miss Goodwin and found her engaged in a deep conversation about birds with Randolph Patterson. To Tiffy's eyes, the two seemed to be enjoying each other's company very much—perhaps too much. Tiffy Rose tamped down a spark of jealousy.

"Miss Goodwin, I apologize for interrupting you," said Tiffy Rose through only slightly gritted teeth.

"What is it, Tifton?" asked Miss Goodwin, her smile innocent, her face clear.

"Is something wrong, Miss Baldwin?" asked Randolph Patterson solicitously. "You look very agitated. Is the heat getting to you?"

"No, it's not the heat. I have something I must give to Captain Thayer. I must give it to him now," Tiffy Rose said urgently.

"Now?"

"In the middle of the picnic?"

Tiffy Rose looked at the only two people she could rely on for help and began to panic. A shy, placid chaperone and a slightly overbearing fiancé. Not exactly great choices for an emergency. Emergency? What gave her the feeling that Captain Thayer might be in danger? The impulse to reach Captain Thayer welled up in her and threatened to swamp her like a maverick wave swamps a small boat on a stormy sea. She fought back her urge to panic.

"Miss Goodwin, Mr. Chatsworth." Tiffy Rose switched to their given names and began again. "Flora, Randolph, I need your help. I must see Captain Thayer immediately. I have something that I must give him. Will you please help me?" Tifton didn't want to beg, but she required their help to leave the picnic without causing anyone to wonder where she was going. To do that, she needed both an escort and a chaperone.

Flora Goodwin and Randolph Patterson looked at each other and came to an immediate and mutual decision. "Of course, we will help," they said in unison.

Elated by their response, Tiffy Rose began to stand up.

"Wait, Miss Baldwin. I understand your desire to dash off in search of Captain Thayer immediately, however, if we don't want to arouse our parents or our hostesses, there are steps we must take to preserve proprieties," cautioned Randolph Patterson. He touched Tifton's hand lightly. "I will make our excuses and return as quickly as possible. Miss Goodwin, I suggest that you prepare for departure."

Within a few minutes, Randolph Patterson returned and offered his hand to Tiffy Rose and helped her up off the blanket. Always a gentleman, he did the same for Miss Goodwin. "That's all taken care of. I have informed both our parents and our hostesses of our plans to take a short, chaperoned, walk to discuss our future. Naturally, our parents agreed to our plan. The Maurices understood and wished us well. However, I sensed that the Rawlins sisters were not pleased when they learned of our departure. Is there something I don't know?" His square-jawed, earnest face showed no guile, only genuine curiosity.

Despite her continued misgivings about Captain Thayer, Tiffy Rose took the time to gently explain Alice's interest in Randolph Patterson as a potential suiter.

Randolph Patterson puffed up with pride and said heartily, "I've become quite popular since this morning's little escapade with the horses and carriage. I will have to thank my coaching instructor when I return home. His lessons served me well."

Tiffy Rose realized how typical it was of Randolph Patterson to give credit for his success to those who had helped him in the past. She regarded his pleasant face. It was then that she noticed a sharper look in his eye, a stronger set to his chin. Right before her very eyes, Randolph Patterson was changing.

"Shall we go?" asked Tiffy Rose with a charming smile. "Time is of the essence." She squeezed the silver watch in her pocket.

Smiling and nodding to their hostesses and their parents, the threesome set out along the riverfront promenade that led from Hollybourne Cottage to the clubhouse. She marveled at how well Randolph Patterson played the role of attentive suiter. To complete the ruse, he occasionally pointed out a particularly attractive flower or interesting plant. Tiffy Rose found it hard to stroll when she wanted to run. Randolph Patterson kept her speed in check by maintaining a firm grip on her elbow.

Once out of sight of the party-goers, the threesome picked up their pace. Tiffy Rose felt a surge of relief when the infirmary appeared in the near distance as they rounded the back of *San Souci* apartments.

"Tiffy Rose, must we walk so fast? People will stare," puffed Miss Goodwin, out of breath from her exertions.

"Yes, we must, Flora. Time is of the essence," repeated Tiffy Rose, staying on familiar terms with her chaperone. "I don't understand why, but I feel compelled to reach Captain Thayer as quickly as possible. I can't explain it, but I fear for his safety."

Suddenly, they were on the porch of the infirmary. Randolph Patterson knocked brusquely on the front door. No one answered his summons despite his continued loud pounding.

"Dr. Martin! Are you in there? Dr. Martin?" he called stridently.

Panic caused Tiffy Rose's head to feel light. She swayed slightly on her feet.

"No time for fainting now, Tifton," said Randolph Patterson briskly. He reached up and felt above the doorframe. Within seconds, he had located the spare key to the front door.

Tiffy Rose and Flora gasped in delight.

"How clever of you, Mr. Chatsworth." Much to Tiffy Rose's surprise, Miss Goodwin actually fluttered her eyelashes at the man. Her chaperone was positively blossoming here on Jekyll Island.

His face flush with success, Randolph Patterson grinned at his audience of two. "The previous doctor shared his little secret with me. It seems that he often locked himself out because he couldn't keep track of his keys. He frequently resorted to using this extra key after partaking in a late-night dinner followed by brandy and cigars."

"Open the door! We must find Captain Thayer!" urged Tiffy Rose.

Randolph Patterson made quick work of the lock and returned the key to its hiding place. Grandly, he held the door open for the ladies. Tiffy Rose raced past him and up the stairs. She threw open the door to Captain Thayer's room and saw—nothing. Captain Thayer was not in his bed. He was nowhere in the room at all.

Flora Goodwin offered an explanation. "Perhaps he has gone back to his own room at the clubhouse."

"No, I don't think so," responded Randolph Patterson. "His things are still here." He pointed to the personal items on the dresser.

"You are right. Here is his watch, his wallet, and his hat and shoes." Miss Goodwin and Randolph Patterson examined the room for any other personal items. They gathered up anything that belonged to Captain Thayer for safekeeping.

"Look, here is my birding journal. I wonder why it was tucked under the mattress? I wouldn't have seen it if I hadn't been looking for Captain Thayer." Miss Goodwin patted the leather cover tenderly and slid her treasured book into her reticule.

Uninterested in Captain Thayer's personal belongings, Tiffy Rose frantically searched the room. Where was Captain Thayer? She couldn't be wrong. The feeling that he needed her was very strong. If anything, it had increased since she first felt it nearly a half an hour ago. Anxiously, her eyes swept the room.

The utilitarian room offered very few places where a grown man could hide. Its furnishings included a bed, a dresser, a small desk, and a wardrobe. Tiffy Rose looked under the bed with no success. She opened the door to the wardrobe. Inside she found a heavy wool coat, the kind a man from up north would wear in the winter. She pushed it aside to look behind it. In doing so, she exposed the monogram on the lining, a large "P". It meant nothing to her. All that mattered was that she locate Captain Thayer. Somehow, she knew he was nearby.

"Don't touch those!" shouted Miss Goodwin suddenly. She reached out and snatched Randolph Patterson's hands away from a vase filled with a great many white trumpet flowers.

"Jimsonweed," she warned. "It is quite common on Jekyll Island, really throughout the South. I saw some growing along the side of the path we took on our carriage ride. It is more deadly than Hemlock. The slightest touch can cause a painful rash. Ingesting it can lead to intense hallucinations or even a sense of floating. Consuming too much of it causes heart failure and eventually death."

Shocked at being in such close proximity to such a dangerous plant, Randolph Patterson jumped back. Though he had not touched the plant, Miss Goodwin's words caused him to rub his hands on the front of his jacket forcefully trying to remove any contamination, real or imagined.

"What on earth is a giant bouquet of the stuff doing in an infirmary?" he bellowed. "Surely, a doctor or a nurse would know of its power to cause death!"

"A doctor or a nurse would certainly be familiar with Jimsonweed's properties. Jimsonweed depresses the central nervous system. In very small doses, doctors use it to alleviate anxiety. Some say that it is an effective remedy for seasickness," explained Miss Goodwin.

"But it causes death." Randolph Patterson let the word hang in the air.

"Yes, it is a very dangerous plant, though its trumpet-like flowers are quite attractive." Miss Goodwin admired the plant from a respectful distance.

Randolph Patterson shuddered in horror. "I will never look at pretty flowers in the same light again."

Miss Goodwin turned her attention away from the plant and to Tiffy Rose. "Come, Tifton, Captain Thayer is not here. It's time we left. It wouldn't do for Dr. Martin to return and discover that we have invaded his infirmary."

"He is here. Captain Thayer is here. I can feel him," Tiffy Rose said with conviction.

Randolph Patterson looked at her oddly and then shook his head sadly.

Tiffy Rose stood in the middle of the room and pivoted slowly around. She felt as if she had missed something vitally important. A stray breeze ruffled the curtains at the window. She ran to it and stuck her head outside. There, huddled above her on the roof next to a chimney, was Captain Thayer. Somehow, he had managed to climb out the window onto a small ledge and from there, up onto the roof.

"Flora! Randolph! He's here! He's out here!" shouted Tiffy Rose to her companions.

Before they could react, she gathered her skirts and climbed out the lower half of the double-hung window. Thinking only of Captain Thayer's safety, she crept along the overhanging roofline to where she could climb up to the second story roof to join him. She slowly made her way over to him. Tiffy Rose looked down only once at the ground so far away and pondered the folly of her action. Careful not to get caught up in her long skirt, she edged her way over to him. Reaching his side, she realized that he was talking nonsense to himself and rocking. His wide-open eyes stared unseeingly at her. Tiffy Rose stretched out her arm to touch him. Abruptly, he pulled away as if he was frightened of her sudden appearance on the roof. She quickly withdrew her hand.

Captain Thayer continued to rock violently back and forth. He seemed lost in his own world. Tiffy Rose didn't know how to cope with the situation.

"Can you fly?" Captain Thayer suddenly asked her seriously. His eyes remained unfocused.

Miss Goodwin and Randolph Patterson stuck their heads out the window.

"Be careful, Tifton," cautioned Miss Goodwin. "I fear Captain Thayer may have ingested some water with Jimsonweed serum in it." She held up a water glass in which a single white flower petal floated in the milky water.

Not wanting to startle the captain, Tiffy Rose responded to her chaperone in a quiet voice. "He just asked me if I could fly."

"The poor man! He is hallucinating. How could the doctor have been so careless with the dosage?"

"Why would Dr. Martin prescribe Jimsonweed for Captain Thayer's gunshot wound?" asked Randolph Patterson. "Wouldn't that new compound from Germany, *Bayer Aspirin*, be better?"

Miss Goodwin disagreed. "Not for his gunshot wound, but perhaps for his head injury, though I don't know how it can help."

"If you don't mind, I could use a little help here," said Tiffy Rose through gritted teeth.

"Yes! Of course! We must focus on getting Captain Thayer off of the roof."

"And you, too, Tifton," said Randolph Patterson, almost as an afterthought.

Both heads disappeared into the room leaving Tiffy Rose alone on the roof with Captain Thayer. Fear began to possess her. She pushed it aside and watched Captain Thayer.

As he became more agitated, he began to shout, "I can fly! I can fly! Watch me fly!" He tried to stand up.

Tiffy Rose wrapped her arms tightly around his waist and pulled him back down. She rocked him gently until he stopped struggling.

He turned his head and stared at her. In his eyes, she could see him struggle to fight his way clear of the drug that had taken over his mind. For a brief moment, they connected.

He said soberly, "Please don't be a dream. I must be dreaming. Please don't be a part of my dream. Don't disappear. Please don't disappear."

"I am not a dream. I won't disappear," she promised.

The moment was shattered by a shout from the window.

"Tiffy, we have a plan! Randolph knows where a ladder is kept. He is going to lean it against the side of the building just below you. That way he will be able to come up to help you. I am going to toss you this rope. You are to tie your end securely around Captain Thayer. Under his arms, preferably. Make sure that you leave a long tail on both ends of the rope. I will wrap my end around the leg of this heavy wardrobe. You will wrap your end around the chimney. When Randolph climbs the ladder, you and I will help lower Captain Thayer to the ground by releasing our ends of the rope slowly hand-over-hand. Once Captain Thayer is safely down, you can crawl back to the window with my help."

Tiffy Rose stared at Flora, contemplating their plan. It could work though it would take a lot of strength to lower a man as tall as Captain Thayer to the ground. Silently, she thanked her mother for encouraging her to take frequent walks, ride, swim, and play lawn tennis. Because she took regular exercise, she was stronger than most women. Tiffy Rose knew she could do it. She hoped that, in his addled state, Captain Thayer would be agreeable to the plan. Maybe he would think he was flying.

"Tiffy, did you hear me?" called Flora from the window. "Can you do it? Are you strong enough?"

"Yes. Yes. It is a good plan—an audacious plan, but I think it will work."

Tiffy Rose caught the rope when Flora tossed it to her. Tiffy Rose wrapped the tail end of the rope around the chimney and tied it.

"Come along Captain, it is time for us to put your wings on."

Captain Thayer submitted willingly to having the rope tied around his chest. Tiffy Rose had just tied the rope under his arms when he suddenly shouted, "I can fly." Abruptly, he stood up and lost his balance. Tiffy Rose grabbed his shirttails and pulled him to her. Together they tumbled toward the edge of the roof. Miss Goodwin screamed. At the last moment, the rope wrapped around the chimney caught and held.

Her hat, which had gotten pulled off, floated down to the ground. Tiffy Rose hoped that she would arrive on the ground just as gently.

Tiffy Rose and Captain Thayer lay entwined together on the edge of the second-story roof.

"Am I flying?" he asked.

"Not yet. We'll try again soon," she promised weakly. She needed a few moments to recover from the near disaster Captain Thayer almost caused.

Randolph Patterson's head popped up over the edge of the roof. "Ready?"

"As soon as I get untangled, we will be." Tiffy Rose tried to smile.

"The rope on the chimney held, thank goodness," said Flora. "Toss me the other end of that rope. I will wrap it around the leg of the wardrobe."

Tiffy Rose still held Captain Thayer; her arms wrapped around his waist. She wondered at the intimacy of their bodies. Yet another social *faux pas* against her, she thought grimly. She noticed that her dress was torn in several places. Would she never get anything right? She sighed.

"Courage, Tifton, courage," said Randolph Patterson encouragingly. He added confidently, "I know that you can do this."

Tiffy Rose blew her hair out of her face and realized he believed in her. He really did. Her heart swelled with something like pride.

"I can fly!" announced Captain Thayer before Tiffy Rose had time to consider her thoughts.

"Randolph, Captain Thayer thinks he is going to fly. It might help if we allow him to continue with his hallucination."

"Point taken," agreed Randolph Patterson. To both women, he said, "Be careful. Despite your gloves, that rope will burn your hands if you let it slide."

Captain Thayer's first step off the roof caught everyone unprepared. He fell about ten feet off of the two-story roof before Tiffy Rose and Flora were able to stop him. The rope slid swiftly through Tifton's hands, tearing her gloves and burning her palms painfully. The pain was like none she had ever felt before. Remembering how stoically Randolph Patterson bore his injured hands, Tiffy Rose wrapped the worst of her rope-burned palms with a handkerchief and picked up the rope again.

"Are you ladies ready to try once more?" asked Randolph Patterson.

Captain Thayer flapped his arms as he swung back and forth about fifteen feet off the ground. "See, I can fly."

"Of course, you can." Randolph Patterson noted the fraying of the rope holding Captain Thayer aloft as it rubbed against the edge of the roof. "We had better hurry. The rope isn't going to last much longer."

Randolph Patterson grabbed one of Captain Thayer's hands when he swung nearer, stopping the motion. "Steady, Captain. We're about to encounter some turbulence."

Despite the injuries to their hands, their daring plan worked better than Tiffy Rose imagined. Soon Captain Thayer was safely on the ground.

"Where is the doctor? Shouldn't we tell him what happened?" asked Flora.

"The first thing that we need to do is to get Captain Thayer back to his room where we can keep an eye on him," said Tiffy Rose firmly. "No more flying for you, Captain." She wagged a finger at Captain Thayer. He grinned at her, completely oblivious to reality.

"How long will it take for the effects to wear off?" asked Randolph Patterson.

"I don't know. I've told you all I know. Unfortunately, I am not a nurse," admitted Flora.

"But I am," announced the newly arrived Miss Pendergrass. "What seems to be the problem? And more interesting, why is Captain Thayer sitting on the grass all trussed up like a Thanksgiving turkey? And more importantly, Tifton, what were you doing up on the roof?"

"This is no time for questions! Captain Thayer has taken an overdose of Jimsonweed!" exclaimed Miss Goodwin.

"Jimsonweed? Are you certain?" asked Miss Pendergrass, her voice tight with concern.

"We found a half-full water glass containing a Jimsonweed flower petal in it upstairs in the infirmary," explained Randolph Patterson.

"Along with an entire plant!" added Miss Goodwin.

Captain Thayer, who up until this moment had been sitting patiently on the ground, suddenly announced, "I can fly!"

Miss Pendergrass focused all her attention on the hallucinating Captain. She quickly took his vital signs, his pulse, and his respiration rate. She noted that his pupils were dilated. "Where is Dr. Martin?"

"We don't know. He isn't in the infirmary. Can you do anything? Can you help Captain Thayer?" asked Tiffy Rose, clearly distressed.

"We will need to act swiftly. Mr. Chatsworth, get us a wheelchair from the infirmary. Miss Goodwin, please bring a large pitcher of fresh water and a glass. Also, please bring some towels. Miss Baldwin, you stay with me. I will need your help."

Miss Goodwin and Randolph Patterson retreated swiftly back into the infirmary.

"Miss Baldwin, I hope you are not faint of heart or stomach. We must force Captain Thayer to vomit out the contents of his stomach."

In response, Tifton Rose Baldwin plucked a feather from her fallen hat and held it out to Miss Pendergrass. "I will hold onto Captain Thayer while you tickle the back of his throat with this feather. That should bring up what remains of the contents of his stomach."

Chapter 28
Burke

Burke awoke with a terrible headache and a raging thirst. He tried to remember where he was and how he got there. By the light of a single lamp, he could make out very little in the otherwise dark room. He could hear someone softly moving about just out of his view.

"Would you like some water, Captain Thayer?" asked a familiar voice.

Burke nodded weakly.

"Don't try to speak yet. Take a moment to gather your thoughts. After what you have been through the past few days, they must be scattered to the winds."

Gratefully, Burke sipped from the water glass offered to him. He fell back against the pillow, exhausted by the effort of drinking. He couldn't remember ever having felt this bad, not even after he had been nearly killed when the Maine exploded.

"Who?" mumbled Burke.

"I am Miss Pendergrass. Do you remember me?"

Burke nodded.

"That is a good sign. I am so very happy that we found you in time."

"Found?"

"Captain Thayer, it would be better for you if you didn't try to talk. You have had a very trying day. The night is still young. Do you feel like going back to sleep? Simply shake your head, yes or no."

Without opening his eyes, Burke shook his head no. He wanted to know what happened. He opened his mouth to speak when Miss Pendergrass spoke for him.

"I imagine that you are very curious about the events of the past six hours."

"Six hours!" said Burke hoarsely. He tried to sit up. Miss Pendergrass placed a firm hand on his uninjured shoulder and pushed him back down into the pillows.

"If you will be patient Captain Thayer, I will enlighten you. Here, take another sip of water. It is not a short tale."

He drank greedily this time.

"Let me start by saying that for a man who just arrived on Jekyll Island two days ago, you have gathered together a loyal cadre of friends. As a matter of fact, without them you probably wouldn't be alive."

Once again, Burke tried to sit up.

"Ah, ah, ah. I am the story-teller here. It is your job to lie still and listen."

Miss Pendergrass waited until Burke had reluctantly settled back into the pillows.

"As I was saying, you owe your friends your life. And yes, I am well aware that Miss Baldwin is not your cousin, though the two of you have everyone else on the island believing you are. Very clever of you both." Miss Pendergrass tapped her chin. "Let's see. Where should I begin?"

Burke tried to control his impatience.

"Do you remember being shot? I see by the nod of your head that you remember at least some of the events surrounding your injury. Do you remember waking up at the infirmary? Yes. That is good. What about your visitors? Mr. and Mrs. Baldwin? J.P. Morgan and Charles Lanier? Superintendent Grob? Yes. Marvelous. I am very pleased that your memory has not been too badly damaged by the drug you ingested. Do you remember drinking anything while you were at the infirmary? Specifically, did Dr. Martin give you anything to drink?"

Burke lay still and gave her questions some thought. Funny, he could remember a lot about J.P. Morgan and Charles Lanier's visit, including their suspicions about the anarchist tendencies of the woman now seated next to him.

While Miss Pendergrass patiently waited for his answer, she dipped a cloth in a washbasin. After wringing out the excess water, she placed it gently on his forehead. Burke had hoped its cooling properties would trigger his memory, but it didn't. He gave up and signaled that, no, he did not remember Dr. Martin giving him anything to drink.

"No. Too bad. It could be very important. The reason I inquire is because you somehow managed to consume a quantity of Jimsonweed. Do you know it? It is a deadly plant that can be found throughout the South. Very pretty actually. However, the slightest touch of the sap can cause a painful rash. Ingesting the sap, as you did, leads to intense hallucinations, which you experienced. Did you know that you actually thought you could fly? Miss Baldwin had to exert herself quite strenuously to keep your feet on the ground—or at least on the roof. Do you remember being up on the roof? No. It must have been very exciting. It's a good thing that Miss Baldwin is not afraid of heights since she was up there with you."

Burke jerked upright in bed. His head spinning, he stared at Miss Pendergrass in disbelief. Him up on the infirmary roof? Miss Baldwin up on the roof of the infirmary with him? He couldn't imagine it.

Reading his thoughts correctly, Miss Pendergrass said, "Yes, you were up on the roof of the infirmary. Lie back down, Captain Thayer, if you want to hear the rest of my—or should I say—your tale."

Jimsonweed? Flying? How he wished he could ask questions. Reluctantly, Burke did as he was told and lay back down. He needed to know what had happened. Miss Pendergrass would not allow herself to be rushed.

"Now where was I? Oh, yes, I remember now." Miss Pendergrass took a deep breath. "As I was saying, consuming a great quantity of Jimsonweed causes heart failure and eventually death. Fortunately, I arrived on the scene just in time to put my nursing skills to work. Even so, for a short while we thought we had lost you. It wasn't until a few minutes ago that I was able to convince them that you had passed the danger point and that they should go to dinner."

Miss Pendergrass turned up the flame on a small kerosene lamp next to the bed. "I don't believe you will recognize where you are. We decided that it would be safest for you to reside for the time being in Mr. Chatsworth's room. Such a charming man." Miss Pendergrass veered back on target. "After all, there have been two known attempts on your life. The third time might be a rather unfortunate charm."

"Your friends managed to get you off of the infirmary roof—very cleverly, if I may say so. Once you were off the roof, they enlisted my help to relieve you of the poison Jimsonweed you had ingested. Nasty business that was. Once again, Miss Baldwin rose to the challenge. What a level-headed young woman. Take my advice. Marry her before she gets snatched up by someone else—specifically Randolph Patterson Chatsworth III—a worthy opponent for her love. She is charming and witty and displays remarkable intellectual agility. Yes, you should definitely snatch her up. She will make you a fine wife and help-mate."

Burke was growing tired of following Miss Pendergrass various segues off the original story line. Marry Miss Baldwin? He was at least fifteen years older than she was. She was a mere child in comparison with him. Miss Pendergrass would be a much better match for him. He paused briefly in his thoughts and considered this interesting idea.

"To make a long story short, after we relieved you of the poison, we bundled you up in a wheelchair and managed to get you to Mr. Chatsworth's room unseen. This fortunate event was more due to all of the servants either being occupied at the Maurices' garden party or having been drafted into helping to hang the red, white, and blue bunting in preparation for President McKinley's visit than to our abilities at playing hide-and-seek." She smiled a self-satisfied smile.

"Speaking of playing hide-and-seek, you are a wanted man, Captain Thayer. J.P. Morgan has been demanding your presence, as have the club president, Charles Lanier, and the club Superintendent, Ernest Grob. I am fairly certain that even that funny little clockmaker, Mr. Horst, is looking for you. Interestingly enough, the only person who doesn't appear interested in what has become of you is Dr. Martin."

Chapter 29
Tiffy Rose

It was Miss Pendergrass who insisted that they sneak Captain Thayer into Randolph Patterson's private room at the clubhouse. She argued that the captain was in danger—that he had been poisoned by the same person who had tried to shoot him earlier in the day. Since her convoluted reasoning could be correct and Dr. Martin was nowhere to be found, they went along with her suggestion. Given his hallucinations and the risk of heart failure from Jimsonweed poisoning, they had decided to keep watch over him in shifts. This proposal was further complicated by the need to keep Tiffy Rose with her parents until her bedtime.

In the end, Miss Goodwin took the first watch during the dinner hour. She sent a message to the Baldwins stating that she was suffering from indigestion having consumed too much rich food at the Maurices' picnic. Given the amount of food consumed by everyone at the picnic, no one questioned this excuse for missing dinner.

Before she departed to take Miss Pendergrass's place with Captain Thayer, Flora helped Tiffy Rose dress for the evening.

"At the rate that you are going through dresses, Tiffy Rose, you'll soon be going out in your nightclothes!" exclaimed Flora.

Both women began to giggle uncontrollably. Tiffy Rose wondered why they had never had fun together before today. The very idea of Flora calling her Tiffy Rose was so novel that she didn't know what to think.

"I have damaged two so far, haven't I?" she asked while wiping tears of laughter from her eyes.

Miss Goodwin began to count. "Let's see, you tore the train of the first one when you stepped on it the night Randolph Patterson knocked down J.P. Morgan."

Tiffy Rose immediately came to his defense. "Randolph couldn't help it. He was looking for me and didn't see Mr. Morgan. Besides, now that I think about it, I think Mr. Rawlins tripped him first."

"Really?" said Flora, hiding a smile. She returned to the original subject. "Don't forget your best gown. Your remodeling of it left it in a fragile state. The lace tore when we took it off of you after you fainted."

"I don't faint," stated Tiffy firmly.

Flora made a small moue with her mouth, but decided not to disagree. "Your best day dress is covered with Captain Thayer's blood."

Tiffy Rose shivered at the memory. "Let's not forget this afternoon's adventure. I tore my second-best dress while wrestling Captain Thayer off of the roof." She looked down at her hands which were still painful. "The rope burned my hands pretty badly. Please hand me my gloves, Flora. I will need to keep them on tonight or my parents will wonder."

"That was a very brave thing that you did, Tiffy Rose. Very brave, indeed."

Unexpectedly, Tiffy Rose realized that the formerly meek, mild-mannered Flora Goodwin had an inner reserve of strength and resolve. She held out her hands to grasp Flora's. "You were very brave yourself, Flora. I hadn't realized you knew so much about plants, especially poisonous ones."

"My grandfather owned a big plantation. I went everywhere with him and soaked up information like a sponge," said Flora in keeping with her quiet, unassuming persona.

"Well, I might have found Captain Thayer, but you saved his life. If you hadn't told us about Jimsonweed; he would have died."

For the first time in their relationship, the two women smiled at each other in friendship.

Timidly, Flora said, "Tiffy, may I tell you something I have never shared with another person?"

"I would be honored, Flora. I solemnly promise never to tell your secret." Tiffy Rose crossed herself over her heart in promise.

Flora glanced around the room as if checking to make sure that they were truly alone. "I was once in love with a wonderful man."

Tiffy Rose looked up, startled. She had never thought of Flora as a woman—a woman who could fall in love. "Go on," she said gently.

"He and I grew up together. We had so much in common. We shared everything. We enjoyed the same things. We laughed together.

Oh, how we laughed together." Flora sighed longingly. "We had an understanding though we were never formally engaged."

"What happened?" asked Tiffy Rose, positively agog with curiosity.

"Life. I suppose life happened," said Flora philosophically. "One day I woke up and we were poor. You remember the panic of 1893, don't you? My father lost everything. And I lost Davis."

"But, why? Why did you lose your young man?" asked Tiffy Rose with feeling.

"Oh, Tiffy. I couldn't expect him to marry me after we lost all of our money. He had such promise. He needed a wife who would help him achieve his destiny. Without any funds, I would only have held him back." Flora sniffed into her handkerchief.

Tiffy Rose thought for a minute before asking, "Which of you broke off your engagement?"

"I did, of course."

"What was his response?"

"He was heartbroken, as was I." Miss Goodwin looked distressed.

"It's been several years. Do you still think of him fondly?"

"Yes, I do." Miss Goodwin put her handkerchief to her eyes.

"Did he ever marry?" Tiffy Rose knew she was stepping outside the boundaries of good taste, but she couldn't stop herself.

"No, never. Neither of us married."

"Have you any contact with him?" asked Tiffy Rose.

"Well, yes, as a matter of fact, I receive letters from him now and again. He holds a wonderful position in Washington. Just yesterday, I received a postcard from him." She sighed wistfully.

"Would you like to see him?" asked Tiffy Rose, gently.

"Oh, yes. Yes, I would. That's why I sent him a telegram. I asked him if he could determine whether or not you and Captain Thayer are really cousins! I hope to hear from him very soon."

Tiffy Rose and Randolph Patterson dined with their parents in the grand dining room of the clubhouse. Naturally their respective parents were very curious about the outcome of their walk together.

"Well, Tifton, did you and Randolph Patterson have a nice walk together this afternoon?" asked Eunice Chatsworth.

"Yes, it was very—enlightening." Tiffy Rose didn't know what else to say. She didn't want to lie to her parents, yet she couldn't tell them the truth either. So, today's adventure with Captain Thayer became enlightening instead of frightening.

She felt as if she was playing a word game with their respective parents. She whispered as much to Randolph Patterson. He smiled indulgently at her which pleased her parents.

"Is there anything special about your walk that we should know about?" Eunice Chatsworth asked her son.

"We saw an amazingly large bird fly." Randolph Patterson grinned at Tiffy Rose.

Tiffy Rose stifled a giggle. She hadn't realized that Randolph could be so amusing. Not only did he possess a fine sense of humor, he showed himself to be useful in an emergency. She had not expected this. He actually shocked her with his adroit handling of the hallucinating Captain Thayer. He had also been very accommodating about sharing his bed chamber with a virtual stranger. The man was positively unflappable. It was too bad that she could never really love him. Or could she?

"What did the two of you talk about?" asked Etta Baldwin.

"Flowers." Tiffy Rose took a quick sip of fortifying wine.

"Flowers?" repeated her mother, clearly disappointed in her daughter's response. "You spoke of nothing but flowers."

"Randolph knows quite a bit about flowers. However, I think that today, we both learned something new about flowers, particularly the white trumpet kind." Tiffy Rose patted Randolph's hand fondly.

Her parents took this as a good sign. Her mother relaxed a little.

"You spoke of nothing else? You were gone such a long time." Mr. Baldwin searched his daughter's face for some kind of sign.

Randolph Patterson smiled blandly. "We talked about this, that—"

"And the other thing," finished Tiffy Rose carelessly.

Randolph Patterson laughed heartily at her little joke. He squeezed her hand affectionately.

Their parents exchanged worried glances. Tifton Rose and Randolph Patterson had never shown any sort of affection or even tolerance of each other prior to this evening. Tonight, they were conversing and laughing together. This was a side of their offspring that they had never seen before. They were not altogether comfortable with it either.

"We were hoping that the two of you have come to some sort of decision," said Patterson Chatsworth, finally taking the bull by the horns.

"Yes, as a matter of fact, we have," announced Randolph Patterson.

Tiffy Rose nearly died of shock. Randolph Patterson took ahold of her hand and smiled at her encouragingly. Their parents looked at the two of them with undisguised joy.

"We have decided that we enjoy each other's company. We have also decided that we would like to get to know each other better before making any life-changing decisions. Whatever we decide it will be our decision. We hope that you will respect our decision, whatever it may be." Randolph Patterson gazed serenely at the assembled people at the dinner table.

"Whatever we decide, it will be our decision." Tiffy Rose could have kissed him. He said just the right thing. Instead, her happiness showed in her face.

"Excuse me," said J.P. Morgan. "We are asking if anyone has seen Captain Thayer. He disappeared from the infirmary sometime late this afternoon. Have you seen him?"

Everyone at the table exchanged confused glances. Given Randolph Patterson's announcement, at the moment, Captain Thayer's whereabouts were far from everyone's mind. Everyone, that is, except Tiffy Rose. She kept her eyes averted. She was certain that anyone could read it in her eyes that she knew where Captain Thayer was.

Randolph Patterson rested his hand reassuringly on hers and answered for her. "Miss Baldwin and I attended the garden party at the Maurices' this afternoon. To our knowledge, Captain Thayer was not present at the party, at least, we did not see him. One could hardly have expected him to be out and about, given his injuries. Does Dr. Martin know where Captain Thayer is? It doesn't reflect well on the doctor if he has lost a patient." Randolph Patterson smiled up at the financier and blinked.

J.P. Morgan's face showed that he had expected this sort of convoluted and unhelpful answer from Randolph Patterson Chatsworth III. The financier nodded curtly to Mr. and Mrs. Baldwin and Mr. and Mrs. Chatsworth before moving on to question the diners at the next table.

"I wonder what could have happened to the captain," said Etta Baldwin.

"Why would J.P. Morgan ask us about Captain Thayer? We don't even know the man," said Patterson Chatsworth.

"He is our distant cousin," offered Franklin Baldwin with somewhat false bravado. "Military man. He's probably out trying to ensure that the president will be safe tomorrow."

"Will you attend the reception for President McKinley at the dock with me tomorrow, Tifton?" asked Randolph Patterson, changing the subject.

"Yes, I would like that very much, Randolph," Tiffy Rose responded gaily. She overheard her mother whisper to her father, "I don't know what happened during their walk today, but it must have been earthshattering."

Her mother couldn't have put it more aptly. Earthshattering. Tiffy Rose had had an earthshattering walk that day. The events of the day had taught her more about herself in a few short hours than she had learned in her lifetime.

Following dinner, there ensued another game of cat and mouse as Tiffy Rose and Randolph tried to escape their respective parents and return to keep vigil over Captain Thayer.

"If I may have your permission, Mr. Baldwin, I would like to take your daughter on a moonlit walk this evening. The air is particularly fine and mild. The moon is full. It is a lovely evening for a walk. We will, of course, ask Miss Goodwin to accompany us. She is sure to be feeling better by now."

With a request phrased like that, how could Franklin Baldwin refuse? "Permission granted, my dear boy. Permission granted." He pounded Randolph Patterson on the back heartily.

Miss Goodwin was rousted from her chambers. A promise to have Tiffy Rose in bed at a reasonable hour so that she would be at her best when the president arrived tomorrow afternoon was extracted and Tiffy Rose was free. It was exhilarating!

Tiffy Rose could see the attraction of being engaged and then married. Freedom. Freedom to come and go as she pleased. Freedom to make her own decisions. Freedom to make her own choices. She spun around happily next to Randolph Patterson as they walked down the crushed shell pathway toward the Jekyll River. The moon cast shadows through the Spanish moss hanging in the live oak trees. Tiffy Rose felt that she would remember the sound of the light breeze dancing in the live oak trees the rest of her life.

She touched Randolph's arm and stopped their progress. She took both of his hands in hers and said fervently, "Thank you, Randolph. Thank you so much for all that you have done for Captain Thayer—for me."

"Anything to make you happy, my dear. Anything."

Tiffy Rose heard the sincerity in Randolph's voice, felt the warmth of his hands in hers. Something inside her shattered. She turned away before her emotions could betray her.

They walked a few yards in silence.

"Tifton, could you fall in love with me?" asked Randolph Patterson.

"I don't know. I've never been in love before," answered Tiffy Rose truthfully. She wasn't sure enough about her feelings to commit to loving him. They were too new. She needed time to examine them. She hadn't expected love him—no, not at all.

"It's not that hard, you know, to fall in love, I mean."

"Randolph, are you in love with me?" she asked quickly before he could say more.

"What makes you think I don't love you?" he asked in an appalled tone. He took her by the shoulders and pulled her closer to him. His eyes met hers. They shone with reflected moonlight. "Can't you tell that I do?"

"How do you know?" asked Tiffy Rose. "How do you know that you love me?"

"If by love you mean that there is no other person that I would rather be with, no other voice that I would like to hear whispering in my ear, no other face that I would rather look upon, then yes, I am in love with you."

"Oh, Randolph."

He sounded so earnest, so very sincere. He really did love her. Tiffy Rose wanted to put her hands over her ears. He couldn't love her. She couldn't love him. Or could she?

In the moonlight, Randolph failed to see her distress. "Tifton, can you look past my clumsiness and see the man inside? You are so intelligent, vivacious, and witty—so alive. I could never expect a woman like you to be interested in a man like me—my money maybe, but not me. But, now, after the events of these past two days, I finally have the courage to ask this question. Answer me truthfully, do I stand a chance with you? Could you ever love me?"

"Oh, Randolph, I don't—"

Randolph Patterson cut off her protests. "I think I knew I had lost you the moment you lied about Captain Thayer being your cousin. Up until then I thought I might have a chance to win your love. I watched you as you cradled his head in your lap despite the blood that ruined your dress. I saw the way you climbed out on the roof and held tight to him when he wanted to fly. If only—"

Randolph Patterson never finished his sentence. Instead, he swept Tiffy Rose into his arms and kissed her as she had never been kissed before. She found herself kissing him back with the same fever. He released her just as abruptly. Tiffy Rose found that despite the warmth of the spring evening, she felt chilled and alone.

"Tifton, dearest Tifton, answer me one last question before I let you go. Would you climb out on a roof for me?"

Tiffy Rose stared deeply into his eyes—his eyes which were as green as the salt marsh grasses in springtime. Her answer came from deep inside her heart. "I'd like to think I would, Randolph. I'd like to think I would."

Chapter 30
Burke

Burke heard a soft knocking at the door. Dawn had not yet come and the last thing that he remembered was falling asleep with Miss Pendergrass by his side. Randolph Patterson opened the door and there she stood, looking fresh and well-rested.

"How are you feeling this morning, Captain?" she asked briskly. She lifted his wrist and took his pulse.

"Better than I expected." Burke still suffered from a headache and felt nauseous but he wasn't about to tell her that.

Miss Pendergrass had eyes like a hawk and noted his wobbly condition and slightly green face. She humored him and said, "That is very good news. You will still need to take it easy today. The ill-effects of the poison are numerous."

Burke sat up in bed and protested, "President McKinley arrives today and we still don't know if he is in any danger."

"While that is true, I'm afraid you won't be of much use to anyone today and perhaps tomorrow," cautioned Miss Pendergrass. "Jimsonweed is strong poison."

Burke began to argue, but was cut short when Randolph Patterson interrupted.

"I'll go and see what I can dig up for us to eat. It's too early for the kitchens to be open, but perhaps I can find someone to fix us a light breakfast. Captain Thayer, I took the liberty of bringing some clean clothing from your room last night." Randolph Patterson pointed to a stack of clothing on a nearby chair.

"Thank you."

Randolph Patterson merely nodded as if such behavior should be expected. He turned and spoke to Miss Pendergrass. "Adelia, now that you have checked on your patient, it might be prudent for you to return to your room now. I will look to see if the coast is clear."

Adelia? Captain Thayer hadn't even considered that Miss Pendergrass had a first name. He found himself admiring how well the name Adelia suited her. Her name had a musical quality not unlike the sound of her contralto voice. A voice he had found so soothing in those first dark minutes when he woke up last night.

Randolph Patterson swung open the door to his room and found Tiffy Rose and Miss Goodwin standing there preparing to knock on the door.

"Tiffy! Flora! What are you doing here at this hour of the morning? Quickly! Get inside before some early riser comes down the hallway and sees you! Your reputations will be in tatters." He took hold of the women's arms and yanked them into the room.

From his bed, Burke turned toward the newcomers in surprise. "Miss Baldwin! Miss Goodwin! What are you doing here at such an early hour?" he asked echoing Randolph Patterson.

"I am certain that they would not be here without a good reason," said Adelia Pendergrass, the voice of reason. "Tiffy, Flora, please sit down on the settee and catch your breaths. You look as if you have run all the way here."

Instead of sitting down, Tiffy Rose went over and straightened Randolph's tie, allowing her fingers to linger longer than strictly proper. Chatsworth wrapped his hand around hers and kissed it.

Miss Goodwin joined Miss Pendergrass on the settee, greeting her by her Christian name, Adelia. Burke was amazed at the familiarity the four people shared. He couldn't grasp what momentous event took place that turned them from individuals into a close-knit team.

Unaware that he had been the impetus for the change, Burke could only watch from the sidelines. He would never have thought that a well-brought-up girl like Tifton Rose Baldwin would enter a man's bed chamber without blinking an eye. And what of her chaperone? Did Miss Goodwin approve of her charge's behavior? Burke couldn't fathom it. They were comfortable with each other. They trusted and depended on each other and their actions showed it. What had he missed while he had been unconscious?

Tiffy Rose hugged her friend. "Adelia, it is good to find you here. It will save time only having to explain this once."

"Explain what once?" asked Randolph Patterson.

"Tiffy and I spent the better part of last night trying to make sense of what has been happening on the island. We've come up with a theory, due in part to this journal." Miss Goodwin held a leatherbound notebook in her hand.

"Isn't that your birding journal, Flora?" asked Randolph Patterson.

"At first, I thought it was. The covers and the size are exactly alike. However, since they are each a journal or diary of sorts, the similarities end at the first page. Apparently, our notebooks got mixed up at the infirmary. When Dr. Martin took my journal away from me and put it in a locked drawer, he said it wasn't mine. He said that it belonged to a previous patient. He got it wrong. He locked up my journal instead of this one which I found while we were looking for you, Captain Thayer."

Tiffy Rose, who had been pacing the room, could contain her excitement no longer. She took the notebook from Miss Goodwin and held it aloft. "This diary belongs to Percival Pratt! Percy. Percival Pratt. The man, the watch, and the journal must be one and the same!" she announced triumphantly.

Miss Pendergrass sat bolt upright in surprise.

"What's wrong, Adelia? You look like you've seen a ghost." Randolph Patterson hurried to her side.

"Tiffy, did you say that the journal belongs to Percival Pratt?" asked Adelia.

"Percival Pratt. He has penned his name on the inside cover. Do you know him?" asked Tiffy. She held up the journal, open to the inside cover, for everyone to inspect.

"I know of him. I was supposed to meet him on the island but he never showed up." Adelia's speech was slow and measured as she contemplated what this discovery meant.

"You were supposed to meet him!" exclaimed Burke. "Why didn't you tell us?"

"I had no idea that you would be interested in my relationship, such as it was, with Percival Pratt. You didn't tell me you were looking for him," Adelia answered sharply. "What is wrong? Why are you all gaping at me?"

They all stood still when they realized that she didn't know about Percival Pratt's fate.

Tiffy Rose walked over and touched Adelia's sleeve. "Oh, my dear Adelia. Percival Pratt is dead. We are so sorry. He died the two days ago on the beach. I found him. So did Captain Thayer."

"Dead? Percival is dead? Who? How?" Adelia sank into a chair.

"We don't know. We really don't know. We just now learned his name." Randolph Patterson's face was filled with kindness and understanding.

"How?" Adelia asked with a trembling voice. "I must know."

Burke said as gently as he could, "He was murdered."

"Murdered? Percival was murdered?" cried Adelia.

"Yes, he was definitely murdered. His face was beaten in with a shovel. I've been trying to discover who did it," explained Burke.

"I see." Adelia stared out the window while the others were respectfully quiet. After a few moments, she spoke. "Percival Pratt was a friend and colleague. He was a good man. It's time we find out who did this."

"You'll want to look at this," Flora remarked gently. She took the journal from Tiffy Rose and handed it to Adelia. "Especially the final entry."

Adelia reached out for the journal that Flora held out for her. She opened the notebook and leafed through the pages. When she reached the last entry, she stopped. "He's made a notation about a remedy for seasickness. He describes Jimsonweed in detail. He even notes that it can kill."

"Do you think that Percy Pratt may have gone to see Dr. Martin about a cure for seasickness?" asked Flora.

Randolph gave Flora's question some thought. "A cure for seasickness? That could explain why Dr. Martin had Jimsonweed in his examination room. He may have been concocting a seasickness remedy for Mr. Pratt."

"Or, he may have learned about the plant's deadly properties from reading Pratt's notebook," said Tiffy Rose ominously.

"Does it really explain the presence of Jimsonweed?" asked Randolph. "Think about it. The doctor had enough Jimsonweed at the infirmary to cause hallucinations in everyone on the island."

Adelia Pendergrass added her own questions to the mix. "Do you think that Dr. Martin murdered Percival Pratt? Why take away his identity by smashing his face? Why would he do that?"

Flora said, "These are all very good questions that we will need to find the answers to before we will learn who killed Percival Pratt and why."

Randolph Patterson tapped his chin as he pondered the implications of what was being discussed. "Jimsonweed? Hallucinations? Enough of the weed to cause everyone on the island to hallucinate? I wonder what Dr. Martin has planned?"

"Good question," responded Tiffy Rose.

"Why would a doctor want to prescribe a drug that can kill people? I thought they were sworn to uphold the Hippocratic oath," said Flora.

"Maybe he doesn't care about the oath. Maybe he is not a real doctor," proposed Randolph.

Tiffy Rose quickly jumped on his statement. "Randolph, what makes you say that?"

"The thought just popped into my mind. What if we are looking at this all the wrong way? What if Dr. Martin isn't really a doctor? He didn't seem all that comfortable bandaging Captain Thayer's arm. At the time, I got the impression that he was relieved to discover it was only a flesh wound."

"I was relieved that it was only a flesh wound, too," said Burke with a harsh laugh.

"Maybe Percy figured out the truth and died because of it," said Flora.

Adelia lifted her head out of Percival Pratt's journal and said, "You know, Randolph, you might have something there. If Dr. Martin wasn't comfortable treating Captain Thayer's wounds maybe he wasn't really a doctor."

Her words brought all conversation to a halt as everyone digested the new information.

"Dr. Martin isn't really a doctor?" Tiffy Rose mulled this idea over in her mind.

"But why?" asked Flora. "Why would a layman want to pose as a doctor on an island in South Georgia?"

"On an island in South Georgia that is expecting the President of the United States to visit this afternoon." Randolph Patterson's mind was already chasing that thought.

"Why was Dr. Martin generating a large quantity of Jimsonweed serum? What possible use would he have for it?" asked Burke, clearly perplexed.

"It is feasible that Dr. Martin could create a large amount of the deadly serum and use it to cause intense hallucinations. However, it would be difficult to meter the dosage. Remember, consuming too much of it causes heart failure and death," postulated Adelia.

Tiffy Rose, who had been standing next to the window, suddenly said, "Look, there he is now! It's just light enough to see him. He is keeping to the shadows but I can definitely see his face."

Randolph stood next to Tiffy and looked out the window. He rested his hand on her shoulder. "It's him all right."

Adelia joined them at the window and asked, "Why is he carrying what looks like a five-pound keg of nails?"

"Perhaps it's not really nails. It is sealed with a cork. Perhaps it contains something else. Something fluid." Tiffy Rose pressed her nose to the windowpane.

"Where is he going?" asked Burke.

Tiffy Rose pointed to a tall slender tower in the distance. Her quick mind made a giant leap. She whirled around and faced them. "To the water tower. He's going to poison the water supply with Jimsonweed when the president gets here."

"How could you possibly know this?" asked Burke in disbelief. "It is quite a jump from a few jottings in the journal of a dead man and a vase of flowers on top of a bureau dresser to poisoning a water supply!"

"We have you! You, Captain Thayer, were his first Guinea pig—his first test case—unless he poisoned Percival Pratt first. If he killed Percival Pratt, he will stop at nothing! I tell you; he is going to poison the water supply with Jimsonweed! We must hurry," urged Tiffy Rose.

Burke thought her imagination to be a victim of dime novels of romance and suspense. Her over-excited behavior was typical in very young women especially.

Flora joined in the general confusion and shouted, "We must stop him!"

"You follow him. Captain Thayer and I will alert the Jekyll Island Club board members and tell them what is afoot," said Adelia firmly.

"Good idea, Adelia. They will listen to you," commented Randolph.

Roused to action, the threesome moved toward the door, each selecting their weapon of choice. Randolph pulled a small revolver out of a drawer and put it in his pocket. Tiffy and Flora both picked up croquet mallets and swung them over their shoulders.

Burke blinked, not believing what he was seeing. His mind must still be under the influence of the Jimsonweed. He called to them before they could open the door. "Wait a minute. Where are you all going?"

"We are going to follow Dr. Martin and find out what he is up to," Randolph announced.

"You?" snorted Burke in disbelief.

"Yes, us," said Tifton Rose Baldwin, tilting her chin up proudly. She slipped her arm through that of Randolph Patterson Chatsworth III and then offered her other arm to Flora Goodwin. Together, they marched out of the room.

"I believe, Captain Thayer, that you have insulted the very people who saved your life. Twice, I might add," said Adelia Pendergrass with a hint of reproach in her voice.

"Look at them! Not a professional among them. They have no proof! They have only their jumbled imagination to guide them! What are they going to do if they catch up to Dr. Martin? Hit him with their croquet mallets?" Burke was certain that the threesome had gone completely off their rockers.

"I remind you again, Captain Thayer, it was on less flimsy evidence than this that they acted to save your live."

"Twice. I know. Beginner's luck," he scoffed.

Adelia Pendergrass remained unmoved. "In all my years as a secret service agent, I have made it a point never to underestimate the capabilities of the general public. When aroused, they can be counted on to act. And recent events certainly have made your friends angry. They are acting on their suspicions. It is that very kind of attitude that made us a nation back in the Revolutionary War."

Burke stared at the woman in front of him as if seeing her for the first time. "You are a secret service agent? Capabilities of the general public? Tifton Rose Baldwin, Randolph Patterson Chatsworth III, Miss Flora Goodwin useful in a dangerous situation? Will the surprises never end?"

"Ah, I see that you have chosen to deal with the simplest question first." Adelia Pendergrass smiled at Burke tolerantly. "Yes, I am a secret service agent. My current position is that of guardian for Mrs. McKinley. I am of course, undercover."

"That explains why you have such an extensive resume in the field of pottery glazes," he said with a tinge of sarcasm.

She shot an annoyed look in his direction and said, "As a matter of fact, I am actually a very talented potter. However, that is neither here nor there. You didn't really think that Mrs. McKinley would have a man to guard her? The privacy issues alone are mind-boggling. Catch-up with the times, Captain Thayer. Women are assuming many important positions in today's world."

Burke had many questions he wished to ask and many feelings he wished to express. Here at last was a woman who, in many ways, was at least his equal if not his superior. How had he not seen this when he first met her?

"Miss Pendergrass, you amaze me."

"That's very nice of you to say, Captain. I find you very interesting. However, now is not the time or place for a meeting of the mutual admiration society. If your friends are correct, we have a killer to catch."

"What are you talking about? Their crazy idea that Dr. Martin is a villainous anarchist who plans to poison the millionaires of Jekyll Island? You can't possibly believe this!"

"Given the evidence, I would say that they are not far wrong in their educated guess. Percival Pratt is—was—an expert in the field of poisons, specifically in the area of chemical warfare. You may not be aware, but many plants are poisonous to humans and beasts: Jimsonweed, Bitter Nightshade, Wild Parsnip, Poison Hemlock, Mistletoe, Foxglove, the list goes on. One of his duties while on Jekyll Island was to determine what types of poisonous plants could be found on the island. Think of it as a kind of chemical warfare. He must have seen the Jimsonweed at Dr. Martin's office and commented on the dangers of Jimsonweed. He would know that the nectar from the white, trumpet-shaped flowers, as well as the leaves and seeds are all poisonous."

"And you believe that Dr. Martin killed Percival Pratt because he cottoned onto his plans?"

"Basically, yes. Your friends believe it, too. They are out doing something about it. Shouldn't we?"

"What do you suggest, Miss Pendergrass? An assault on the doctor's office at dawn?"

"No, I suggest we pool what we know and wake up J.P. Morgan and the rest of the board."

"And what about our croquet-wielding friends?"

"You would do well to keep in mind that the very people you are deriding, saved your life two times in the past twenty-four hours." Miss Pendergrass pointed to the pile of fresh clothing on the chair.

Burke hesitated momentarily, but then, reading the expression on her face, gave in and got dressed.

Chapter 31
Tiffy Rose

Randolph, Flora, and Tiffy Rose walked as nonchalantly as they could through the hallway and down the stairs to the lobby. As it was still before dawn, there was no one about to ask unanswerable questions about their presence, croquet mallets in hand, at such an early hour. Once outside, they picked up their pace. Without consulting each other, they all chose to stay in the shadows as much as possible.

Tiffy crept along beside Randolph and Flora brought up the rear. She couldn't see Dr. Martin ahead of them. The doctor, if he should still be called that, had had a head start. They had been delayed by their circuitous route out of the clubhouse.

When they reached the water tower, Dr. Martin was nowhere to be seen. A small moan of disappointment escaped Tiffy.

"Don't give up yet, my dearest," murmured Randolph in her ear. "What do your instincts tell you this time?"

Tiffy Rose looked at the big man beside her, startled that he trusted her abilities. She stood completely still and put her mind to it. Randolph and Flora watched her and patiently waited. Then, the answer came to her.

"He won't want to be seen," she whispered. "He won't use the ladder on this side of the water tower. It is too visible from the clubhouse windows. He has another plan."

In the deep quiet that accompanies the dark time before dawn, they heard the sound of metal striking metal.

"He's got a grappling hook," said Randolph quietly, instantly understanding how the doctor planned to reach to the top of the tower. "I recognize the sound. He intends to climb the tower using a rope. I noticed how fit and muscular he was when I first met him. He must be a rock climber. He must plan to carry the cask in some sort of backpack."

"Quickly! We must stop him from dumping poison in the water tank," cried Tiffy Rose. "People will die!"

"Shouldn't we go and wake up Superintendent Grob and J.P. Morgan?" asked Flora, her voice barely above a whisper. "We will need reinforcements. Perhaps they will listen to us."

They all paused and absorbed that sobering thought.

"Do you really think that Superintendent Grob and J.P. Morgan will listen to us?" asked Tiffy Rose in a small voice.

Flora answered hopelessly, "I don't think so. Captain Thayer did not believe us and he knows us—sort of. It's not yet dawn. We are virtual unknowns to these powerful men. I don't think we have even a remote chance of seeing these men this morning. Even if we did eventually see them to plead our case, it will be too late. Dr. Martin will have poisoned the water supply. People will die if we don't do something now."

"I agree," said Randolph Patterson. Unshaven and disheveled, Randolph looked very young and vaguely raffish.

"So do I." Tiffy Rose stuck her chin up and gazed at her companions defiantly.

"I will go up and deal with this madman," said Randolph Patterson, his pleasant face suddenly looking rather grim and white.

A tiny shriek escaped Tiffy Rose. She clutched his arm, realizing how much he had come to mean to her in the past twenty-four hours.

Misinterpreting her distress, Randolph Patterson said, "One of us has to do it. There is no other way." In an unexpected gesture, he gathered Tiffy Rose into his arms and kissed her as if it were the last thing on earth that he was going to do. Tears stung in Tiffy's eyes as she returned his kiss. Perhaps it would be the last thing he would do. Her arms went around his neck. She pulled him down and kissed him again. For a moment, they shared the inexpressively wonderful feeling of sustaining each other against the world.

Randolph released Tiffy Rose and began to climb the ladder before she could catch her breath.

Watching him climb, Tiffy Rose remembered what Randolph had asked her in the moonlight just a few short hours ago. "Would you climb out on a roof for me?"

She looked up at his receding figure and the realization that she loved Randolph Patterson Chatsworth III swept through her and carried her off like a warm wave. Though he couldn't hear her, this time she answered his question correctly. "Not a roof, but a water tower. I will climb a water tower for you, Randolph."

Standing nearby, Flora Goodwin applauded silently, a look of happy approval on her face. She whispered, "I will stay here in case you are unsuccessful and Dr. Martin comes back down. He won't escape me." Flora swung her croquet mallet menacingly.

Tiffy Rose caught Flora's mallet mid-swing and hushed her. "Dear courageous Flora. You are brave and true. Thank you for being my friend." She embraced her chaperone tightly.

"Come on! Up the ladder you go!" urged Flora. Quickly, she helped Tiffy Rose adjust her skirts to make the climb possible.

Tiffy, her skirts tucked into her belt, her mallet tied with a sash and slung over her shoulder, started up the ladder.

Randolph felt her presence on the ladder and looked down. He smiled at Tiffy Rose and mouthed a single word. Courage.

It was a long climb up to the top of the water tower. They climbed as silently as they possibly could. Despite having a ladder, their progress was slow. Her rope-burned hands throbbing, Tiffy Rose wondered how Dr. Martin was faring with his grappling hook and rope.

The tower consisted of two sections. The lower two-thirds of the water tower was constructed of tabby. Perched atop of this base sat a circular metal holding tank. Rotating on the roof of the tank was a windmill that generated the power necessary to pump the water where it was needed. It looked like a lighthouse with a weathervane on top.

Tiffy Rose recognized that Martin would need to mix his deadly concoction into the holding tank's water from the top of the tank. This meant that after reaching the top of the four-story tabby tower, he would still need to climb another twenty feet to the top of the tank. The roof of the tank had a slight pitch to it which would make it difficult to maintain one's footing. Tiffy Rose did not relish climbing up on the roof to apprehend Martin. She hadn't enjoyed her experience on the infirmary roof and this was much higher.

Randolph must have had similar thoughts because once he reached the narrow walkway around the holding tank, he moved toward the other side of the tower, the side where Martin had just pulled himself up. Instinctively, when she reached the top, Tiffy Rose ran around in the opposite direction and sandwiched Martin between them.

"Hold it right there, Martin. We know what you are up to," Randolph shouted.

Martin looked up in surprise. Completely caught off-guard, he was shocked to see Randolph Patterson Chatsworth standing there.

Since he had assumed that everyone would be out looking for Captain Thayer, he blurted out an obvious question. "Why aren't you looking for Captain Thayer? He's suffering from hallucinations and stumbled out of the infirmary hours ago. He is probably out in the swampy marsh dying as we speak."

The instant Martin spoke the words, Tiffy Rose knew that he had intentionally poisoned Captain Thayer with Jimsonweed.

"Rest assured that Captain Thayer is safe," said Randolph.

Whatever his thoughts were at that particular moment, Martin recovered quickly. He lunged at Chatsworth and struck him a glancing blow on his face with the small axe that he carried in order to open the cask when the time came. Randolph cried out in pain. He covered his bleeding face with his hands.

Tiffy Rose moved swiftly to Randolph's aid only to find herself jerked to a stop when her skirts got caught on a protruding piece of metal. Cursing silently, she yanked on the material trying to pull it loose. Nearby, the battle raged on.

Wiping away the blood, Randolph struck back with his fists. A champion boxer at his university, many of his blows connected with Martin's face and torso, disorienting the man.

Tiffy continued to skirmish with her truculent skirt. She watched, horrified, as a life and death struggle between Randolph and Martin unfolded.

Having gained the advantage, Randolph threw the smaller man against the building. Martin dropped the axe at some point during the fight. Their battle intensified. Despite the lack of space to maneuver on the narrow walkway surrounding the water tower, Randolph managed to grasp one of the straps holding the backpack with its deadly contents. He yanked it off of Martin's shoulder. The weight of the cask caused the backpack to slip off the man's other shoulder. It landed between his feet and hindered Martin's ability to fight. This gave Randolph an edge over his opponent.

Randolph pressed the attack. He managed to trap Martin against the railing that ran waist-high around the water tower. From this precarious position, it would have been a simple matter to launch Dr. Martin and his evil concoction over the railing to his death.

But Randolph wasn't a murderer. Martin read this in his opponent's eyes and knew he had won. Martin made a calculated decision to take at least one life in exchange for his. He heaved himself toward Randolph in one great effort. The maneuver caught Randolph off guard. His head struck the water tower, disorienting him.

As Tiffy Rose watched, Martin pulled a vial of poison out of his pocket, opened it, and prepared to throw it into Randolph's eyes. In one enormous tug, Tiffy Rose tore her skirt free. Martin failed to notice Tiffy Rose swiftly approaching from his rear.

Wielding her croquet mallet with a strength she did not know she possessed, she swung the mallet at Martin as hard as she could. The man took the blow squarely on his back, knocking the wind out of him. Randolph leapt up and swung Martin around and gripped his arms firmly behind his back.

Tiffy Rose swooped down and picked up the barrel.

"Look out below!" she shouted at the top of her lungs. Following her warning, she sent the cask of poison over the side of the water tower.

"Look Martin! There goes your poison!" said Randolph through gritted teeth.

"Noooooo!" cried Martin as he watched his poison plunge to its own death.

A few seconds later, they could hear the satisfying crunch of the cask splintering apart when it impacted the earth below.

Martin leaned over the railing, cursing. He turned and shook his fist at Tiffy Rose and Randolph. "I am not beaten yet," he shouted. He snapped a rappelling line to the railing and leapt over the side.

Tiffy screamed. Randolph pulled her to him and held her face against his shoulder. Together they listened for the sound of Martin's body making contact with the earth. When they didn't hear it, Randolph moved over to the railing and looked down. What he saw amazed him.

"Look Tiffy. Martin's hanging by his harness and rappelling line. He must be about fifteen feet in the air. His rappelling line is too short. If we move quickly, we may be able to reach the bottom before he cuts himself loose."

"Hurry!"

Randolph and Tiffy arrived at the base of the ladder in time to see Martin cut himself free and drop the remaining fifteen feet. Winded by his fall, he was ill-prepared to fend off the croquet mallet wielding Flora Goodwin. One or two good whacks later, the man lay dazed at their feet.

Chapter 32
Burke

It had taken Burke and Miss Pendergrass several hours to awaken and assemble the Jekyll Island Club board members in the grand dining room. By the time the men were willing to meet with them, Tomas Martinez had been captured by Tiffy Rose, Flora, and Randolph Patterson. Thankfully they thwarted his poisonous plan. Burke still smarted from the realization that his chief role in this adventure occurred when he tried to fly off the roof of the infirmary.

The board members began questioning the hostile witness.

"Why? You ask why? I will tell you why I wanted to poison the Jekyll Island water supply. My name is Tomas Martinez. I am Castilian Spanish and proud of it," announced Martin In a thick Spanish accent.

The men around him gasped in disbelief. They had trusted him as their doctor. They had consulted him in important matters of health. They had treated him as an equal. He betrayed them. He tried to poison them. It was unbelievable. It was incomprehensible.

Noting the shock on the faces around him, Tomas Martinez switched to an American accent and sneered, "You, Americans, are so innocent and gullible. You believe anything that you are told. You didn't even check my credentials when I said I was on the island to replace Dr. Merrill. Instead, you welcomed me. You even threw me a party. How easy it was to fool you." His disdainful expression left little doubt of his feelings toward the people present in the room and Americans in general.

Murmurs of consternation could be heard throughout the meeting room.

"I am no doctor. Dr. Thomas Martin was a ruse to achieve my goal of killing President McKinley and as many millionaires as possible. President McKinley declared war on my country." Martin glared at the men surrounding him before continuing his rant. "The wealthy club members on Jekyll Island—you—supported the war effort with your endless wealth. You destroyed my country's economy. You took away our colonies, all because of the sinking of your precious battleship. You must be punished!"

Martinez switched his attention to Randolph Patterson Chatsworth and Tiffy Rose Baldwin. "You are responsible for my failure!" Hatred burning in his eyes, Tomas Martinez rose from his chair and flew at Randolph Patterson screeching, "You must be punished! You have destroyed everything that I have worked for!"

Tiffy Rose stepped in front of the heavily bandaged Randolph Patterson and swung at Martinez with her croquet mallet. The head of the mallet connected with his chest with a satisfying thump. Martinez fell backward into his chair.

Sheriff Higgins handcuffed the anarchist to his chair. "We'll have none of that now," he commanded. "I should have done that in the first place."

"Would someone please explain the events that led up to the capture of Dr. Martin—I mean—Tomas Martinez?" bellowed J.P. Morgan, clearly at the end of his patience. "President McKinley is due here in a few hours. We need to know what happened."

"Perhaps the five of us can explain," began Captain Thayer.

"It takes all five of you to explain what happened?" asked the financier, puffing out his cheeks.

"The events ebbed and flowed like the tide here on Jekyll Island, sir. It will make more sense if each of us told you about the parts we were most involved with," explained Randolph Patterson.

J.P. Morgan eyed Randolph Patterson suspiciously as if he were uncertain that this man standing before him was the same young man who had knocked him so clumsily to the floor just two nights earlier. Even Morgan could sense that something had changed about him. Despite his bandaged face, Randolph Patterson looked strong and sure of himself. There was a solidity and composure about him that hadn't been present before. And, indeed Chatsworth had changed, thought Burke. He wasn't the same man that he was just forty-eight hours ago. After their experiences, none of them were truly the same.

"If you will allow me to begin, Mr. Morgan," said Tiffy Rose politely.

Having had his sleep disturbed in the wee hours of the morning, J.P. Morgan was less than gracious when he signaled for Miss Baldwin to proceed.

"I was horseback-riding on the beach with my friends when I came across a dead body. At almost the same moment as my discovery, Captain Thayer arrived on the scene."

Burke took over. "I sent Miss Baldwin back to her friends and asked her to secure help, which she did. The body was transported back to the Jekyll Island Club where it was examined by the members of the Jekyll Island Club board, Martinez, and myself."

"You tricked me! I needed to find that pocket watch! I saw you take it, yet I couldn't find it. Where is it? The watch is the only thing besides his notebook that would tell you the identity of the dead man. Without his name, you would still be floundering around in the dark!" raved Martinez.

"Shut him up!" growled J.P. Morgan.

Burke ignored them both. "I kept the pocket watch and took it the next morning to the clockmaker, Mr. Horst," continued Burke. "After he opened it and we discovered the first name of the owner, I left the watch with him for repair."

"Only the first name?" asked J.P. Morgan.

"Percy."

"Were you able to determine who Percy was?" asked the financier.

Miss Pendergrass answered Mr. Morgan's question. She summarized things neatly by leaving out the details of looking for Captain Thayer and where they found the journal. "We did not learn his last name until early this morning. Miss Goodwin discovered Percy's journal. From it, we learned the victim's full name. Percival Pratt."

From the audience came a sharp gasp. Though he looked around, Burke couldn't identify who had made the noise.

"Percival Pratt? Who is—excuse me—who was Percival Pratt?" asked J.P. Morgan.

Adelia Pendergrass also fielded this question. "Percival Pratt was a secret service agent for the United States government. Specifically, he is attached to the Secret Service staff protecting the president. Under the guise of an avid bird watcher, Percival Pratt traveled to different locations scouting for security problems. His field of expertise was poisons."

"Percival Pratt was a birdwatcher. That explains why he carried a pair of binoculars and a compass in his pockets. If his notebook had been left with his body, we would have been able to solve this case much more quickly," added Burke.

"Wait a minute! Did Martin or Martinez kill Percival Pratt?" asked J.P. Morgan, growing excited that this mystery might be solved.

Martinez began shouting, "I did not kill Pratt! He drank some Jimsonweed. But I did not kill him! He was alive when he left the clinic. I swear to you, he was alive."

"He's an anarchist! They lie! He killed Pratt!" screamed Mr. Rawlins.

"Don't believe him!" shouted Mr. Barnes. "He's lying!"

"I am not lying! I did not kill Pratt!" shouted Martinez.

"Quiet! Quiet!" shouted J.P. Morgan. "Martinez, you'll have your turn in court."

Eventually the room quieted down and Tiffy Rose picked up the story. "The next morning, Mr. Horst, the clockmaker, brought the watch to me because he couldn't find Captain Burke."

"I was out checking the island for weak spots in the security," explained Burke.

"And we all know where that got you!" Martinez laughed triumphantly. "Shot. You got shot," he taunted.

Randolph Patterson pointed accusingly at Martinez. "You shot Captain Thayer with a rifle."

"No! You're wrong! I did not shoot Thayer! I had other plans for him. First, I had to get the pocket watch back!" shouted Martinez. "I did not shoot at Captain Thayer! I did not kill Pratt! I gave Pratt some Jimsonweed. I wanted to test its potency. I needed to know what the effects were in order to prepare my greatest triumph—poisoning the Jekyll Island water supply!"

"You didn't shoot Captain Thayer?" asked Mr. Barnes. "If you didn't, who did?"

His question was on the lips of many of the men in the room.

"How could I have shot him? I have no gun." Martinez smiled confidently at his accusers.

"You could have taken one from my gun room," said Mr. Maurice. "One is missing."

"One of your guns is missing? Why didn't you say so?" asked J.P. Morgan. "When did you notice it was missing?"

"I discovered my gun was missing yesterday afternoon," answered Mr. Maurice. "I spent the remainder of the day looking for it. This morning is the first opportunity I have had to speak with you or the sheriff."

"I tell you; I did not steal a gun from anyone. I did not shoot Captain Thayer. Ask Superintendent Grob. He knows that I was still on the club grounds when Captain Thayer rode off yesterday morning. I saw him as I went to the laundry to care for an injured employee," said Martinez in a more normal voice. "She had burned herself with scalding water. Superintendent Grob saw me there. I had no time to shoot the captain. I may have tried to poison everyone, but I did not kill Pratt or shoot Captain Thayer."

"Don't believe him! The man is a lunatic!" said Mr. Maurice.

"An anarchist!" said Mr. Barnes.

"You cannot believe a word he says. An anarchist will lie, steal, and kill to achieve his goals!" Mr. Rawlins said forcefully.

"If Martinez didn't fire the rifle, then who shot Captain Thayer?" asked Mr. Maurice.

"I told you that it was a stray hunter who didn't follow the club rules," said J.P. Morgan, satisfied with his conclusion.

"That needs to be proved," said Burke, still uncertain about the incident. He couldn't decide if Martinez was telling the truth or not.

"It isn't necessarily germane to the issue at hand, which is: how did you know to pursue Martinez?"

"Yes! How did you know that Martinez planned to poison the water supply?" asked Mr. Rawlins, much calmer now.

"We must admit that our reasoning is not airtight. It was after we found and rescued Captain Thayer from the infirmary roof—remember he had been poisoned with Jimsonweed—that things began to fall into place," explained Randolph Patterson Chatsworth. "Miss Goodwin located what she thought was her journal, but it actually belonged to Percival Pratt. Miss Baldwin and Miss Goodwin spent most of last night studying the journal in search of any clues about Pratt's death. The only notes of interest that they found were related to Jimsonweed. They brought the journal and the pocket watch to my room this morning."

"May I see the watch?" asked J.P. Morgan. He looked at Captain Thayer who shrugged his shoulders and pointed to Tiffy Rose.

"I have it, Mr. Morgan." Tiffy Rose held out the watch to him.

Taking the pocket watch into his hands, Morgan ran his fingers over the gold tracings. He snapped open the front of the case and then the back. As he did so a small photograph fell out of the case. He bent over and picked it up. After taking a minute to study the face in the photograph, he handed it to Mrs. Rawlins and said quietly. "I believe this is yours, Millicent."

"Millicent?" asked Burke, Tiffy Rose, Adelia, Flora, and Randolph at the same time. "'*To my beloved Percy, Your sweetheart Milly*'."

Much to everyone's surprise Millicent Rawlins began a terrible keening. She said her lover's name over and over again like a litany. "Percy. My beloved Percy. Percy. My beloved Percy."

Mr. Rawlins stepped closer to his wife and said sharply, "Pull yourself together, Millicent. Haven't you made enough of a spectacle of yourself for one day?"

At first it appeared as if Millicent Rawlins was going to leave the dining room, her face buried in her handkerchief. Suddenly, she pointed at her husband and screeched, "You killed him! I know that you did! You couldn't stand to see me happy! You knew of my plans to leave you! You wouldn't have cared except for the money! My money! Money you've been living off of for years without earning a cent yourself! You killed him! You have ruined my one chance for happiness! You killed Percy!"

"I have always said that money can't buy happiness," whispered Adelia to Tiffy Rose.

Tiffy Rose shot Adelia a look and then asked the obvious question. "Mr. Rawlins, did you kill Percival Pratt?"

Had the question come from a man, Rawlins would have fielded it without batting an eye. The fact that a woman asked it caught him off-guard causing him to answer truthfully and with a great deal of disdain. "The man was sleeping with my wife! He deserved to die! I beat his face in with a shovel!"

Realizing what he had said, his wife erupted in a fresh wave of tears. The noise brought Rawlins back to his senses. Seeing the looks of horror on the faces of the men around him—his contemporaries—his equals—he turned swiftly and stalked out of the room. The Glynn County sheriff followed closely on his heels.

Several of Millicent's women friends escorted her from the room.

The silence in the room was complete until Martinez gloated, "I told you I didn't kill the man. I bet once Rawlins is questioned, he will confess to stealing a gun from Maurice's gun room and shooting Captain Thayer, too. All because of a pocket watch."

Chapter 33
Tiffy Rose

"Tifton, what have you done with your clothes? I can't help but notice that three of your dresses and an assortment of undergarments have gone missing. Do I need to speak with Superintendent Grob about his staff?" Mrs. Baldwin stood at the foot of Tiffy Rose's bed, tapping her foot.

Horrified at the thought of Superintendent Grob investigating the disappearance of her undergarments, Tiffy Rose nearly shouted 'no'. She struggled to remain calm as she offered an explanation to her mother. "No, ma'am, that won't be necessary. Miss Goodwin and I sent them off to be cleaned and pressed. I am sure that they will be back from the laundry soon."

Her mother heaved a great sigh. "Tifton, as a child you always were one for getting your clothes dirty. I had hoped you would grow up to be a lady. What on earth will you wear to meet the president at the pier today? And the reception tomorrow? You only have the one dress left! You simply cannot wear it to both events. Everyone will talk."

Her mother stopped speaking and considered what she had just said. Then her face brightened. "Everyone is already talking, aren't they? Your exploits this morning are well-known around the Jekyll Island Club. After what you did this morning! Imagine! My daughter and her fiancé are responsible for saving the president's life—saving everyone's life! Climbing a water tower! Tossing poison over the side! Capturing an anarchist! Very heroic! Very cheeky of you!"

Mother and daughter smiled at each other. Their smiles grew wider as each acknowledged their mutual respect for each other. Suddenly they were in each other's arms, laughing.

"I am so very proud of you, Tiffy Rose."

"I am so very proud of you, Mama."

"Tifton! There you are," said Randolph Patterson when he found her sitting in the shadow of the wide veranda that overlooked the Jekyll River. He went to her with his arms outstretched.

Tiffy Rose felt a lump in the back of her throat. She blinked back tears. She had hidden herself away in this forgotten corner of the veranda in order to think. Yet, he had found her. Had he come looking for her or had he just happened upon her? She studied his cheerful face and decided that he had come looking for her—for her alone. That was the only explanation because of all things, Randolph was kind. He was always kind. He was loyal and generous, brave and sensible. Tiffy Rose found it a very pleasing combination of attributes in a man.

But did she love him? This morning, she had climbed nearly to the top of the water tower and saved his life. Had she been caught up in the heat of the moment or had she really feared for his safety? How would she know that Randolph was the right man for her? Was he the man she wanted to wake up to every morning? Would he ever kiss her again as he had at the base of the water tower? Or had he kissed her in a never to be repeated fit of passion brought about by the dangerous situation? Despite the circumstances, she had thoroughly enjoyed that kiss. Tiny smile formed on her lips.

And what did Randolph think of her? Did he find her worthy of his attentions? Was it her money that he found attractive? Or was he just being kind? He had said he was in love with her, but he had yet to say the words, 'I love you.'

"Tifton, you are looking rather serious and thoughtful this afternoon," commented Randolph. "I hope that this morning's events have not distressed you greatly. You know I prefer to see you gay and laughing."

So, he still called her Tifton, not Tiffy, not even Tiffy Rose. She felt unbearably sad. She lifted her eyes to his and said, "I know you do, but today—"

He cut her off as if he didn't want to hear what he might say. "Perhaps you are merely overtired, my dear. We are all exhausted by our efforts."

"Perhaps." She reached toward his hands and took them in hers. She saw hope begin to grow in his eyes. "I have been thinking—about us."

"Good thoughts, I hope." His battered and bruised face serious, Randolph Patterson leaned forward and closed the distance between them.

"Randolph, please forgive me. I have been so confused, but I am not now."

"Please, tell me, Tiffy, have I any hope that you will come to love me as I love you? Is there hope—like a flickering candle shedding its light at the end of a long tunnel?"

She wanted to apologize for all of her selfish behavior. She wanted to tell Randolph that her feelings toward him had changed. She wanted him to take her in his arms and hold her like he was never going to let her go. She opened her mouth but the words would not come out. All she could think of was that she didn't deserve his love. "Randolph—I'm sorry—"

Abruptly, he released her hands and turned away from her. Randolph smiled his sad, sweet, smile. "Don't feel sorry for me. I wouldn't have missed this adventure for the world. The fact that you played a role in it makes it all the more special. I can understand that you would prefer I leave you now."

His words felt like a hot knife had been plunged into her heart. In a blinding moment of clarity, she realized that, without Randolph Patterson, her life would be a very bleak indeed.

So, this then, was love.

Her confusion and indecision vanished. "Randolph!" she cried as she held her arms out to him. "Please don't leave me. Please don't ever leave me alone without you."

He spun around and swiftly gathered her into his arms. He held her with arms that once were clumsy but now were strong. He kissed her with lips that once were cool but now were warm with passion. Tiffy Rose had come home.

Releasing her with much reluctance, Randolph Patterson tamped down the flames of his ardor. He resumed his normally bland expression. Only this time, it held a hint of a smile in his eyes and at the corners of his mouth.

Tiffy Rose smiled up at him, her eyes brimming with joy.

"President McKinley's boat is about to dock at the pier. Would you like to go and join the crowd now or would you prefer to make a dramatic late entrance? I must say that there is nothing like taking your seat in the middle of the overture for attracting the gaze of all of the opera glasses in the house."

"Shall we go for the dramatic, just this once, Randolph dear?"

"Anything to bring a smile to your face, Tiffy, my heart's delight."

Always a gentleman, Randolph Patterson offered his arm to Tiffy Rose. Together, they walked toward the pier.

The scene that greeted them at the pier took their breath away. The residents of the Jekyll Island Club turned out to greet President McKinley. In fine style, women wore their most attractive afternoon dresses with full-length skirts and tight-fitting corsets. All manner of hats perched on carefully coifed hair. Men looked dignified in top hats and neatly pressed morning suits. Servants dressed in their best clothes. Even Mr. Horst, the clockmaker, stood nearby watching the festivities.

"Tiffy Rose! Tiffy Rose! Over here!" called the Barnes twins. They waved them over.

"Shall we grace them with our presence, my dear?" asked Randolph Patterson, shamelessly proud of their accomplishments.

Catching his buoyant mood, Tiffy Rose answered, "Most definitely."

In a complete abandonment of decorum, Becca Barnes squealed and threw her arms around Tiffy Rose. "Oh, Miss Baldwin! How frightening for you! How very brave of you! Climbing up a four-story ladder!"

"All to save dear Mr. Chatsworth's life!" squealed her sister, Beverly.

Tiffy Rose managed to successfully extricate herself from Becca's grasp. Craving the protection he offered, she moved nearer to Randolph.

"We want to have you over for tea," said Beverly earnestly.

"I know! We'll host a lawn party for you as soon as the president leaves!" Becca's eyes glazed over as she imagined the party hosting the heroes of the day.

"Yes! That is a lovely idea, Becca." Beverly nodded in agreement.

"Everyone knows what good friends we are. They will expect it of us!" said Becca.

"Good friends?" questioned Margaret Maurice, her tone dismissive. "Why you hardly know Miss Baldwin! It should be our responsibility to host a party for Mr. Chatsworth and Miss Baldwin. Afterall, we are the club members of the longest standing."

"And Hollybourne Cottage is perfect for a party," said Cornelia Maurice.

"So much nicer than the clubhouse," added Emily Maurice.

"I know! Tifton Rose, why don't you come and stay with us for a while?" asked Marian Maurice. "Hollybourne Cottage has so many rooms. We're sure that you will find staying with us delightful."

"Positively delightful!" gushed Emily. "You simply must call me, Emmy."

"And call me, Meg," said Margaret Maurice.

"The family calls me, Mamie. I want you to, too," added Marian.

"And I'm Nina," finished Cornelia.

Other young women joined them and began asking a flurry of questions.

"Did you really go out on a roof to rescue Captain Thayer?"

"I heard that you climbed a water tower to save Mr. Chatsworth's life!"

"Tiffy Rose, you are so very brave."

"I would have fainted!"

Tiffy Rose kept a firm grip on Randolph's arm as she tried to cope with all of the young women chattering at her at once. She whispered in his ear, "How did we go from virtual outcasts to most popular guests in one climb up a water tower?"

"I'm not entirely sure," he said, his lips brushing her cheek.

As he did so, Tiffy Rose watched as, several feet away, Alice Rawlins began to sob. Her sisters, May and Grace, surrounded her and took her a little apart from the crowd. Tiffy Rose, understanding the reason for Alice's distress, said a little prayer that Alice and her sisters find happiness. Things would not be easy for the Rawlins girls from now on. Their parents' little scene and their father's guilt would make life very difficult indeed.

Just beyond the threesome, the clockmaker stood with a large object wrapped in chamois cloth in his arms. Tiffy Rose wondered if it was the French ormolu clock. She hoped he had repaired it in time for Mrs. Baker's dinner that evening.

Mrs. Baker suddenly appeared as if Tiffy Rose had conjured her up merely by thinking of her.

"Good afternoon, Miss Baldwin. Mr. Chatsworth, it is good to see you up and about." Mrs. Baker surveyed the damage to Randolph Patterson's face. Fortunately, the worst of it was hidden under a clean, white dressing placed there by Miss Pendergrass after she had stitched his wound closed.

"Tonight, we are hosting an intimate dinner for President McKinley, his wife, and their party. President McKinley has specifically asked that you, Miss Baldwin, Miss Goodwin, Miss Pendergrass, and Captain Thayer be invited."

"How kind of you to invite us, Mrs. Baker. If it weren't for the president specifically asking for us, we wouldn't dream of interfering with your carefully planned dinner," said Randolph Patterson graciously. "Hopefully, the president's request won't inconvenience you very much."

Mrs. Baker smiled and responded, "You are too kind. Thank you for understanding. I assume you will be coming."

"Yes, we will be there. We will all be there," answered Randolph Patterson.

"Good. See you at seven, then."

After Mrs. Baker had turned away and gone in search of Captain Thayer and the others, Tiffy Rose stifled a small cry.

Randolph Patterson turned to her and asked gently, "Tiffy, dearest, what is the matter?"

Tiffy Rose wailed, "I haven't anything to wear!"

Chapter 34
Burke

Burke watched as the crowd parted for Miss Baldwin and Mr. Chatsworth. People greeted them like royalty. He remembered her charm, her vivacity. He remembered Randolph Patterson Chatsworth's clumsiness. He remembered the brief interludes he had shared with such a delightful young woman. And to think, he gave Chatsworth advice on how to win her. Burke felt a twinge of jealously in his breast.

"They look well together, don't they?" asked Miss Pendergrass who had magically appeared at his elbow.

He glared down at her and then back at the couple who were shaking hands and receiving congratulations. Congratulations that should have been his! A beautiful woman who should be standing next to him right now!

"I can see the green-eyed monster of jealously has taken ahold of your sensibilities. In our profession, it is best that we stay out of the spotlight and in the shadows. We are much better playing the supporting roles rather than the leading ones," Miss Pendergrass said wisely.

He continued to stare glumly at the handsome pair.

"He'll take good care of her and she needs him. He can offer her something that you cannot—freedom. Freedom to make her own decisions. Freedom to act. Freedom to be herself."

"I could offer her that!" he said, finally finding his voice.

"Could you? Or would you be too busy chasing the next crisis all over the world? By focusing on your career exclusively, you would relegate her to the background of your life. This would smother her. Randolph knows that. He will watch over her and let her take center stage. People like you and me are too busy to love and marry, unless it is to each other?" She gazed at him meaningfully.

Burke studied the handsome woman standing in front of him, speaking softly to him in her soothing contralto voice. She held his eyes, mesmerizing him. She would be a worthy partner in his life. He looked back at Tiffy Rose, sweet, young, whimsical, and brave Tiffy Rose and made his decision.

William McKinley, the most popular president since Abraham Lincoln, projected a genuineness and warmth that other government officials lacked. Everyone present at the pier hoped to shake hands or exchange a few words with their beloved president. Though the president enjoyed interacting with the public, his secret service agents did not. Protecting the president was a nightmare in crowds of any size. Burke, Adelia, and the other agents would have to be on their toes.

While waiting for President McKinley and his party to arrive, the onlookers sorted themselves out into groups and talked. Rested and out of his wheelchair, Burke felt more like his old self. He and Adelia shamelessly eavesdropped while keeping a professional eye on the crowd.

"Anarchists are a threat to our American way of life," said one man fervently. "Look at what happened here this morning. What a catastrophe that would have been. Thank heavens for Chatsworth and his friends."

"Every day, you read about bombings and shootings throughout big cities everywhere. These terrorists reject authority in every form. They even preach the downfall of the United States government! When will this reign of terror end?" asked another.

"I am amazed that President McKinley isn't more worried about his own life. I read a quote in the newspaper that said he believes that 'no one would wish to hurt me'."

"He's a brave man. Look at what happened here this morning. Tomas Martinez was only pretending to be Dr. Martin. He almost succeeded at poisoning our water supply! All because he did not like the outcome of the war against Spain."

"Isn't a dissatisfied factory worker more likely to be an anarchist than a professional man?"

"Was Martinez a professional man or was he merely pretending?"

"What does it matter? The man was an anarchist."

"Putting poison in our source of drinking water reeks of anarchy."

"If it hadn't been for Randolph Patterson Chatsworth, he might have succeeded! Brave man, that Chatsworth. Very brave."

Burke wanted to break in and remind the speaker that Chatsworth had help. Lots of it. But Adelia tugged on his sleeve and pulled him away to listen to a different conversation.

"Why use poison? Why not use a bomb? Just the other day, I read in the paper that anarchist newspapers provide step-by-step directions for creating a bomb!"

"From what I understand it is fairly easy to make a bomb. All that you need is a fuse or detonator and an explosive like dynamite. Dynamite is readily available and stable, unlike nitroglycerin."

"What if the anarchist doesn't want to be around when the bomb goes off?"

"Then he will need a timing device."

"Timing device?"

"Yes, a timing device is sort of like a clock. The anarchist sets the dial to the time he wants the bomb to detonate and starts it ticking. Electrical wires are attached to both the clock and the explosives will act as a circuit. When the circuit is closed by the striking of the hour or half hour, the bomb will go off."

"Too complicated for me."

Burke and Adelia listened carefully to what the man was saying, but the speaker soon moved off onto other, more mundane, topics.

Adelia and Burke joined another conversation, this one focused on President McKinley.

"McKinley will always get my vote. When the Philadelphia and Reading Railroad failed so suddenly in 1893, I got worried. The financial panic that followed never seemed to end. I began to wonder if the U.S. banking system would collapse."

"Do you remember how prices for consumer goods fell?"

"I wonder how many hundreds of financial institutions and businesses shut their doors. Unemployment in our town reached nearly twenty percent. Industrial activity virtually came to a halt."

"It was McKinley's election in 1896 that calmed the nation and brought on the recovery. Factories opened their gates and workers got back to work. Yes, sir, McKinley's got my vote."

The sound of boat horns filled the air. President McKinley's motor launch, the *Colfax*, pulled up to the Jekyll Island Club pier. A few moments later, President McKinley stepped ashore. Burke was surprised to see that the president was a short man, no more than five feet six or seven inches tall. He was also a robustly large man, a man who partook in little exercise beyond a short walk now and again. When he smiled, he was particularly handsome with a square jaw and strong cheekbones. He projected an air of confidence and affability at the same time. He was a nice man—a kind man. His eyes shone with a genuine goodness of spirit.

The president got off the boat and turned to help his wife disembark. The welcoming committee stepped forward and presented Ida McKinley with a bouquet of flowers. Mrs. McKinley stood near the president and behaved with quiet dignity. Burke thought the woman looked a little frail and unnerved by the boisterous welcome.

He turned to Adelia and asked, "Adelia, is Mrs. McKinley comfortable with crowds?"

"No, she is not. Actually, she doesn't like noise and commotion at all. Her husband appears to revel in it."

People crowded the crushed shell road and overflowed the barricades. Miss Pendergrass pointed to the president who was shaking hands with nearly everyone within reach. "Watch how he shakes hands. He is a master at it. I once heard that he could shake hands with fifty people per minute."

Burke watched as McKinley worked the crowd. The president extended his hand and clasped the other person's fingers so that his own hand couldn't be squeezed in a tight grip. With his left hand, McKinley grasped the person's elbow and pushed the person right along—all the while preparing to greet the next person in line.

"He's a master, all right," agreed Burke.

The president didn't spend much time at the pier. After saying a few words of greeting, he began to move toward the waiting carriage.

Speaker of the House of Representatives, Thomas Reed, stepped forward and courteously raised his hat and said, "How do you do, Mr. President?"

President McKinley bowed and responded, "How do you do, Mr. Speaker?"

The two men parted company. President McKinley boarded the carriage for the peace and quiet of Solterra. The speaker of the house walked in the direction of *San Souci* where he was staying with John Moore.

"So much for the mud-slinging we expected from these two bitter enemies," said Burke, slightly let down by the meeting's lack of excitement.

"Yes, after the nationwide stir about their feud over colonization created in the newspapers, I thought they would at least snub each other if not come to blows," replied Adelia wryly.

They stood for a minute, watching the crowd disperse.

Rocking back and forth on his heels, Burke spoke. "May I escort you to the dinner tonight?"

Taken aback, yet flattered, Adelia Pendergrass stuttered slightly. "Yes—yes—that would be very nice."

"I will meet you at 6:45 in the lobby?"

"Fine."

Burke watched her go, noting the graceful swing to her hips and the way she held her head high. He could like Miss Adelia Pendergrass. He could like her very much.

Chapter 35
Tiffy Rose

"Mama! Stop fussing! For heaven's sake, getting dressed with you in attendance is more difficult than climbing a water tower!"

"Don't smart mouth me, young lady! I will not be compared with a short, squat building!"

"Tall and slender building is more like it," laughed Tiffy Rose. She hugged her short, though willowy mother and wiped the grimace off of her face.

"You, my dear, are the tall and slender one." She turned her daughter so that she could see herself in the full-length mirror. Her voice and demeaner softened. "Look at you. Just look at you. You are especially lovely tonight."

Tiffy Rose's eyes misted with tears.

"Don't make me cry, Mama. I mustn't meet the president with red eyes."

Mrs. Baldwin handed Tiffy her handkerchief. "No, you mustn't." She paused and then added, "Tiffy Rose, tonight might be the most important night of your life."

Tiffy interrupted, "Do you think Randolph will propose tonight? Really propose?"

"I was referring to meeting President McKinley, but, yes, Randolph's bound to propose sometime. Everyone already thinks you are engaged. You might as well make it official."

"Aren't you happy, Mama? You don't sound happy."

"It's all happening so very quickly. One minute you were so unhappy that my heart literally ached for you. Now you are on a course to marry Randolph. Are you happy? Really happy?" Her mother searched Tiffy's face looking for an answer. "You aren't just doing this because your father and I believe it is a good match for you, are you?"

"No, Mama." Tiffy Rose paused for a minute, considering her words. "Mama, I think our stay on Jekyll Island has changed us—Randolph and me—for the better. We've had the opportunity to spend time together, to work together, and even to laugh together. He's not the man I thought he was. He is a good man—a truly good man. He is strong, loyal, brave, and true. He is generous of spirit." As an afterthought, she smiled and added, "He has a delightful sense of humor, too."

Tiffy Rose went to her mother and took her hands in hers. "Mama, I love Randolph. I truly love him. I only hope that he loves me in return."

Mrs. Baldwin burst into tears. "I did so hope that you would grow to love each other as your father and I have. I do so want you to be happy." She clung to her daughter fiercely.

Wiping her eyes, her mother's face became serious. "Tiffy, you have placed yourself in great danger on at least three occasions since we have arrived on the island. We still have two days left in our stay. I sometimes wonder if we can keep you safe that long. Promise me that you will stay safe. Promise me that you will avoid dangerous situations in the future."

"The excitement is all over. I promise I won't go chasing after any new dangers. Besides, I have Randolph and Flora to protect me."

"I'm not sure I can count on them to keep you out of trouble. Where is Miss Goodwin? I haven't seen her all afternoon."

"Come to think of it, neither have I. I wonder where she could be."

"Surely she will be at dinner with the president tonight, won't she?"

"I sincerely hope so. Why would she miss such a glorious opportunity? Dinner with the president! And he specifically asked for us!"

"Turn around once more and let me see your hem. Oh, where is Miss Goodwin when I need her? She was always so good at making the final adjustments that are needed."

"I'm sure that she will turn up."

At precisely half past six, Randolph Patterson met Tiffy Rose in the lobby of the clubhouse. Her parents marveled over the fact that for the first time in her life, Tiffy Rose was ready on time. Randolph's parents exclaimed over her dress, one that she and Flora had remodeled earlier in the day, and fussed about happily. Tonight, indeed, was an important night. Not only would their children be meeting President McKinley in a very private setting, this was to be their first function without chaperones or their parents present. To top it all off, there was love in the air.

Taking Tiffy Rose firmly by the elbow, Randolph Patterson bid everyone goodnight. They strolled down the short path to Solterra. He guided them to a small gazebo.

"Tiffy dearest, I don't remember ever seeing you look so lovely," said Randolph Patterson.

Tiffy Rose smiled beguilingly at Randolph, wondering why she had hesitated to love him. He stood before her tall, confident, and adoring. Her heart fluttered with joy.

"I love your smile almost as much as I love you," he said gallantly.

She blushed becomingly, snapped open her fan and fluttered it coyly.

"What a darling flirt you are!" he exclaimed.

Tiffy Rose lifted her hand and touched Randolph's bandaged face. "Oh, Randolph, he hurt you. I am so sorry. I should have prevented him from harming you. I couldn't get my dress unstuck. I tried so hard. I was nearly too late. I am so sorry, my love."

"Courage, my dearest, you have so much courage. I cannot imagine my life without you."

Randolph drew a small black velvet bag from his pocket and said nervously in a rush of words, "Tiffy, I don't know how to say this. I don't know where to begin. I only hope that you will recognize the sincerity of my words. Please accept this simple gift as a token of my love for you. I hope that you like it. It seemed fitting at the time, but now I'm not so sure. I didn't have time to have it wrapped. As it was, I had to summon the jeweler over to the island in a rush. He was given instructions to bring his best pieces. I hope you like this piece I have selected for you, Tiffy dearest. It is a very simple piece, yet nothing could explain how I feel about you better than this." He held out his gift to her, looking just for a moment, unsure of himself.

His expression endeared him to Tiffy Rose more than anything else. She put a finger to his lips and said firmly, "Randolph Patterson Chatsworth III, I am certain to like anything you choose for me. I just hope that you realize that it is you that I want, not gifts."

Randolph Patterson looked at her as if she was a wonderful prize—a jewel rarer than anything on earth. "Hold out your hands," he said softly.

She held out her cupped hands, but kept her eyes focused on his. He poured out the contents of the bag. She gasped when she felt the delicate necklace slide into her hands. She held it up and admired the dime-sized stones set equidistant from each other, connected by a fine gold chain. The necklace was long in the fashionable manner of the time. It hung down to her waist when he took it from her and looped it around her neck.

"Study the stones carefully, dearest. See if you can cipher their meaning."

Tiffy Rose named each of the stones out loud, starting at the gold clasp. Diamond, emerald, amethyst, ruby, emerald, sapphire, and tourmaline. She laughed in surprise. "It spells 'dearest'."

"You are very clever, Tiffy dearest. I know it is fashionable to give one's fiancée a *Regard Ring*, but I feel more than regard for you. You will always be my dearest Tiffy."

"It is lovely. Absolutely lovely. I will cherish it and wear it with honor."

Randolph Patterson smiled contentedly. "The diamonds represent passion. The rubies symbolize eternity. Emeralds symbolize love and amethysts stand for modesty and honesty. I hope you like it. I do love you, Tiffy dearest."

"And I love you, Randolph." Tiffy Rose bestowed a kiss on his cheek.

"I know you do, dearest. You climbed a water tower for me."

"I climbed a water tower *with* you." She stood on her tip-toes and kissed him full on his lips.

"Tiffy dearest, will you marry me?"

"Yes. I can't think of anything that I would rather do."

The look they exchanged spoke of their intense affection and regard for each other.

A passing matron noted their intimacy and remarked, "Be careful, my dears, it is quite unfashionable in today's society to love one's husband or wife."

Tiffy Rose and Randolph Patterson laughed happily, knowing they had found each other.

Chapter 36
Burke

Burke and Adelia stood near the mantlepiece in the large, comfortable sitting room at Solterra. Introductions complete, the invited guests were making conversation while waiting for dinner to be announced.

"Here comes the happy couple," said Adelia Pendergrass under her breath as Randolph Patterson and Tiffy Rose approached. "You must admit, they do make a nice couple."

"I don't remember him being so confident," commented Burke. He eyed Chatsworth suspiciously.

"Nothing gives a man more confidence than a good woman standing by his side." Unexpectedly, Miss Pendergrass winked at Burke.

Wordlessly, Burke stared at her in surprise.

Unfazed by the mischief her wink had brought about, she continued, "I think Jekyll Island has worked its magic on both of them, don't you?"

"I'm not sure what to think," Burke finally managed to say.

"Good evening, Adelia. Good evening, Captain Thayer. Are you enjoying yourselves this lovely evening?" asked Randolph Patterson cheerfully.

"Good evening," Burke greeted his friends. "Are you looking forward to meeting the president?"

"I must admit that I am more than a little nervous." Randolph Patterson ventured a shy smile.

Burke smiled at Randolph. He couldn't help but like the self-effacing young man. His charm lay in his total lack of egotism.

A flustered Mrs. Baker rushed over and joined them. At her side stood a rather handsome man of about thirty.

"Excuse me, Captain Thayer, Mr. Chatsworth, Miss Baldwin, Miss Pendergrass, I would like you to meet Davis Ewing. He is serving as attaché to President McKinley. He is also an acquaintance of Miss Goodwin."

Mrs. Baker hovered nervously while they all exchanged greetings. The minute the formalities were complete she said, "We seem to be missing Miss Goodwin."

"Isn't she here?" exclaimed Tiffy Rose. Her chaperone was never late, ever.

"No! President McKinley will be down soon and he will expect to speak to the five of you. As you can see, only four of you are present," Mrs. Baker said, nervously stating the obvious.

"Do you mean to say that Miss Goodwin hasn't arrived yet?" asked Burke. He cast his eye about the room but did not find Miss Goodwin among those at the dinner party.

"No. She has not arrived nor has she sent word about what could possibly be delaying her. I must admit, I am very concerned. Meeting the president, and to be thanked by him, is a great honor. A once in a lifetime honor. An honor that someone in Miss Goodwin's position would not want to miss."

"Most definitely not," asserted Miss Pendergrass.

Always polite and correct from an etiquette point of view, Randolph Patterson asked his hostess, "Would it be appropriate for us to go in search of her? We would need to leave your lovely party in order to do so. Would you mind?"

Picking up on his lead, Tiffy Rose added, "Mrs. Baker, would it be possible to delay the president for a few more minutes in order to give us time to locate Miss Goodwin?"

Mrs. Baker dithered. "I don't know. I just don't know. What do you think, Mr. Chatsworth? What should I do?"

Burke fumed slightly at how, once again, his status as a government official was overlooked in favor of club membership. What an exclusive enclave Jekyll Island was proving itself to be.

Randolph reassured his hostess, "Dear lady, do not fret. Your dinner party will be a smashing success this evening. We will return within the half hour with Miss Goodwin."

"If you don't mind, I would like to accompany you," said Davis Ewing.

"Certainly. We could use the extra set of eyes," said Randolph.

"You know Miss Goodwin?" asked Tiffy Rose.

"Yes, she and I grew up together. At one time, we had an understanding." Davis Ewing spoke with purpose. "I came to Jekyll Island specifically to see her. I kept my arrival a secret in case my presence here didn't please her."

Burke wondered where this young man's rambling monologue was leading. Tiffy Rose seemed to understand, though.

"Mr. Ewing, did you recently send Flora a postcard?" asked Tiffy Rose.

"Yes, as a matter of fact, I did."

"Well then, Mr. Ewing, based on the private information Flora shared with me last night, she will be thrilled to see you. Shall we go?" Tiffy Rose asked her companions.

All that was missing was their croquet mallets, thought Burke meanly.

"We will need to fly if we are to beat the president to the party," exclaimed Miss Pendergrass. "Tiffy, you know Flora best, where do you suggest we look?"

Tiffy Rose thought for a moment as they walked quickly out of Solterra and toward the front of the clubhouse. She looked up at the window that she had earlier determined was the room she shared with Flora.

"Randolph, please be a dear and tell me what time it is."

Ever eager to please his fiancée, Randolph Patterson drew out his pocket watch and said, "It is ten minutes past the hour of seven."

"It was only twenty minutes ago that I was in my room. Flora was not there. My mother had to help me get dressed." Tiffy Rose paused. "As a matter of fact, Flora had not been there for quite some time. I have not seen her since she took my dresses to the laundress to be cleaned and repaired. I did so want to show her my dress." She touched her skirt gently.

"Then there is no sense us looking for her in your rooms," stated Miss Pendergrass with authority.

"To the laundry, then," said Randolph Patterson. He pointed to the row of buildings lining Pier Road.

They walked swiftly toward the laundry building.

Tiffy said, "Perhaps we will find someone there who has seen her."

Burke could hear the worry in her voice.

"Steady on, dearest," encouraged Randolph Patterson. He took Tiffy Rose by the elbow and helped her along.

Burke watched the protective gesture and decided he would see if Miss Pendergrass would react favorably. He drew nearer to her and touched her elbow. She turned toward him, surprised. Apparently pleased with his gesture, she slowed her pace slightly and fell into step with him.

At the laundry, they wasted a few minutes looking around trying to find someone to ask about Flora. Eventually, they unearthed a young woman who was up to her ears in mending. Tiffy Rose recognized her dresses.

"Those are my dresses!" she exclaimed.

The tired young woman forgot her place and said, "A right fine mess they are too. What did you do to them, roll around on the shell road?"

"Actually, it was a roof that did that one in," Tiffy Rose admitted.

"When you find one with a large rip in it, that one is due to a slight mishap on the water tower." Randolph Patterson pointed to his bandaged face and smiled briefly.

"Do you remember the woman who brought these dresses in to you?" asked Miss Pendergrass, getting to the point of the matter.

"Of course, I do. She was here about two hours ago," responded the laundress.

"Did you happen to see what direction she went when she left you?" asked Tiffy Rose, becoming excited.

"Back to the clubhouse where she belongs," said the girl.

"How long ago was that?" asked Burke.

"Like I said, about two hours ago. Now if you want these dresses mended any time soon, you'd best be on your way." The laundress gave them a brief nod of dismissal and went back to her work.

Stepping outside, the disappointed searchers looked toward the clubhouse.

"She simply disappeared." His face lined with worry; Davis Ewing looked around at the other buildings.

"Two hours ago," said Adelia.

"Between here and the clubhouse," added Randolph.

"Where could she be?" wailed Tiffy.

Burke checked his pocket watch. "We've only got another fifteen minutes to find her before we will be late for the president."

"What should we do?" asked Tiffy.

As one, they began to walk back toward the clubhouse.

Out of the corner of his eye, Burke saw a white shape being moved in the window of the clockmaker's workshop. He grasped Adelia's elbow and pointed. "Do you see what I see?"

At the same moment, Tiffy Rose cried, "I see her. I see Flora!" She raced over to the clockmaker's workshop. "She's in there. There in the clockmaker's workshop!"

The others ran to the door of the small workshop. Burke tugged at the door knob to no avail.

Gagged and tied to a chair, Flora struggled to free herself.

"Flora! Is it really you?" asked Davis Ewing though the window.

Flora stopped struggling. She sat frozen, staring with wide open eyes at the man who had once represented all her happiness.

Davis Ewing rattled the doorknob in frustration. "Is there a door around back?"

"No. This is the only door," responded Burke.

"What about the windows?" asked Davis.

"I tried," cried Tiffy Rose. "They have been nailed shut from the inside."

"The door and window frames are very sturdy. I don't think we can easily break them," admitted Burke.

"Hang on, I think I've got this," said Randolph Patterson cheerfully.

Burke turned and glared Chatsworth. Why was it that the man was inevitably cheerful? He watched as Chatsworth withdrew a small bundle from his pocket. Once unrolled, it revealed a wide variety of small clockmaking tools.

"Look!" cried Tiffy Rose. "They look just like the set we saw in the clockmaker's workshop."

"They are identical. I purchased them today from the jeweler," said Randolph proudly.

"A jeweler?" asked Adelia, her curiosity aroused. She noted for the first time Tiffy's beautiful *Regard* necklace as it sparkled in the setting sun.

"Move aside and let me work," said a grinning Randolph Patterson. He gave Burke a push.

"Don't tell me that lock-picking is one of your hidden talents," said Tiffy Rose. She gently rested her hands on his shoulders.

Randolph smiled up at her. Kneeling down, he eyed the lock. "Yes, I just had to have the set. I've been practicing all afternoon on just about every locked door on the island. Such fun! I've actually gotten quite good at it."

Within seconds Randolph had successfully picked the lock and opened the door. Tiffy Rose gently removed the gag from Flora's mouth.

"Davis? Is it really you?" Flora's voice filled with tears.

"Yes, beloved. It is truly me." Davis Ewing carefully removed the ties that bound her to the chair. He pulled her into his arms and kissed her.

Suddenly, Flora pushed him away. Stroking his face lovingly, she said, "Davis, dear Davis, there will be time for tender kisses later." She turned to her friends and addressed them. "I thought you'd never find me in time! We've got to get to the clock! It's timed to explode at seven-thirty!"

The others gaped at her.

"What is timed to go off?" asked Davis.

"A bomb! The clockmaker planted a bomb in the Bakers' mantlepiece clock!"

"A bomb!" exclaimed Tiffy in horror.

Randolph Patterson checked his watch. "It's seven-twenty now!"

Flora pushed them out the door. "Quickly! There is enough dynamite in that clock to blow up all of Solterra as well as the president!"

"But—"

"I'll tell you along the way. There is no time to waste." Flora gathered up her skirts and set off at a good pace toward Solterra.

The others ran after her.

Flora called over her shoulder, "After I dropped Tiffy Rose's torn clothing off at the laundress, I walked past the clockmaker's workshop, much as you did. He was coming out the door to his shop. I must have startled him. He dropped the clock he was carrying. The base cracked open. I could see dynamite sticks inside. I must have cried out and pointed because the next thing I knew he had thrown me into his shack, gagged and tied me up and locked the door. I've been trying to get out ever since."

"Whose clock?" asked Davis Ewing.

"Which clock?" asked Adelia.

"What did the clock look like?" asked Burke.

"It was a gilt statue of Psyche holding a clockface. It's mounted on a wooden base," said Tiffy Rose almost to herself.

"How did you know?" asked Flora.

"I saw him at the pier, holding the something bulky under his arm. I could tell by its shape that it was the same clock we saw the day before yesterday."

"Where is the clock now?" asked Burke.

"It's on the mantel in Solterra!" cried Adelia. "I saw it there tonight."

"When is the bomb set to go off?"

"Seven-thirty!"

Burke, Randolph and Davis sprinted off leaving the women and their movement-hampering skirts behind.

Minutes later, Burke and Randolph burst into Solterra's parlor, startling the guests. Davis Ewing began to quickly usher people from the parlor and toward safety. While Randolph ran interference, Burke snatched the clock off the mantel and ran out the French doors into the garden. Together they heaved the clock as far away from Solterra Cottage as they could. Just as the clock struck the half-hour, it exploded with a horrific blast that blew out the riverside windows of the cottage.

Burke felt himself being blown backward in much the same manner as the explosion on the Maine. Fragments of the clock struck the ground near him. Bits and pieces of singed palm fronds floated down from the sky. Women screamed. Men sounded the alarm.

Adelia appeared out of the smoke. She knelt down and cradled his head in her arms. Into his addled brain crept one very clear thought. He could love this woman.

"Adelia, may I call on you when we both return to Washington?"

"Of course, Captain Thayer. Of course." She smiled with pleasure.

Several hours later...

Tiffy Rose, Randolph, Adelia, Flora, and Davis, sat with Burke on the terrace at Solterra. Much had happened during the intervening hours.

"And what of the others? Is anyone hurt?" asked Tiffy Rose.

"No, we arrived in time. No one has been hurt," answered Burke.

"Good. That's good." Her relief evident.

"Yes, it is. By the way, Captain Thayer, Mr. Ewing brings proof positive that you and Miss Baldwin really are third cousins twice removed." Flora gave a little laugh and cast a look of adoration toward Davis Ewing.

"Are we really cousins? Imagine that!" exclaimed Tiffy.

"Apparently, you really did know each other when you, Tiffy, were a small child and you, Captain Thayer, were completing your studies."

"There are so many Tifts, it is hard to keep track of them all." Burke smiled at the thought of having Tiffy Rose as a cousin. He changed subjects when a thought came to him. "And what of Mr. Horst, the clockmaker?"

"He has been captured. Apparently, he forgot he was on an island and did not plan a suitable escape," answered Davis Ewing. "I can't believe that anyone who appeared so civilized could be a murderer."

"Why did he attack the president with a bomb?" asked Flora.

"Apparently Mr. Horst has been writing the president for years," explained Davis Ewing. "It seems that he wants to stop the electrification of the United States. He fears it will bring the end to traditional clocks. People would no longer hear the comforting tick-tock of a pendulum clock and be doomed to use only electric clocks. Apparently, Horst foresees a future in which every useful device relies upon switches that are set in either an on or an off position. These switches are driven or set by electrical impulses. He calls it 'the digital age'."

"The digital age?" Randolph rolled the word around on his tongue. "That's an interesting concept. Not possible, but still interesting."

"Were there other bombs in other clocks?" asked Flora.

"Morgan has sent men from house to house and room to room. No more bombs have been found, thank goodness. It seems Horst only held a grudge against the president."

Randolph tuned to Flora and smiled. "What about you, Flora? What is the reason behind your very happy countenance?"

"I've brought news from Flora's father," answered Davis Ewing. He reached over and took Flora's hand. "Should you tell them or would you prefer that I did?"

"I will let you tell them."

"Flora's father recently made an investment in internal combustion engines with a man named Henry Ford. Apparently, it is paying off already."

"Flora, that is wonderful news!" exclaimed Tiffy Rose.

"Yes, the stumbling block to our marriage has been removed. Knowing that his daughter's happiness lies with me, he approached me shortly before I came to Jekyll Island. He has set aside a substantial dowry for Flora."

"We are going to be married! We want you all to come to our wedding!" exclaimed Flora.

"Will you be married here on Jekyll Island like we plan to be?" asked Randolph. He cast a loving glance at Tiffy Rose.

"What a lovely idea," said Flora.

Tiffy Rose said, "I see Mrs. Baker waving at us from the parlor. Shall we go and meet the president?"

End Notes and Interesting Facts

McKinley Assassination

On September 6, 1901, at the Buffalo New York Pan American Exposition, President William McKinley was assassinated by Leon Czolgosz. He was 58 years old. An avowed anarchist, Czolgosz fired two bullets into the president, one in his chest and one in his abdomen. The president died September 14, 1901.

The death of William McKinley resulted in Vice President Theodore Roosevelt becoming president. His rise to power brought about the end of the Gilded Age and the Robber Barons. Roosevelt and the presidents who followed him enacted laws and established taxes that effectively ended an age. Americans would no longer see men rise from nothing to stupendous wealth.

The Sinking of the Maine

Further investigation into the sinking of the 6682-ton second class battleship Maine has brought up several conflicting theories concerning what caused the explosion. It is now believed that a fire started a storage room and ignited the ammunition stocks. The Maine was built in the New York Navy Yard and commissioned in 1895.

Anarchists

Anarchists believe in 'propaganda by the deed'. They take violent action to make a point. Armed with newly patented dynamite, the world's first widely available weapon of mass destruction, anarchists conducted riots, bombings, and assassinations. In other words, they are terrorists. Anarchists believe that there should be no government, no accumulation of property, and the right to bear arms. In what has been called "The Golden Age of Assassination" (1892-1901) more monarchs, presidents, and prime ministers were murdered in any time before or since. What follows is an incomplete list of assassinations that can be laid at the feet of anarchists:

1881 Czar Alexander II of Russia
1881 President Garfield
1892 Henry Clay Frick (unsuccessful attempt on life of Andrew Carnegie's second in command)
1894 French President Marie Francois Carnot
1897 Spanish Prime Minister Antonio Caravan de Castillo
1898 Empress of Austria-Hungary Elizabeth Hapsburg
1900 King of Italy Umberto I
1901 President William McKinley
1912 Former President Theodore Roosevelt (unsuccessful attempt)

The 1893 World's Fair

Prior to the 1893 World's Fair in Chicago, a battle raged between General Electric (Edison and Financier J.P. Morgan with direct current (DC)) and Westinghouse (Nikola Tesla and George Westinghouse with alternating current (AC)). Each company thought that they had the best system for bringing electricity to people across the nation. Westinghouse and AC current won. The fair also introduced the Ferris Wheel (George W.G. Ferris Jr.), Scott Joplin, "moving walkways", and fluorescent lights. New foods included: Cracker Jack snacks, Quaker Oats, Cream of Wheat, Shredded Wheat, Milton Hershey's chocolate, and the hamburger.

New Products at the turn of the century

At the turn of the century, consumer goods flourished along with the increased ease of manufacturing. Never before had so many new products become available in such a short period of time. New products included: Coca-Cola soft drink, Pabst Blue Ribbon beer, Kellogg's Shredded Wheat, Cream of Wheat, Juicy Fruit gum, Quaker Oats, Aunt Jemima's pancake mix and others.

Immigration

In the late 1800s, an unprecedented number of people came to the United States—the land of opportunity. During the last decade of the 19th century, an estimated nine million people came in search of a brighter future.

Robber Barons

The fifty years prior to McKinley's assassination witnessed the rise of the self-made man. These men through ingenuity, insight, innovation, hard work, and sheer force of will, amassed unbelievable fortunes. Robber Barons is a term which is unfairly applied with a wide brush to all wealthy industrialists and financiers during the Gilded Age. Though there are always examples of bad apples, these were nearly all self-made men who used their ingenuity, innovative ideas, and hard work to move the United States into the Industrial Age. They were tough competitors who played by the rules of their time which were few. And, yes, they amassed enormous personal fortunes.

With great wealth comes even greater responsibility. Some of these men gave away their fortune to establish foundations, libraries, and educational institutions, others lost their fortunes when depression gripped the nation as it did in 1893. A majority of these men were generous with their wealth, setting up foundations to disperse money to the needy. Most believed in fair wages, healthcare for employees, safe working conditions, and voting rights for women.

The Gilded Age

The era of the Gilded Age extended from approximately 1870-1900. It was characterized by rapid economic growth, the development of new manufacturing processes and new products, and the accumulation of wealth. Critics consider the Gilded Age a time defined by gross materialism, blatant political corruption, and corporate greed. Mark Twain coined the term when he published a book under the same name.

The End of the Gilded Age

Many historians say that the Gilded Aged ended with President McKinley's assassination. Following his death, Theodore Roosevelt became president. Known for his dislike of business, especially monopolies, no one was surprised when, as president, Roosevelt used the Sherman Anti-Trust Act to file multiple anti-trust suits against a number of companies. With the end of monopolies and the implementation of taxes, business changed forever.

The Panic of 1893

The primary cause of the financial panic of 1893 was the failure of the Philadelphia and Reading Railroad. Its bankruptcy placed so much strain on the U.S. banking system that it nearly collapsed. A run on gold occurred when people exchanged silver certificates for gold. Over-production caused prices for consumer goods to fall. Hundreds of financial institutions and thousands of businesses shut their doors. Unemployment in some areas was as high as twenty percent. Industrial activity virtually came to a halt. J.P. Morgan helped out the government financially saying that he had faith in men and faith in the country.

From Farms to Factories

Steamships were the first use of mechanical (or steam) power. The use of rivers and steamships enabled goods to be shipped more easily to markets, allowing producers to market their goods to a wider audience. However, steamships had one major constraint—they could only go where the water allowed them to go. Enter the railroads. With the advent of railroads, goods could be shipped to an even broader area, essentially wherever track could be laid and maintained. The discovery of oil opened up a whole host of new product applications including a relatively safe fluid for to provide light: kerosene. To build all these factories to make all the new consumer products required iron which eventually was refined into steel. Electricity replaced kerosene. The next big thing? Gas-powered internal combustion engines and the automobile. It was through the efforts of these men that changed the

United States from an agrarian society to an industrial one in a mere fifty years.

Personal Hygiene

Diseases like tuberculosis, also known as consumption, were rampant during the 1800s. Toward the end of the century, doctors and people began to understand their causes. While cures were still in the distant future, personal hygiene was modified to curb the spread of disease.

For example, doctors encouraged men to remove their facial hair. The advent of the safety razor in 1903 made shaving much easier and safer.

For women, fighting disease involved changes in fashion. When women realized that dragging their skirts through the mud and spittle on the street brought disease right into their home, shorter skirts became the norm. Since feet and ankles could now be seen, shorter skirts lead to a desire for fashionable shoes. For more information, see *How Tuberculosis Shaped Victorian Fashion*, **Smithsonian Magazine**, May 10, 2016.

Jekyll Island

On March 9, 1914, Solterra Cottage burnt to the ground. The fire was believed to have started in the attic or perhaps a faulty flue. Fortunately, much of the furnishings and paintings were saved.

In April 1909, Mrs. Charlotte Maurice fell ill from typhoid fever which she contracted while visiting the island. She died in August of that same year. It wasn't until 1912 that Dr. William W. Ford concluded that the disease was caused by eating oysters from beds that were located too close to the sewage disposal area.

In the early 1900s, Cyrus Hall McCormick went on to consolidate several farming equipment businesses (including McCormick Harvesting Company and the Deering Company) in order to create International Harvester Company.

The Charles Stewart Maurice family is the only Jekyll Island Club family to have been club members from its inception in 1886 to its closing in 1947. Hollybourne was built 1890-1891.

Charlie Hill served as the Maurice coachman. He took the family on a buggy ride nearly every day.

Furness Cottage is better known as the Infirmary. Built by Walter Rogers Furness in 1890, it was first located to the south of Moss Cottage. In 1896, Joseph Pulitzer bought it from Furness and had it moved straight east from its original position. He used the building to house his servants. Frank Goodyear had it moved again in 1930 to its current location at the corner of Plantation Road and Riverview Drive. He donated it to the club to be used as an infirmary.

Recipes for an Afternoon Tea

Mustard Dill Sauce for Seafood

½ cup mayonnaise
¼ cup of Dijon mustard
½ tablespoon of freshly chopped dill
½ teaspoon of honey (if desired)

Mix ingredients together well, chill, and serve. Makes 4 servings.

Fruit Salad

2 Georgia Peaches sliced into bite-size pieces
1 pint raspberries, rinsed
1 pint strawberries, rinsed and hulled and quartered
1 pint blueberries, rinsed
4 tablespoons of honey
Pinch of cinnamon

Combine fruit with honey and cinnamon. Toss gently. Chill if desired. Different fruits may be used, depending on season.

Chilled Shrimp Salad

2-3 cups of fresh Georgia shrimp
¼ cup of chopped Vidalia onions
1 cup celery, diced
¾ cup of mayonnaise
2 tablespoons of sunflower oil
1 tablespoon of apple cider vinegar
Salad greens
Add curry powder to taste if desired.

Boil shrimp until ready to eat. Chill. When shrimp is chilled, peel and cut up into bite-sized pieces if desired. Combine other ingredients. Mix lightly. Chill to blend flavors. Serve on salad greens.

Candied Sweet Potatoes

4 sweet potatoes
1 cup orange juice
1 small can of Dole pineapple tidbits
¼ cup honey
1 teaspoon cornstarch
1 tablespoon of melted butter
1/3 cup of packed brown sugar

Bake sweet potatoes in the oven until soft (350 degrees for approximately one hour). Allow to cool. Peel to remove skins. Dispose of skins. In a baking dish, lay sliced sweet potatoes. Mix in pineapple tidbits. In sauce pan, combine remaining ingredients: cornstarch, butter, brown sugar, orange juice, and honey. Mix and heat. Stir until thickened. Pour over sweet potatoes. Cover and bake at 350 degrees for 20-30 minutes until hot enough to serve.

Pink Lemonade

6-10 lemons (enough to squeeze 2 cups of fresh lemon juice)
1 package of frozen raspberries
1 cup of white sugar
1 cup boiling water
5 cups of cold water
Lemon slices

Squeeze lemons until you have 2 cups of fresh lemon juice. Defrost frozen raspberries until soft. Open package and pour out one cup of juice. Boil 1 cup of water. Take water off the heat. Stir in sugar. Keep stirring until sugar dissolves. Pour cold water into a pitcher. Add lemon juice and raspberry juice. Carefully add hot sugar water (which should be fairly cool by now). Garnish with lemon slices. Serve over ice.

Bibliography

Bagwell, Tyler, The Jekyll Island Club, Arcadia Publishing, 1998.

Balsan, Consuelo Vanderbilt, The Glitter and the Gold, St. Martin's Press, 1953.

Dedman, Bill and Newell, Paul Clark Jr., Empty Mansions, Ballantine Books, 2013.

Fish, Tulla, Once Upon an Island: The Story of Fabulous Jekyll, 1959

Hutto, Richard Jay, Crowning Glory: American Wives of Princes and Dukes, Henchard Press, 2007.

McCash, June Hall and Brenden, Martin, The Jekyll Island Club Hotel, The Dunning Company Publishers, 2012.

McCash, William Barton and McCash, June Hall, The Jekyll Island Club: Southern Haven for America's Millionaires, University of Georgia Press, 1989.

Miller, Scott, The President and the Assassin, Random House, 2011.

Mueller, Pamela Bauer, Splendid Isolation, Pinata Publishing, 2010.

Rauchway, Eric, Murdering McKinley, Hill and Wang, 2003.

Smithsonian Magazine, *How Tuberculosis Shaped Victorian Fashion,* May 10, 2016.

Stuart, Amanda Mackenzie, Consuelo and Alva Vanderbilt, Harper, 2008.

Twain, Mark (Samuel Clemens), The Gilded Age, Harper and Brothers Publishers, 1873.

Vanderbilt, Arthur T. II, Fortune's Children: The Fall of the House of Vanderbilt, William Morrow and Company, 1989.

Hollybourne Cottage

Death on Jekyll Island

A Postcard from the Gilded Age

Book Club Questions

1. Does the premise of this story appeal to you? Why?
2. Were you aware of the political and social tensions of the early 1890s?
3. What did you enjoy most about this book?
4. Where you aware of the activities of anarchists in the 1800s? Did their activities surprise you? Why? Why not?
5. This book delves into women's roles in society and the societal norms they faced. How do you think their experiences match those of modern women?
6. There are three strong female characters sharing the pages of this book. How are they similar? How are they different?
7. Does Randolph Patterson Chatsworth III make a believable hero? Did he surprise you?
8. Does Tifton Rose make a believable heroine? Did she surprise you?
9. Which character did you like the best? Why?
10. Would you like to meet any of the characters? Which ones?

The Postcard Mysteries

By Carol Tonnesen

www.postcardmysteries.com

carol.tonnesen@postcardmysteries.com

available on www.amazon.com

Do you have a craving for mysteries that mix romance and mystery with places and history? In each Postcard Mystery, a postcard serves as the catalyst that catapults ordinary people into adventures that change their lives. Written to appeal to people who believe a person can change, these books feature strong men and women who throw caution to the wind in order to open themselves up to mystery, adventure, and finally, love.

Available on Amazon.com

The Red Bus: A Postcard to an Assassin. Can two strangers, linked only by a postcard, race across Europe on the Orient Express in time to prevent an assassination?

The Fishing Bridge: A Postcard to a Traitor. British agent Charles Littleton longs to be a cowboy. Hot on the trail of traitors selling atomic bomb secrets, he finds himself in Yellowstone National Park. With the help of Trudy and Bandit, a talented Border collie with all the answers, Charles proves he has what it takes.

The Highlands: A Postcard to Deception. Set against a backdrop of Scotland's Sheep Dog Trials, veterinarian, Iain copes with deceptions and murder that threaten to destroy his veterinary practice. Can Aylee and her unexpected Border collie help him?

Angels' Share: A Postcard to a Dead Man. A postcard to a dead man sets in motion a clever scheme to destroy a family business. With his whisky distillery under siege, a missing will, and rampant thievery, can Rory set things to rights? Or does he need the help of a clever young woman and a pig?

Rumrunner's Reef: A Postcard to a Smuggler. The sight of a nearly naked man emerging from the waters of Florida Bay provides an interesting start to Lizette's vacation. But, are the Florida Keys really different from Chicago?

The Zephyr: A Postcard to a Thief. Follow rancher Charlie on his train ride from Denver to San Francisco on the California Zephyr. Can he prevent the theft of precious jewels?

The Golden Isles: A Postcard to Fear. April 1942, a time of German U-boat attacks, torpedoed ships, and fear in coastal Georgia. A postcard, a message, a life changed. Can Ray and Helen prevent the sabotage of the Liberty ships the U.S. merchant marines so desperately needs?

Paris Souvenir: A Postcard with a Secret. 1918—A world at war. Vivienne, a French nurse, and Fletcher, a German-American, are thrown into a web of espionage, mechanized warfare, and black-marketeers. Can the secrets shared through postcards unite them against a common enemy?

See No Evil: A Postcard to a Burglar. Citizens of mid-century America found themselves caught between two polar opposites. On the one hand, the nation's citizens, experiencing post World War II abundance, saw themselves as prosperous, safe, and full of hope. On the other hand, the nation faced the threat of nuclear war leaving its citizens fearful and full of dread. One summer morning, Eve Akins wishes for the kind of man who came along once in a blue moon. Instead, fate sends murder and mayhem to her small village of Lebanon, Ohio. (First in the series)

Speak No Evil: A Postcard from a Con Artist. In the midst of seemingly imminent nuclear holocaust, the nation, encouraged by John Glenn's orbital success, saw itself as prosperous, safe, and full of hope. Though bomb shelters lurked in the corners of backyards, out of sight and temporarily out of mind, citizens of 1962 America enjoyed themselves at barbeques, card parties, and outdoor activities. If only life could be that simple for Riley and Eve Wills of Lebanon, Ohio. (Second in the series)

Hear No Evil: A Postcard on a Party Line. In the 1960s, the citizens of the United States tuned in, turned on, tripped out, dropped out, blew up and grew up. Revolution, counterculture, and hallucinogens were all part of the scene. The small town of Lebanon, Ohio, is no exception. In July of 1969, NASA put a man on the moon, providing a bright spot in an otherwise turbulent decade. Will man's greatest achievement be eclipsed by murder and mayhem in Lebanon, Ohio? (Third in the series)

The Westerner: A Postcard to the Girl He Left Behind. Based on the real lives of two Lebanon, Ohio citizens in the 1870s, this East meets West story is about the love between a girl from the East and a soldier stationed in the West. Lieutenant James Madison Burns meets the lovely Lebanon native, Caroline Corwin Sage, at a party hosted by the owners of Glendower Mansion. As tensions mount between the United States and the Indian Nations, James is sent West to serve under the command of General George Armstrong Custer. Letters never enough, Caroline is determined not to become the girl he left behind...

The Lake House: A Postcard from the Shadows. 1927. Speak-easies, hot jazz, sky scrapers, bootleggers. The stock market is booming, necklines are plunging, and hemlines are rising. In the summer time, life slows down and everyone who can goes to a lake house—borrowed, rented, or owned—to beat the heat. Unfortunately, Sunny Fiske and her brother are in for a summer storm that promises to bring more than heat lightening to their lives.

ABOUT THE AUTHOR

I am an avid collector of postcards. I began writing the Postcard Mystery series the very day I found a postcard of a red bus in a stack of postcards labeled 'Old European Postcards 50¢'. This became ***The Red Bus: A Postcard to an Assassin.*** Often the right postcard falls in my lap and when looking at it I know what needs to be written. Once a postcard is selected, I meticulously research the topic and location. Whenever possible, I visit the area and conduct face-to-face interviews with people appropriate to the story. I live on a farm with my beloved husband and an assortment of animals, including two Border Collies.

Made in the USA
Monee, IL
16 April 2025

15913584R00134